Easing up on tiptoe, Abbie kissed him softly.

It was remorse for something she couldn't fix, but also a plea to forgive and move on.

"I don't want your pity," Jace said.

"It wasn't pity."

He searched her eyes. "Then why?"

"Because you're a good man, and I wanted to kiss you," she whispered.

He didn't nod. He didn't smile. He didn't even tighten his arms around her. He merely lowered his head, gently kissed her back and Abbie felt a chunk of her heart tear away.

They stood there for a time when it ended, feeling the March air cool their lips and ruffle their hair, last night's memories curling in their bellies and imaginations. Then Jace's gaze dropped to her mouth again.

Somewhere far away a voice whispered that this was another mistake Abbie would regret. But it drifted off like morning fog the second his lips found hers

Dear Reader,

My husband, Mike, and I love to visit the places where I set my books—and since I'm a big chicken when it comes to flying, we travel by car. Silly phobias aside, it really is the best way to experience the sights, sounds and textures that make locales interesting and exciting.

We've visited Arizona's prehistoric cliff dwellings, the Montana Rockies, the Maine coast and more, and each place is beautiful in its own way. But for us, there's no place like the rich, wooded Allegheny Mountains of Pennsylvania—especially in early spring, when the creeks are thawing, the air is indescribably fresh and the trees are just beginning to green. This is our pretty part of the world—and the setting for *Just a Whisper Away*. I hope you'll like it, too.

Peace, love and happy reading,

Lauren

LAUREN NICHOLS

JUST A WHISPER AWAY

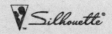

INTIMATE MOMENTS™

Published by Silhouette Books

America's Publisher of Contemporary Romance

 SILHOUETTE BOOKS

ISBN 0-373-27491-2

JUST A WHISPER AWAY

Copyright © 2006 by Edie Hanes

Visit Silhouette Books at www.eHarlequin.com

Printed in U.S.A.

Books by Lauren Nichols

Silhouette Intimate Moments

Accidental Heiress #840
Accidental Hero #893
Accidental Father #994
Bachelor in Blue Jeans #1164
Run to Me #1271
Deadly Reunion #1374
Just a Whisper Away #1421

LAUREN NICHOLS

started writing by accident, so it seems fitting that the word *accidental* appears in her first three titles for Silhouette. Once eager to illustrate children's books, she tried to get her foot in that door, only to learn that most publishing houses used their own artists. Then one publisher offered to look at her sketches if she also wrote the tale. During the penning of that story, Lauren fell head over heels in love with writing fiction.

In addition to her novels, Lauren's romance and mystery short stories have appeared in several leading magazines. She counts her family and friends as her greatest treasures, and strongly believes in the Beatles' philosophy—"All You Need Is Love." When this Pennsylvania author isn't writing or trying unsuccessfully to give up French vanilla cappuccino, she's traveling or hanging out with her very best friend/husband, Mike.

Lauren loves to hear from her readers. You can contact her at www.laurennichols.com.

For Bob, Kevin and Ernie, brothers extraordinaire.
And for the wonderful women who love them,
Deb, Shelley and Kathy.
And always for Mike.

Acknowledgments

My thanks to Tom Shields for the tour of his lumberyard
and sawmill during the preparation of this book, and to
Carmella Manno who took me through the kiln drying
process and was always there to answer my
goofy questions. I owe you.

Chapter 1

A powerful jolt of recognition hit Jace Rogan as he crossed the country club's crowded dining room. He stopped dead in his tracks, his eagerness to leave the faux, day-early Mardi Gras celebration forgotten. For an instant he simply stood there, feeling his nerves vibrate and adrenaline pulse through him. Then the night, the music and the costumed crowd all faded to a blur as he watched a good-looking couple join the other partiers on the dance floor.

It couldn't be her... Yet when his gaze fell to the smooth, graceful slope of the woman's bare back in her plunging gown, he knew it was.

Jace drew a cautious breath. He'd touched that back...kissed the sweet, sexy small of it...held those hips in his hands and slid his fingers through that long auburn hair.

The memory lasted only a second before a bitter one took its place. Jace jerked his gaze from the side-slit in Abbie Winslow's dress to scan the lavishly decorated room.

It didn't take long to spot an old enemy.

Wearing a powdered wig and the fancy brocades of an English lord, Abbie's perpetually controlling father stood beside his table, beaming as the new surgeon in town kept his daughter smiling and engaged.

Morgan Winslow's venomous tirade thundered in Jace's mind, as clearly as if it had happened yesterday, but he blocked it out. The words didn't hurt anymore because he'd used Morgan's humiliating rant to succeed beyond the banker's wildest expectations—beyond the town's expectations.

And suddenly he wanted Abbie to know that, too.

Cutting through the crowd, he tapped Abbie's partner on the shoulder, all the while enjoying an unobstructed view of the shimmering, halter-style gown that clung like liquid silver to her body. Small diamond earrings winked at her lobes when she jerked her head up in surprise.

"Mind, Doc?" Jace asked with a smile when the surgeon turned around. "We're old friends."

"Not at all," he returned amiably, then grinned at Abbie. "Okay with you?"

Jace met her wide brown eyes and startled features. "How about it, Abbie? Care to dance for old times' sake?"

For a second, she didn't seem capable of uttering a word, and Jace found some pleasure in that. Then she murmured, "Of course," and turned to the doctor. "I'll see you back at the table, Paul."

"I'll be there. Enjoy."

"Thanks."

Then Jace opened his arms and Abbie stepped into them for the first time in fourteen years. The first time since her father had caught them locked intimately together in the gazebo behind the Winslow's country home. Unexpectedly, some of his bitterness faded as her uneasy gaze searched his, and he silently—reluctantly—admitted that it felt good to hold her again.

"Hello, Jace," she said quietly. "It's nice to see you again. You look wonderful."

The dress code for this shindig was always costume or black-tie, and for the first time tonight he was glad he'd worn a tux—the lesser of the two evils. It made a statement that he'd come far since that night in the gazebo.

"So do you," he returned as she pinned her gaze to his shoulder, and they began to move. "California living seems to agree with you."

He stole a glance over her head at the crowd. Morgan Winslow's face had turned to stone, and, sophomoric as it was, Jace's pleasure doubled.

He spoke close to Abbie's temple, inhaled the light floral scent of her perfume. "I see you're not into costumes, either."

"Not the one my dad chose for me," she said. But there was a vulnerable look in her chocolate-brown eyes, and Jace knew she was wondering why they were dancing after fourteen years of silence. Her voice softened. "I found this dress in a trunk in the attic. It was my mom's."

Jace heard the loving, the *missing* in her reply and the kid in him empathized with that, but he didn't comment. Because a dozen feet behind Abbie, his fun-loving baby brother was grinning up a storm and dancing his partner their way. He'd told everyone at the Rogan Logging & Lumber table that he was cutting out early to get some work done—which surprised no one. Now Ty was on his way to see who'd convinced him otherwise.

Jace spun Abbie off in another direction. The last thing he wanted now was small talk from someone wearing a plumed hat and a Cyrano nose. "So, how's the legal eagle business?"

"You know what I do?"

"Hard not to. Your dad brags you up every time you win a case." They'd talked a lot back when they'd cared about each other. Fourteen years ago, Abbie the Crusader had wanted to practice law more than anything in life—much more than she'd wanted a roughneck logger with a past people still loved to talk about. "Not that I get the news firsthand," he added, managing to keep an edge out of his voice. "I do my banking elsewhere."

Abbie held back a sigh, but kept her thoughts to herself. Anything she said would bring up that wonderful-then-terrible night in the gazebo, and she already had more anxiety in her life than she could handle. That included the dewy warmth radiating between them and the sudden return of libido as Jace's leg insinuated itself between hers and they moved to the slow, moody rhythm of "The Way We Were."

How appropriate. Lifting her gaze, she took in Jace's strong jaw and handsome features. He was more power-fully built now, more attractive in a sexy, rugged...maybe even cynical way. His feathery black hair was long by Cal-ifornia attorney standards, but it was neatly trimmed, and his compelling storm-gray eyes held a look of confidence that he'd never had at twenty-two.

The gentle pressure of his hand on her bare back made her tremble as he guided her away from another cou-ple...and suddenly, feelings and regrets she'd thought she'd put aside returned with heart-tugging poignancy. Swallow-ing, she searched for conversation, but everything she came up with felt awkward. "I'm surprised to see you here tonight. I wouldn't have guessed you'd like this sort of thing."

"People change," he replied, a shrug in his voice. "I guess you're home for a visit?"

"Yes, I got in yesterday afternoon."

His smile held a trace of sarcasm. "And already you're partying at the country club. How long are you staying this time?"

How long? Abbie suppressed a shudder as sniper fire echoed in her mind again. Hopefully, until the Los Angeles Police Department uncovered enough evidence to keep the young man she'd defended last month behind bars. The one who'd sent her the musical greeting card.

The one who wanted her dead.

Forcing Danny Long's genial choir-boy features from her mind, she answered, "I'm not sure. At least until my dad gets back from his honeymoon. They'll be gone for two weeks."

"Morgan's remarrying?"

"Yes, this Friday night."

"I hadn't heard. Then again, it's not as if we move in the same circles."

No, she supposed not.

It had been nearly seventeen years since her mother's death from meningitis, and though Abbie had adored her mother, she was glad her dad had found Miriam to share his life. At sixty—and with Abbie living and working in Los Angeles—her father wouldn't be alone.

"Actually," she said, acutely aware of Jace's leg between hers again, "I tried to back out, but Dad insisted that Paul—Dr. Bryant—needed a dinner date."

"And how like you to oblige him."

Abbie jerked her gaze up to his, hearing what he hadn't said. *Sweet little Abbie, always doing her daddy's bidding.* And finally she knew what this dance was all about.

"All right," she returned quietly. "Let's get this over with. Does your asking me to dance mean that the cold war is over, or that it's just regaining stre—"

With a loud crack, something exploded behind them, and Abbie lunged forward, her arms circling his neck in a stranglehold.

"Abbie?" Shocked by her reaction and more concerned than he wanted to be, Jace stilled, then slowly tightened his arms around her. "Hey," he said softly as laughter and apologies erupted behind them. "You're okay. That was nothing. One of the waiters just lost a bottle of champagne from his tray."

It took more than a moment for his words to sink in. Then, flushing deeply, she seemed to regain her composure and put some distance between them again. "Well," she murmured, "that was embarrassing. I'm sorry. I was just a little startled."

Jace searched her dark eyes as they began to move to the music again. "That's not true. You're shaking. And if that was startled, I'd hate to see terrified. What are they doing to you in L.A.?"

"Nothing," she replied brightly. "I told you, I was just surprised." The band finished to a smattering of applause, and Abbie put her hands together, too—a little too energetically, Jace thought.

Smiling again, she backed away. "I should get back to my table and let you get on with your evening. Thank you for the dance."

"You're welcome," he replied, still disturbed by the fear he'd seen in her eyes and damning himself for caring. "Enjoy the rest of your visit."

"I will. And it really was nice to see you again."

He should've let her walk away. That would've been the smart thing to do—the *intelligent* thing to do. Then Jace caught sight of Morgan's black eyes and beet-red face, and the past came roaring back. Tossing good sense out the door, he called her name, caught her fingertips…and drew her back to him.

Then his mouth was covering hers, and a tingle he hadn't counted on was sweeping through his system. Jace jerked away. For a second their gazes locked, and that old breathless current flowed between them. The same snap and sizzle they'd fought from the moment they'd met so long ago. Then he pulled himself together, forced a smile and started away. "See you around," he called. "Give my regards to your dad."

He'd barely stepped into the crisp March air when he heard the country club's door bang open again.

"What was that all about?" she shouted, swiftly closing the distance between them as he strode to his SUV.

He glanced behind him. A thin coating of old snow crunched beneath her strappy open-toed high heels as she crossed the parking lot.

"Was it payback? Restitution for something that happened *fourteen years ago?* My God, Jace, when are you going to get past that?"

Ignoring her, he pulled his keys from his pocket and pointed the remote at his black Explorer. The taillights flashed as the doors unlocked.

"Because if ticking off my dad was what that kiss was about," she continued when he faced her, "it was one of the most asinine displays of childishness I've ever witnessed!"

"Yes, it was," he agreed calmly, opening his door. "But

I must say it felt good. Now, you'd better get back inside before you freeze."

"I intend to. But you need to know something before you leave." She held his gaze in the amber spill of the light poles. "If you wanted to poke my father with a stick, dancing with me would've done the trick. You didn't have to kiss me. And that makes me wonder why you felt the need to do it."

Sending her a dry look, Jace climbed into his SUV. "Believe me, I wouldn't have if the only thing he'd done to me was run me off the night I stole his little girl's virginity."

Some of the anger drained from her face. "What did he do?"

Jace fired the engine, lowered his window and shut the door.

"Tell me," she insisted, her breath clouding before her. "You can't drop something like that in my lap, then leave."

Shaking his head, he dropped the SUV into gear. "You'll have to ask him. Then ask him if it made a damn bit of difference."

Minutes later, she was pulling her father away from his plumed and ruffled fiancée and doing just what Jace had suggested. She didn't let go of him until they'd reached a vacant back table littered with coffee cups, confetti and sparkling Mardi Gras beads. "What did you do to Jace?"

Morgan Winslow stared down at his daughter, tension still glinting in his dark eyes. At nearly six feet, with a thickening jaw and midsection, he appeared to be in no mood to be cross-examined by his only child. "I don't know what you're talking about, and I'm still angry with you for running after that presumptuous wood hick. He may have cleaned up on the outside, but underneath that rented tuxedo he's still trailer trash."

"Dad, stop it. What did you do to him? And don't say nothing, because I know better. He's still angry, and that anger's directed at you, not me—though God knows I deserve it."

"It *was* nothing. He came to me for a business loan, and for the sake of the stockholders, I had to act responsibly. He simply resents the fact that I turned him down."

"No. There's more to it than that. *How* did you turn him down? What did you say to him?"

For a moment she doubted that he'd reply. Then he said in a righteous tone, "I told him that my bank didn't loan money to people who couldn't pay it back—that his background made him a bad credit risk, and that he wouldn't get the money from any other bank in town, either."

Abbie's jaw sagged. "And you made sure of that?"

He didn't answer, but Abbie knew it was so. Then she took into account Jace's bearing, his clothing, the new SUV he drove and the high price tag on this annual charity event…and she knew he'd done well with his life. "He got the loan anyway, didn't he?" she said. "Somewhere out of town? And his credit was flawless, wasn't it?"

Morgan's gaze hardened. "I don't know a thing about the man *or* his business."

Abbie released a tattered breath. "Dear God, no wonder he's angry. You're still making him pay for that night in the gazebo."

"I prefer not to think about that night, if you don't mind. Now, let's return to our table. Dr. Bryant, Miriam and the others will be wondering what's keeping us."

Abbie shook her head. "You go ahead. Suddenly I don't feel much like partying. I'm going back to the house."

"*Now?* It's not even ten o'clock. And how do you propose to do that? This isn't Los Angeles. You won't find a cab here."

She knew that. Laurel Ridge, Pennsylvania, wasn't large enough to support a taxi service. "I'll walk."

Anger flashed through her father's eyes again. They both knew she couldn't walk the three miles to the Winslow home in the dark, especially dressed the way she was.

Taking the keys to his Lexus from his pocket, he spoke impatiently. "I'll tell the others that you're not feeling well, and ride back with Miriam."

Abbie accepted the keys. Everyone would know that was a lie, but at this point, she didn't care. Suddenly her mind was reeling with questions, and they all concerned Jace. "I'll see you in the morning, Dad."

Twenty minutes later, Abbie had reset the security system, pulled on a robe and was curled in the deepviolet chair beside the white nightstand in her bedroom. Eagerly, she pulled the phone book from the drawer. Her mother had decorated the room when she was in high school, and it was still lovely. Over the years, her dad had suggested that they remodel, but Abbie had steadfastly refused. She loved the white walls and violet-sprinkled pattern on the fussy voile curtains, bedspread and pillow shams. Loved the plush, deep-violet rugs on the hardwood floor. Not because she still gravitated toward the frilly. She loved it because her mother had worked so hard to make it pretty for her, and sometimes she still missed her mom terribly.

Abbie flipped quickly through the phone book's pages to the Rs, and seconds later, found a listing for Rogan

Logging & Lumber. The location was the same as the company Jace had worked for right out of high school. *The place they'd met her senior year.* She'd needed information on the lumber industry for a term paper, and the company's owner, Jim Freemont, had assigned Jace the job of answering her questions and showing her around.

The chemistry between them had been swift, nerve-thrumming and irresistible. To his credit—and Abbie's frustration—while she was in high school, Jace had never let it go beyond a few hungry kisses. He was older and blue-collar, he'd told her. She was Morgan Winslow's college-bound princess.

Swallowing, Abbie turned to the yellow pages and read his ad.

Wholesale Timber and Kiln-dried Lumber. We Deliver Locally.

Below that, in smaller print, it read:

Owned and Operated by Ty & J.C. Rogan.

A warm run of satisfaction moved through her. He'd bought out his boss. And he'd done it despite her father's best efforts to stop him.

Abbie slipped the book back into the drawer, her mind turning back to that warm August night before she'd returned to college to start her sophomore year. How far Jace had come since then. How far they'd both come.

She'd tried not to think about that night after she'd gone back to school. It had hurt and shamed her too much to dwell on what she'd done.

She'd never regretted making love with him; that part

had been wonderful, because after the quick flash of pain, she'd been awash with such feelings of tenderness and completion, she'd wanted to stay in his arms forever. But it wasn't to be.

The room blurred as tears filled her eyes and suddenly Abbie saw her father step through the patio door to see why the pool lights were on. *"Abbie? Abbie! Are you out here?"*

Oh, yes…she'd been there. Forty short yards away in the gazebo, she'd pressed a horrified finger to Jace's lips and prayed that, without an answer, her dad would go back inside and they'd have a chance to dress. Then her father started up the knoll toward them, and she'd had to beg him not to come any closer.

Her dad's disillusionment when they finally appeared turned to rage when he saw she'd been with Jillie Rae Rogan's bastard son. Especially since weeks before, he'd seen them talking at the fair and warned Abbie to stay away from him. *When you lie down with dogs, you get up with fleas.*

"You knew I'd be home by eleven," Abbie heard her father thunder again, speaking as if Jace wasn't there. "You wanted me to see this! Dammit, Abbie, you deliberately dragged that kid back here to rub my nose in it!"

The betrayal in Jace's eyes nearly destroyed her. "Jace, he's wrong!" she'd cried. "I swear it!"

"Am I?" her father raved on. "You've been rebellious all summer. Well, fine. From now on you make your own choices and to hell with what I think. But if you ever see him again, you'll never get another dime from me for your education. You want to go back to college? You want to go to law school? It's your choice. Just remember that his mother was a whore and he'll never be anything better!" Then, swiping a dismissing hand in the air, he'd stalked back to the house. A moment later, Jace was gone, too.

Abbie lolled her head back in the violet chair, tears running from the corners of her eyes, feeling as spent tonight as she'd felt fourteen years ago. He'd never let her explain. Not then, not when she'd phoned him and not when she'd tried to see him at work. Now, when she considered her father's financial blackballing, it was easy to see why he'd acted the way he had tonight.

Abbie touched her lips. She could still feel the tender pressure of his mouth…still feel the rise in her stomach, still feel the strength of his arms after that champagne bottle smashed. He'd been her friend, her lover. And she'd hurt him terribly.

Her cell phone rang. Slowly, Abbie left the chair to remove it from the charger on her dresser. After wiping her eyes and clearing her throat, she checked the caller ID window. And for the second time that night, fear rippled through her. Unfolding the phone, she spoke quickly.

"Stuart, what's happened?" She'd already spoken to him today, and a second call—especially this late—was unusual.

The elderly senior partner of her law firm replied in a kind, soothing voice. "First, calm down. What I have to say is nothing for you to be concerned about."

But it had been important enough for him to contact her well after ten o'clock, and that made her question his statement. Abbie drew a breath, then swallowed. "Okay, I'm calm. Tell me."

"They had to release him, Abbie. They couldn't hold him any longer. Detectives Powell and Rush searched his apartment from top to bottom and found nothing to link him to the shooting or the greeting card you received."

Abbie's heart raced. She'd been dreading this, but she couldn't say she hadn't expected it. "I guess that means they didn't find Maryanne Richards's gold cross and chain, either."

"No."

"Is he still under surveillance?" Since the trial had ended, Powell and Rush, the officers who'd originally arrested him, had blatantly dogged Danny Long's steps, hoping he'd do something to justify locking him up again. They'd yanked him in for lineups on every peeping, rape and homicide case in the past four weeks. And Danny had smiled sweetly through all of it.

"Yes, he's still being watched. I understand that at the moment, he's tucked away in his apartment." A hint of discomfort entered his tone. "Unfortunately, Mr. Long's new attorney has threatened the city with a harassment suit if Powell and Rush don't back off, so your friends in the department will be watching him from a distance now."

When she didn't reply, Stuart seemed to read her mind. "Abbie, you're safe where you are, and getting him off the street has become a priority with many officers who respect what you—" he halted abruptly, then finished cautiously "—what you might have done."

Abbie sighed, guilt joining her anxiety. Stuart knew she'd done it, but he'd never asked because he also knew she wouldn't lie to him. To admit her sin, and have him do nothing would put him in a grave position with the bar. "Please thank them for me," she murmured.

"I already have—for both of us. I want that sick animal behind bars as badly as you do."

Abbie doubted that. Stuart was the dearest, most supportive man she'd ever known. But he wasn't being stalked by a disturbed twenty-three-year-old in a red baseball cap who'd raped and murdered, and he hadn't been the target of sniper fire. She had—two nights ago, outside her apartment, on the same day she'd received the pretty musical greeting card with the cheery—and chilling—sentiment. *Can't wait to see you again.*

They weren't the exact words her client had used as he left the courtroom a free man, but they were close enough to stop her heart. Danny's blond hair, glassy blue gaze and saccharine smile coalesced in Abbie's mind, and goose-flesh prickled over every square inch of her.

Stuart's voice gentled. "Have you heard from Collin?"

She nearly laughed. "Stuart, he didn't have time for me when we were married. Why would he contact me now?"

"Simple courtesy?" he returned, obviously annoyed. "He lives and works here in the city, so he's aware you've had trouble."

"Believe me," she said truthfully, "I'm not losing sleep over Collin's lack of courtesy." Tires crunched in the circular driveway below. Moving to her bedroom window, Abbie peered down and saw headlights approach. "Stuart, I need to say good-night now. My dad and his fiancée just came home, and I'd rather not be discussing this when they come inside."

"You haven't told them?"

"I haven't told anyone—especially them. I didn't see any reason to put a damper on their wedding or their honeymoon cruise, especially since they aren't at risk. My dad can be impossible, but he loves me in his own way. If he knew there'd been an attempt on my life, he'd cancel the cruise and sit on me until the danger had passed—even though he and Miriam have been looking forward to this for months."

Stuart's tone held a hint of reproach. "As a father and grandfather myself, I don't believe he should be kept in the dark. But, of course, that's your prerogative. Now…try to enjoy this time with your family, stay there where you're safe and trust that we'll handle things on this end."

"I'll try. Good night. And thank you for being such a good friend."

"You're very welcome, my girl," he murmured, then hung up.

Abbie closed her phone and returned it to the charger, a shiver racking her as her mind overflowed with thoughts of courtrooms and juries and friendships and bullets… And then, finally, Jace. She'd thought often about how a meeting between them would go if they ever spoke again. But in her imagination, she'd always made sure it went well. Tonight…tonight had hurt.

There was nothing she could do about the situation in L.A. but wait and hope. But maybe she *could* do something about this fourteen-year-old mess.

Really? a small voice inquired. *Or do you just want to see him again? You're still thinking about that kiss.*

"Shut up," she muttered. She had enough to deal with right now without hoping for more than an uneasy truce. And it would be uneasy. He wasn't the type to forgive and forget fourteen years of resentment at the drop of an apology.

There was a light knock at her door, followed by her father's low voice. Though it was gruff, she heard a faint softening in it. "Abbie? Miriam's putting a pot of decaf on. If you like, you can join us downstairs for coffee and dessert."

They'd just had dessert at the country club, but earlier, Miriam had mentioned buying petits fours so they'd have something to nibble after the gala.

Abbie crossed the oak floor and opened the door. After more courtroom confrontations than she could count, she did her best to avoid them in her personal life, and tonight was no exception. Besides, this was the closest her father was ever going to come to an apology.

He was still in costume but, wigless now, his thinning salt-and-pepper hair stuck to his scalp.

"Coffee, huh?" she said.

"Yes, some damn thing called chocolate-raspberry truffle. If you're game, she's grinding the beans now."

Abbie worked up a smile she didn't feel, determined to salvage at least part of the night. Determined to put Danny Long out of her mind. "Of course, I'm game. I live in the nutcase capital of the world. Just give me a minute to jump into sweats, and I'll be down."

Grinning, Danny clicked on the light beside his unmade sleeper sofa and turned up the volume on his thirteen-inch TV—just in case the cops sitting at the end of the street felt like ignoring the order to keep their distance. Then he slipped his black hoodie over his T-shirt, pulled the hood over his hair and slung the strap of his crammed duffel bag across his chest.

He crossed to the rear window in his second floor efficiency apartment.

It was dark now, but the moon was high. Luckily, the only people in his neighborhood who went out after eleven o'clock were the druggies and the hookers who worked the streets. Raising the window, Danny eased himself through the opening, stepped onto the sloping back porch roof, then pulled the window shut. Usually, he left it open a crack, but tonight he wouldn't have to. He wouldn't be coming back.

Backing off the roof, he reached into the rainspout for the plastic sandwich bag he'd taped there, stuffed it in his pocket…and dropped soundlessly to the grass below.

Then he headed for the shack where heroine addict Eddie Parker lived with his girlfriend Leticia. Last year, he'd caught Eddie shoplifting cold medicine for resale at Danny's ex-workplace but hadn't turned him in. Two-time loser Eddie had been so grateful he hadn't gone to jail, he'd promised Danny the moon. He'd phoned Eddie earlier from one of the three track phones he'd bought at a discount electronics place and, big surprise, Eddie needed money again. Which worked out great for both of them because Danny needed Eddie's crappy yellow ninety-four Olds Cutlass.

He also needed a favor and knew Eddie wouldn't refuse.

When he got there forty minutes later, Eddie was in a bad way, chewing gum hard and talking fast as Danny clued him in behind Eddie's whitewashed block bungalow.

Eddie swiped at the perspiration over his lip, light from inside the house illuminating his small, fidgety build. "Okay. Yeah, I can do that," Eddie said. "When do you want me to go by your place?"

"Tomorrow—after dark. Use the side stairs. Walk around in front of the windows, turn on the TV. Then, around midnight, shut off the lights like you're going to sleep. The unmarked cop car I told you about will be sitting at the end of the street. Don't leave until it does—and don't let anybody see you up close."

Reaching into his duffel, Danny handed over one of his track phones, his red San Francisco 49ers ball cap and a box of hair bleach that would turn Eddie into a blonde. "Keep the phone with you," he ordered. "I'll call you the next time I need your help. Every time you do me a favor, I'll send you one hundred dollars. But don't go wearing the hat and showing yourself around unless I tell you to. And don't say you did what I asked if you didn't, because I'll know."

Nodding, licking his lips, Eddie took the five one hundred dollar bills Danny separated from the wad in his jeans pocket, then turned over the keys to the Olds.

"It's all gassed up, Danny."

"Good. One more thing. Don't tell Leticia about this." Then Danny remembered to smile—be charming and caring. "Hey, Eddie?"

"Yeah?"

"Take care of yourself while I'm gone, buddy."

Two hours later, heading east on I-15, the breathless tickle in his belly became too much, and Danny pulled to the side of the road, stripped off his sweatshirt and took a roll of clear utility tape from his pack. Then he reached in his pocket for the sandwich bag. His pulse quickened as two shiny gold crosses and chains slid out and curled into his palm.

Suddenly, tears welled in his eyes, and he eased his head back against the seat. Maryanne had seemed so pure, so sweet, so perfect for him. But, like his mother and Prudence, she'd betrayed him, singing like an angel in church…then giving it up to any guy who bought her a burger and fries when the last note left her lying lips.

He stopped crying immediately and raised his chin. He'd loved her—loved her blindly, just like he'd loved Prudence—but she'd lied, and she'd gotten what she deserved. Clicking on the dome light, Danny slipped Prudence's chain and cross around his neck and felt that excitement in his blood again. Then he reexamined the broken chain he'd torn from Maryanne's throat. He'd fix it later, but for now…

Lifting his white T-shirt, he ripped off a section of tape, then pressed the necklace above his left nipple and sealed it to his skin. A tingle moved through him.

Yesterday, he'd found out that his lying, betraying bitch of an ex-lawyer had left town and it could be weeks until she came back. The whiner in the next cell had made a big stink when somebody else from Braddock and McMillain showed up to take his case. The whiner wanted *her* and only her.

Danny pulled his sweatshirt back on, then dropped the Cutlass into gear and eased out on the road again. Too bad for the whiner.

He had a few things to do first—plans to make and information to gather. But when he was through with Abbie Winslow, there wouldn't be enough of her left over for an autopsy.

Chapter 2

At eight o'clock the next morning, skinny little Ida Fannin swept through Jace's always open door as he was searching his desk for a file he'd misplaced. Her cheeks were cherub rosy and specks of glitter from last night's festivities still sparkled in her curly gray hair.

"Good morning," she sang out happily, then placed a mug of coffee beside the one already sitting on his desk. "How are you this crisp, lovely day?"

Jace stared curiously, wondering what had put the extra spring in her step this morning. Whatever it was, he needed some. He was exhausted. He'd been awake half the night thinking about things he shouldn't give a damn about. Eventually, he'd given up on sleep and come into the office, just in time to help pull Farr Canada's seventy-two thousand board feet of red oak out of the number three kiln and slide the next load in.

"Morning, Ida. I'm okay. Did you enjoy yourself last night?" At nearly seventy, his office manager still wore makeup, and today, pale blue eye shadow and pink lipstick picked up the colors in her polyester pantsuit.

"Oh, my, yes," she exclaimed. "The decorations were so bright and pretty, and the music was delightful. I'm eager to see what the food bank's take will be."

"Same here. There's a chance we could know by tonight's meeting." For the past five years—since he and Ty had bought the business—they'd reserved a company table for the annual charity ball. Jace usually passed on the event, but this year, it had benefited the food bank, and he was on the board. A lot of years had passed since his childhood in Jillie Rae's trailer, but he still remembered what it was to go hungry.

Ida continued to grin expectantly, almost as though she were waiting for an announcement. Just before she launched into another spate of happy chirping, Jace realized what it was, and cringed inside.

"I couldn't help noticing that *your* night took a better turn as you were leaving. Before that, I expected you to bolt every time someone opened a door."

Hoping to change the subject, he rolled his chair away to check a drawer in the filing cabinet behind him. "Ida, have you seen—?"

"The Farr Canada paperwork? Yes, it's right here in your Out tray." By the time he'd shut the drawer and turned around, it was on his desk blotter. "They'll be picking up their load on Tuesday."

Smiling, he wondered again why he even bothered to double-check these things. "Anything else going on that I should know about?"

"Nope."

But she still refused to move a happy little muscle, and he finally decided to just get the interrogation over with. "Okay, what?"

"I didn't realize you knew Morgan Winslow's daughter!"

Paging through the work order and documentation on drying time, he grumbled, "I don't."

"I see," she bubbled gleefully. "Then you just stumbled into her last night and landed on her lips." Ignoring the bland look he sent her, she added, "You know, I heard she married a California attorney a few years ago, but that must over now, because—"

He sighed. "Ida, I really need to look these over."

"—because she's waiting to see you."

Jace jerked his head up. "What?"

"Abbie Winslow. She's waiting in the reception area. Such a pretty thing. The coffee I brought in is for her."

Adrenaline prickled over every bone, muscle and hair follicle Jace owned as the image of Abbie in that backless gown filled his mind, and the unexpectedly visceral sensation of kissing her again hit him like a sledgehammer.

Slowly, he unrolled the sleeves of his pale blue oxford cloth shirt, buttoned his cuffs and stood to grab his olive corduroy jacket from the back of his chair. There was no point in telling Ida that she should've told him sooner; she was the glue that held the place together, and did things in her own sweet time. Some days he and Ty felt like they worked for her. "Send her back, Ida."

She gave him another of her tickled-pink looks as he walked around his desk to stand beside the door. "I'll just do that."

The polished pine hall beyond the door wasn't long, but when Abbie appeared a moment later, Jace still had time for a good look. Topped by a long, snow-white knitted scarf, her knee-length black-and-gray herringbone coat hung open, and beneath it she wore black wool slacks and a pearl-gray turtleneck. Parted in the middle, her long auburn hair curved around her forehead and high cheekbones, then fell sleek and shiny on either side of her upturned collar. She looked expensive. And very beautiful.

"Hi," she said quietly, and Jace decided she'd come bearing white doves and an olive branch.

"Hello, Abbie." When she'd stepped inside, he closed that always open door.

"The place looks good, Jace. Bigger, more organized. I'm happy for you."

"Thanks. We're doing all right." Even when he'd worked here as a logger, the company had been a viable business. Now, with all the improvements and newly erected kilns, Rogan was quickly becoming one of the most respected logging and lumber companies in Northwest Pennsylvania. And, thank God, profits were good. Between Ty's talent for finding new customers, and a cherry-, oak- and maple-hungry public, they'd never had a problem meeting their mortgage payments.

But he'd bet their new skidder she wasn't here to check out the place.

"What's on your mind?" Her dark eyes looked a little tired, and considering the night he'd spent, Jace felt a run of satisfaction.

"You know why I'm here. That business last night was awkward."

"If you want an apology because I used you to get to your father, you're not going to get one. I figure we're even now. You used me, I used you; quid pro quo." He returned to his desk, then nodded toward the chair and the white mug on her side of it. "Have a seat if you want. The coffee's yours. Ida brought it in."

"Thank you, but I won't be here long enough to drink it. I came to apologize for a very stupid thing I did well over a decade ago. I tried to explain then, but you wouldn't hear me out."

"Abbie, it's been way too long to get into all of this again."

Her soft tone nearly got to him. Nearly. "Has it? It didn't seem that way last night. It's time we put this thing behind us."

Jace felt his nerves knot. He thought he *had* put it behind him. Then he'd seen her father's smugly approving smile as she'd danced with an *acceptable* suitor, and his old outcast status had risen up and grabbed him where he lived.

"Whatever. I don't feel the need to go into it, but if you have something to say, the floor's yours."

Frustration lined her face for a second, then she let it go and moistened her lips. "You know what a control freak my dad's been since my mother died."

He nodded, thinking that was putting it mildly.

"I needed some space from that. I know raising a daughter alone had to have been an enormous responsibility. But I was just so tired of being told what to think, what to say and who I could and couldn't see that I had to make it clear to him that I was an adult now—and I was going to live my life in my own way."

"So you decided to bed me in your gazebo and wait for your dad to come home."

"No! Maybe I did coax you back to the house so he'd find us together. But not consciously, and not in the scheming, conniving way you think. I cared about you, Jace. I wouldn't have slept with you just to spite my father. In fact, once we started making lo—" She halted before she finished the word. "Well," she said, dropping her voice, "my father was the furthest thing from my mind." She glanced down at the black leather gloves she held, then met his eyes again. "And, if you'll recall, I only suggested that we take a swim."

Yes, that's what she'd said that night. She'd said there were spare swim trunks in the cabana—that he didn't even have to go home to get his. Then she'd given him the tour of the picnic grotto and gazebo behind the Winslow's fancy estate, and they'd never made it to the pool.

His intercom buzzed. Holding her gaze, Jace depressed the button. "Yes, Ida?"

"I wouldn't have disturbed the two of you for the world, honey, but there's a lawyer on the phone."

"Our attorney?"

"No, one of those personal injury lawyers. It's about the accident."

Jace swore softly. "Get his number and tell him I'll call him back."

Abbie watched him break the connection, then briefly massage the tension over his eyes. "Trouble?"

"Maybe. One of our men was hurt yesterday, and it looks like he'll be laid up for a few months. The thing is, we're friends. It's not like him to latch on to an ambulance chaser."

Abbie let the reference slide. By now, she was used to snide remarks and lawyer jokes. "If you're covering his medical expenses, and the equipment he was using wasn't faulty, you probably don't have much to worry ab—" She stopped herself. "Sorry, occupational hazard. You have your own attorney. It's not my place to comment."

"That's right," he said glibly, "it isn't. God knows I wouldn't want you to do anything unethical." But despite his words, the implication was that she had. Fourteen years ago. And to her chagrin, it hurt.

Abbie drew a breath and let it out silently. All right, she'd tried. Now it was time to go. He still believed she'd orchestrated that awful night, but with all the turmoil in her life now, she had to take her own advice and let it go, no matter how much she wanted to resolve this. She just didn't have the energy to fight wars on two emotional fronts.

Clearing her throat, she buttoned her coat and pulled on her gloves. "Know what?" she murmured. "I should have my head examined for coming here. Lately, everything I do with the greater good in mind backfires badly. Goodbye, Jace."

Jace watched her open the door and walk to the front of the building. Then the illogical urge to follow her pushed him out of his chair. He still didn't believe her story, but he could've treated her better.

Ida buzzed him again as he rounded his desk. He jabbed the intercom button.

"It's that lawyer again, Jace. He wants the name of the company's attorney. He said he doesn't have time to sit on his hands waiting."

"Tell him I'll call him back in ten minutes," he returned impatiently. "If he gets nasty, hang up on him, and if he phones again, don't pick up. Check the caller ID before you answer." Then he strode out to the reception area, and stood at one of their new plate-glass windows.

Outside, two six-foot-high, carved-wood grizzlies flanked the door. The wind gusted around them, picking up clouds of snow and nearly obscuring the mammoth steel buildings housing the kilns and sawmill. Then taillights flashed red in the grainy mist and Jace knew he'd missed her.

Swearing under his breath, he retraced his steps, picking up curious looks from their staff forester and a couple of guys from the mill.

"Ida," he said, approaching her desk, "get our new friend on the phone for me, please. Then track down Ty. If he's not at his place, he's probably with the girl from last night."

"Ginger."

"Yeah, her," he said, annoyed with Ty's cavalier lifestyle and wondering why his equipment hadn't fallen off yet. "I know this is his late day, but tell him I need him now. Playtime's over."

You're just ticked off because it's been six months since you got laid.

Probably, he decided, entering the rear office and dropping into his chair. But that wasn't the reason for the clutching in his gut this morning. Then his gaze settled on that mug full of coffee, Abbie's big doe eyes and full mouth came to mind…and he had to admit that maybe it was. He'd been a total ass, but she and her father had damn near eviscerated him that night and the pain had lasted a very long time.

Ida buzzed him. "Mr. Cleaver's on the line."

Cleaver. How appropriate. "Thanks," he said, then picked up the phone and tried to be civil. "Mr. Cleaver. What can we do for you?"

An hour later, with Ty overseeing things, Jace tore out of the lot and headed for their lawyer's office. They needed to nip this thing in the bud. He doubted Cleaver could make a suit stick because there was no way Jace could see that the company had been negligent. But the price Cleaver had named for an out-of-court settlement was robbery, and he had to know for sure. Damn lawyers.

More to the point, damn lawyer, because he couldn't get Abbie out of his mind. Worse, every time he thought of her—disturbing as it was to admit—memories rose, his blood heated and he felt that old gut-gnawing pull again.

That night, still disturbed over her morning meeting with Jace, Abbie locked her dad's SUV and strode quickly across the windy lot to the fire hall. After hearing Miriam mention that help was needed with the town's annual Friends Without Families Easter dinner, Abbie had decided to attend tonight's meeting and offer her services. She'd be back in L.A. before Easter, but she'd worked the event when she was in high school and looked forward to doing whatever she could while she was here.

She tucked her chin deep into her collar. Situated near the river on the town's outskirts, it was a low, sprawling red-brick building, recently erected after a long fund-raising drive. According to Miriam, it was paying for itself nicely with rentals from weddings and other community events. Coming inside, Abbie wiped her boots on the mat, got her bearings in the reduced lighting, then headed for the room at the end of the corridor and the low hum of voices.

The cell phone in her shoulder bag rang. Taking it from the side flap, she frowned at the Number Unavailable message in the ID window, flipped it open and said hello.

A chillingly familiar voice stroked her ear, and the bottom fell out of her stomach.

"I just came from your place, counselor, but you weren't home." Danny Long's laughter raised gooseflesh the entire length of her. "Where are you?"

Abbie dropped the phone and it clattered and skittered over the tile floor. Quickly retrieving it, she stabbed the

End button to break the connection, then stabbed it again to shut it off permanently.

For a moment she couldn't do anything but shake. Then, spotting a haven of sorts a few yards away, she hurried into the ladies' room, locked the door and wilted against it.

She should have changed her cell number! Why hadn't she thought of that? She rarely gave the number to clients, but Danny had been—no, *had seemed*—so fragile and ruined over Maryanne's death, she'd made an exception in his case. In doing that, she'd given him a pipeline directly to her.

But not for long.

Trembling, she turned her cell back on, then speed-dialed Stuart, knowing he'd still be at the office.

"I just heard from him," she said when he answered. "He called my cell phone. Stuart, he said he was at my apartment today. Is that possible? Could he—" She shook her head. "I don't know. Could he have *done* something in there?" She lived in a secure building, but Danny was a manipulative charmer, and he was capable of fooling people. He'd certainly fooled her.

"Anything's possible," the elderly attorney returned, his agitation evident. "But I suspect he was lying. Did he threaten you in any way?"

"No." And that meant there was no crime. Stalking was a difficult charge to prove. She'd given Danny her number willingly, which gave him the right to use it, and there was no law against a former client calling to say hello.

Stuart spoke again. "I'll have security check your apartment and get back to you. In the meantime, you need to change your cell phone number."

"I'll do it first thing in the morning."

"Good." He paused then, his voice lowering in grandfatherly concern. "Abbie, are you all right?"

"Yes. Yes," she repeated through a breath. "I'm fine. At least, I will be in a minute." Then again, how fine could she be when she was hiding out in a restroom? "But now that I'm thinking more clearly, I feel like a fool for bothering you with this. I'll call building security myself."

"As you wish," he said gently. "But it would've been no trouble. I want to help in any way I can."

"I know," she murmured, "and that means more to me than I can say." She inhaled deeply. "Stuart, I need to make that call now."

"Call me back."

"I will."

Minutes later, after she'd learned that Danny *had* lied about going to her apartment, they'd spoken again. Stuart had made a phone call, too, bringing the detectives up to speed, though they'd said there was little they could do. Then Stuart had pressed her again to put the whole thing out of her mind and do something that would make her smile.

Smiling was a stretch, she decided. Especially when seven pairs of eyes turned from the table when she entered the meeting room—but only six of them were welcoming.

She nearly walked back out.

Ida Fannin rocketed out of her seat and rushed to greet her. "Abbie, what a lovely surprise! How nice of you to join us! Give me your coat, then help yourself to the coffee and donuts. Sorry, but they're all glazed. I don't like making food decisions when I'm in a hurry."

Feeling a bit glazed herself, Abbie slipped off her coat and Ida wrestled it from her hands. Could this night get any worse? "Ida, I'm afraid I'm late. Maybe I should—"

"Go? Goodness, no. We're just trying to decide who's going to handle publicity for the event. Everyone," she called out, crossing to the coatrack, "this lovely young woman is Morgan Winslow's daughter, Abbie. A few of you might remember her. She lives and works in Los Angeles now, but she's come home for her daddy's wedding."

Then she made the introductions, and before Abbie could draw more than a half dozen breaths, Ida had her in a seat across from Jace.

Her frazzled nerves frayed a little more. Few men could look darkly dangerous, sexy and utterly delicious all at the same time. But as Abbie took in his thick, collar-skimming black hair, compelling gaze and the grim curve of his mouth, she had to admit that Jace pulled it off without breaking a sweat. Then again, in her mind, he always had. Tonight he wore an open-throated black polo shirt that clung to his broad shoulders and drew her gaze to the muscular arms that had held her last night.

"Hello, again," he said politely, then pushed to his feet. He scanned her jeans and hip-length burgundy sweater. "How did you hear about us?"

"My dad's fiancée. Miriam knows I like to be busy, and she thought volunteering would give me something to do while I was in town."

His mouth twisted with irony, and his dark brows lifted. "Imagine that."

"Yes," she murmured. "Imagine."

His gaze shifted to Ida, who was pulling her pen and tablet close again. The next words that passed his lips made Abbie wish she'd stayed in the ladies' room.

"Ida, Abbie and I can handle the publicity. She'll only be here for a short time, and that's a job that can be completed early." He faced her again, but continued to speak to Ida. "Having her on board could be a nice bonus for us. She's connected. She might be able to convince a few of her

country-club friends to make big, tax-deductible donations."

Abbie felt herself pale as all eyes slid her way. "I—I'm
not sure I'm the best person for the job. I've been away
for years, and I'm afraid I don't have many contacts in
town anymore."

Grinning in delight, Ida reached over to pat her hand.
"Then won't it be lovely to get reacquainted, dear? And
if you have questions or problems, Jace will be there to
help."

An hour later, feeling shell-shocked and uneasy, Abbie
said good night to everyone and hurried through the
grainy, swirling snow toward her dad's car. For the life of
her, she couldn't fathom why Jace would suggest they
work together when they needed their own public rela-
tions guru just to keep them from sniping at each other.
Had he done it because they needed the money he
assumed she could get for them? Or was the reason more
personal than that?

Clouds scudded overhead, nearly concealing a handful
of stars and the white quarter-moon. As Abbie hunched
deeper into her upturned collar and knitted scarf, she heard
the crunch of footsteps behind her. After feeling his eyes
on her for the past hour, there was no doubt that those footsteps belonged to Jace. Reaching the SUV, she turned to
see what he wanted.

"You don't have to work with me," he said soberly, his
breath clouding as he approached. "It seemed like a good
idea at the time, but you obviously have reservations. I'll
find someone local who wants to help."

"I didn't say I didn't want to help."

"Neither did I."

"I think you did, and you're wrong. I have no

problem helping with the dinner. You're the reason I have reservations."

"Why?"

"Why?" she repeated. Was his memory that bad? Abbie stared at him for several seconds, then sighed. "Never mind. I have to go."

Pulling up on the door lever, she tried unsuccessfully to open it—tried again, but it still wouldn't budge. "Wonderful," she breathed.

"It's unlocked, right?" he said from behind her.

Irritated that he'd even ask, she kept tugging. "Yes, it's unlocked. It's frozen shut."

"Then stop trying to force it before you break the handle. Let me try."

"No, I'll do it." She was quite sure she could open a door on her own.

"Fine," he replied, "but if you're going to snap a handle, snap a rear one. It'll be less frustrating to deal with while you're waiting to get it fixed."

Shoulders slumping, picturing her dad using one of the other doors to get into his car, she backed away and motioned for Jace to have at it.

In a moment, he'd pounded a fist around the back door to loosen it and opened it easily. Then he crawled inside and shoved the front door open.

"Okay, you're set," he concluded, backing out and waiting for her to slide behind the wheel. "But you'd better put a can of deicer in your purse if you're planning to be here a while."

Nodding, she started the car, then met his gray eyes. To her chagrin, that man-woman thing zipped between them, totally unexpected on the heels of her annoyance. "Thank you—for this, and for keeping me on my feet last night when that champagne bottle hit the floor."

"You're welcome," he returned after a startled second. "Be careful going home."

Abbie nodded. He'd felt that current of awareness, too, but he seemed determined to ignore it, so she would, too.

He was nearly to his own vehicle when she called his name. "Jace, wait."

He walked back, turning up the collar on his brown leather bomber jacket and thrusting his hands into his pockets. Then, somehow, memories of their one unforgettable night together rose in her mind, and Abbie saw him smiling and shirtless, her naive fingers stroking his chest hair.

Her stomach floated. "What do you want to do about the publicity thing? Would you rather partner with someone you'll find it easier to work with?"

"That depends," he replied, managing a small smile. "Are you planning to be difficult?"

Bristling, she lifted her chin. "No. Are you?"

"No."

"All right, then. Where do we go from here? Easter isn't that far off."

Even in the faint moonlight, she saw a challenge rise in his eyes. "I'll phone you at your dad's place and we'll set up something." He paused. "Then again, it might be better if I called your cell. No stress. On anyone."

"If you want to know something, ask."

"All right. Are you planning to tell your dad we'll be seeing each other again?"

"I'm not a child anymore, Jace. Of course I'm going to tell him, and how he handles it is up to him. Now I have a question. Why did you suggest that we work together?

Because of the money you think I can get for the food bank? Or did you just want to take another virtual poke at my father?"

"What do you think?"

She didn't know—or maybe she didn't want to know. "My dad's number is in the book," she replied, already tired of sparring with him. "If I'm not there, leave a message. As for my cell…" Danny's voice came back to her and she felt another pinch of anxiety. "That number will be changing. I'll give you the new one in a day or so."

Then she closed her door, backed out of her parking space and left, a shivery truth once more making itself known. Whether they were fencing with each other, merely breathing the same air…or kissing on a dance floor…the attraction between them was still strong.

Last night at the country club their lips had barely touched, yet something about that kiss had been so tantalizing and provocative, Abbie had felt the power of it in a hundred different places.

An airy thrill moved through her, and she didn't try to discourage it. It had been so long since a man had affected her this way it felt good to know that she was still able to respond. Toward the end of her marriage, she'd begun to worry.

Reaching the downtown area, she passed a short block of businesses, the mini mall, then the movie theater where she and Jace had once snuggled in the dark munching popcorn…and each other. Her nipples hardened.

And suddenly she wondered if her relationship with Collin would've worked if they'd had even a quarter of the chemistry that she and Jace still generated.

Chapter 3

The phone rang Wednesday evening as Abbie lit the tapers on the formal dining room table and called into the family room for her father and Miriam. She'd spent the morning changing her cell phone number and shopping, and the afternoon in the kitchen preparing dinner for the three of them. Now the house was filled with the tangy aromas of baked ham with raisin sauce, yams, chunky homemade applesauce and green beans with slivered almonds. Chocolate mousse was chilling in the refrigerator.

Grumbling that the caller had better not be a telemarketer, her dad veered into the hall, choosing the alternate route to the kitchen phone while Miriam joined Abbie in the Winslows' dining room.

Miriam Abbot was a tall, attractive widow in her late fifties with fashionably short salt-and-pepper brown hair, brown eyes and a winning smile. Two years ago, she'd moved to Laurel Ridge and opened a travel agency in the building across the street from Morgan Winslow's bank, and they'd quickly found enough common ground to form a friendship. Today she wore chocolate-brown wool slacks, topped by an off-white cashmere sweater, gold chains and a silky patterned scarf. Small gold hoops glinted at her earlobes.

"Everything looks and smells wonderful," she said graciously. Her admiring gaze took in the steaming bowls and platters…the fresh flowers and the formal place settings…the gold-edged tea roses on white bone china. "You've gone to so much trouble. I just wish you would've let me help you."

"Believe me," Abbie replied, "I enjoyed being busy." It had been a relief to concentrate on something other than her troubles in L.A. Though security had assured her that nothing had been disturbed in her apartment, hearing Danny's voice last night had started an uneasy feeling in Abbie that wouldn't go away. Meeting Miriam's eyes, she continued. "Besides, I wanted to do something special for the two of you."

"Well, thank you," she returned. "You know, your dad loves having you home. Especially tonight, when you've made his favorite meal."

Scowling, Morgan reentered the spacious dining room and said gruffly, "And I'd prefer to eat that meal while it's hot." Crossing one of the long Persian rugs on the gleaming hardwood, he handed the cordless handset to Abbie. "It's for you," he said brusquely. "Guess who?"

Feeling a rush of nerves, she accepted it and stepped away from the table. She didn't have to guess. The red blotches on her father's cheeks told her that the next voice she heard would be Jace's low baritone.

"You two go ahead and start," she murmured. "I'll be right back." Then she stepped into the pretty oak kitchen and raised the receiver to her ear. In the background, scattered laughter and conversation mingled with bouncy country music. "Hello?"

"Sorry for interrupting your dinner," he said, and Abbie knew instantly that he was either put off by something her father had said, or he hadn't wanted to make the call in the first place. "I won't keep you long."

"No problem, we hadn't started yet."

"Good. I just called to ask when you're free to discuss the publicity for the Friends dinner. As you said, Easter isn't far away."

Abbie drew a breath, startled by the jittery feeling in her chest. She visited jails on a regular basis, faced criminals in interrogation rooms and held her own against the legal sharks on the other side of the courtroom. Yet maintaining her poise around Jace was becoming a real problem. "I'm free anytime, so we can schedule around your day."

"Days won't work. I'm at the business or checking logging sites until after five. But if you'd like to have dinner somewhere or come to my place, I can arrange to be free tomorrow, Saturday after our noon closing or any night next week."

Abbie moved deeper into the kitchen to lean against the butcher-block work island. Conversation had ceased in the dining room, and she could picture her dad doing a slow burn as he tried to eavesdrop. Not that his opinions swayed her anymore. She loved and respected her father, but she was no longer that eager-to-please, motherless teenager. "Which would you prefer?"

"Doesn't matter. It would be more convenient if you came to the house. Then I wouldn't have to drag a folder full of last year's fliers and lists with me—and you wouldn't have to squeeze a notebook in between your coffee cup and water glass." He paused. "But maybe you'd feel more comfortable meeting me somewhere else."

Abbie silently counted to ten. "You really enjoy baiting me, don't you?" The truth was, she wouldn't feel comfortable anywhere with his doubting gray gaze boring into her, but she'd signed on to help and she had no intention of bailing out.

"I'm not baiting you. I'm just trying to arrive at a meeting place, a date and a time."

"All right," she replied evenly. "I'll see you at your place tomorrow night. Seven o'clock. How do I get there?"

Her father's stern voice came from the dining room. "Abbie, we'd like to say the blessing soon." But she didn't answer.

"I'm in the book. It's a log house outside of town on Maxwell Road. You'll know it when you see it. There'll be sap buckets hanging on the maple trees."

He was gathering sap? For maple syrup? Despite the fact that his work revolved around trees and timber, she wouldn't have thought he'd be interested in that sort of thing. Or maybe the interest wasn't his, she thought. Maybe he was gathering it for someone else. Someone female.

An illogical pinch of jealousy bit her and, annoyed, Abbie shook it off. He was entitled to a life. Giving him her virginity fourteen years ago didn't give her any special hold on him—not that she wanted one. He was too stiff and unyielding. Too…something.

"I'll find it," she replied, still curious about the music and noise in the background, still wondering where he was calling from. "I'll see you at seven."

When she walked into the dining room a moment later, her father's cheeks were still red, and Miriam was wearing a wary and confused look. Abbie took her seat, her father said the blessing and she began filling her plate.

Her dad extended the platter of sliced ham. "What did *he* want?"

Abbie took a slice, then drizzled a bit of raisin sauce over it. "I'm helping with the Friends Without Families Easter dinner."

"What does that have to do with him?"

"Jace is on the board of the local food bank, and they're organizing the event."

Abbie caught the sharp surprise in Miriam's eyes. She'd wondered if Miriam had been playing matchmaker when she suggested getting involved in the project, because she'd asked about that kiss. But apparently, her stepmother-to-be had been as clueless about Jace's involvement as Abbie had.

Smiling, but speaking firmly, Abbie glanced at her father again. "We're working on publicity together. I'm seeing him tomorrow night."

His eyes went dead and he sent her a long, steady look that was easy to interpret. *You're thirty-three years old, and I can't tell you what to do anymore. But this does not please me.*

Forty minutes later, when her dad had returned to the family room off the formal living room to read the evening paper, and she and Miriam were straightening the kitchen, Miriam sent Abbie a skeptical look. "Want to tell me what's going on between you and your dad?"

Abbie met her eyes for a moment, then returned the salt and pepper shakers to the cupboard beside the built-in microwave. She wiped a damp dishcloth over the pale blue countertops. "He didn't tell you about Jace and me?"

"When I asked about the kiss at the Mardi Gras party, he muttered something about ancient history. But from his mood tonight—and that phone call—I'm thinking that it's not so ancient." She smiled. "I don't mean to pry—truly. Your business is your business. I'd just rather not spend my honeymoon with a grumpy bear without knowing *why* he's grumpy."

Abbie rinsed the cloth then draped it over the divider in the stainless double sink. Her dad hadn't gotten bullheaded and left the table after Jace's call, and he'd complimented Abbie on the meal. But conversation had been strained despite Miriam's best efforts to shake her father out of his funk. "It's a long story," she murmured.

Miriam smiled. "They're my favorite kind. I don't have anything to do for a while, and we both know that in a matter of seconds, your dad will be reading the newspaper through his eyelids."

Abbie glanced toward the doorway leading to the dining room and the living and family rooms beyond. She wasn't ashamed of what had happened with Jace all those years ago. And she didn't mind telling Miriam about it because she was easy to talk to and they'd already begun to form a relationship based on mutual admiration and respect. But now that the tension in the house was ebbing, she didn't want to be discussing that night in the gazebo if her father came in. This was his home, he'd be getting married in two days and he didn't need to get all worked up again.

Miriam seemed to read her mind. "Know what? I was about to suggest we have another cup of tea, but I don't think either of us is all that thirsty."

Abbie waited through her pause.

"When your dad picked me up after work, he said he'd

had a horrific day. I'm going to tell him that you're driving me home. Unless you'd rather not?"

Abbie knew she meant, *unless you'd rather not tell me the story.* But at this point, she *wanted* to talk about it. "I'd like to drive you home. Unless Dad's not dozing and he'd prefer to do it."

Miriam grinned. "Oh, he's dozing, all right."

Thirty minutes later, Abbie drove west on Maxwell Road beneath an onyx sky and a sparkling canopy of stars. She'd dropped Miriam off in town, and they'd talked the whole way. Though Miriam had given Abbie a few things to think about, she'd consider those things later. Right now she was searching for a log home surrounded by trees dressed in sap buckets. She'd told herself that since he wasn't at home—and she was out and about, anyway—it wouldn't hurt to make a dry run past his house so she could find it easily tomorrow.

But, though a sliver of moonlight reflected off a new dusting of snow, it was hard to see into the wooded landscape where leafless trees were interspersed with towering hemlocks and pines.

Two miles outside of town on the left side of the bumpy, unpaved road, she spotted the first sap bucket just inside the tree line. In a moment, several others glinted in the car's headlights and a rural mailbox appeared.

Rolling to a stop beside his driveway, Abbie lowered her window and peered down the sloping lane. The faint odor of exhaust mingled with the fresh scents of pine and winter, and a faint breeze carried it inside.

Situated in a carved-out section of the woods, his log home stood, its peaked, glass-walled frontage and wide wraparound porch impressive in the glow of roof- and pole-mounted spotlights. Inside, a lamp burned dimly beyond the open drapes, and behind the house and to the right, several outbuildings melted into the trees.

Gripped by curiosity, Abbie continued to stare. They'd gotten a dusting of snow around four o'clock, and Jace's long, plowed driveway was smooth and white, devoid of tire tracks. Obviously, he hadn't returned yet. And now that she'd located his home…she had to turn around somewhere, didn't she?

Shushing the tiny voice that said she was just being nosy, she made a sharp left turn and drove down to the property.

She'd barely reached the wide plowed area around the garage when headlights appeared at the top of the drive and adrenaline jolted through her.

Dammit, dammit, dammit! *Couldn't he have waited five more minutes to come home?*

Quickly, Abbie pulled up to the garage door, backed around, straightened her dad's SUV and shoved it into Park. Then she waited, because there was nothing else she could do.

In a moment, he'd pulled in beside her, their vehicles pointing east and west, driver's-side windows parallel to each other's. Jace lowered his window.

Feeling like the intruder she was, Abbie met his gaze across three feet of cool air.

"You're twenty-two hours early," he said.

"I know. I had to take my dad's fiancée home, and as long as I was out, I thought I'd try to locate your house. I was just turning around."

His brow lined. "Your dad's fiancée lives on this road?"

Abbie understood his confusion. She'd only seen three houses on the way, and they were all at the far end of Maxwell. Except for the dilapidated barn she'd passed a quarter mile down the road, Jace's home was the only building on this stretch of road. "No, she lives in town, but it was a pretty night, and I was at loose ends."

"Why is that?"

"I don't know. I guess I'm still on Pacific time. Everyone else's night is winding down, but it feels like mine's just beginning." She paused as the realization that there wasn't another car, home or person in sight made her feel weightless—made her nerve endings dance. Again, she wondered why she'd never felt this way with Collin.

"Your home's lovely," she said when he didn't move to fill the silence. "Living out this far, I'm surprised that you don't have a gate or a chain across the drive."

"Why?" he asked, faintly amused. "To keep nosy people from invading my space? Gates and chains only make thieves think there's something worth stealing inside."

"Is there?"

"I don't know. What do you consider valuable?"

Life without fear, Abbie thought instantly, recalling why she was a continent away from her life and her friends. "I think the things we consider valuable change from day to day."

"I think you're right." Then he smiled a little and nodded toward the house. "Would you like to come inside? It's a little warmer and more comfortable if we're going to have a philosophical conversation."

Abbie shook her head. "Thanks, but I can't. I told Dad I'd be right back. He'll start thinking I buried his car in a snowdrift if I'm late."

The mention of her father made Jace's smile fade, and suddenly Abbie needed to tell him that she knew about her dad's financial blackballing. "I asked him what he'd done to you."

"Oh?"

"Yes. The night of the gala, you said there was more between the two of you than the gazebo incident."

"It wasn't an incident, Abbie, we had sex."

"All right, we had sex. I just want you to know that I asked, and he admitted that he'd turned down your application for a loan—and the rest of it." She felt a sharp twinge. He hadn't deserved any of the humiliation her father had dished out. "I'm so sorry for that, Jace. But I really don't understand why you'd go to him for money. You had to know how he'd react."

"His bank was advertising low interest on business loans, and I assumed he was a businessman first and a father second. I also assumed I wouldn't be requesting a loan from the bank president, but from a loan officer."

Abbie filled in the rest. As soon as her father saw the name on the loan application, he'd called Jace in and put him in his place. Again.

"I'm glad he didn't derail your plans. The changes I saw when I came by the other day were amazing."

"We're growing. With the kilns we put in two years ago, we employ thirty-five people now. I oversee the lumber end of it and Ty handles the logging. He's turned into a savvy businessman."

"I suspect Ty's big brother knows what he's doing, too," she returned quietly. "I'm happy for both of you."

"Thanks. We're happy for us, too."

Another uneasy silence stretched between them then, and Abbie dropped her father's Ford Expedition into gear. When conversation deteriorated into stock replies, it was time to go. But, hopefully, addressing a bit of the past tonight would make tomorrow night easier on both of them.

She glanced at the digital clock on the dashboard, then back at him. "See you in twenty-one hours and forty-five minutes."

"Yeah. See you then."

Twenty-one hours and forty-five minutes, she thought, following her tracks back up to the road. That was something lovers might say to each other, lovers eager to relive warm, liquid kisses and shivery touches in the dark. Lovers who knew how to smile at each other and never ran out of things to say.

Abbie pressed down harder on the gas pedal as an old longing welled up inside of her, surprising her with its poignancy. Obviously, some lovers were better at those things than others.

Jace unlocked the front door and stepped inside the house, then shrugged out of his leather jacket, kicked off his boots and wandered into his home office. The light on his answering machine was flashing. The first message was from Ty, saying that he was headed to a local watering hole for a beer and a burger and he'd be at Candy's Bar if Jace wanted to join him. The second was from their foster mom and dad who were wintering in Florida.

Betty Parrish's musical laughter spilled from his machine. "Hi, Jacey."

Jace smiled. He'd been Jacey to her ever since he and Ty had gone to live with Betty and Carl after Jillie Rae cut out.

"I just called to give you a weather update," she went on. "It's seventy-four and sunny." She laughed again. "You know, you and Ty could be enjoying some warmer temps, too, if you'd scoot down here for a few days. Now, the campground's having a luau next Friday night and I need a head count. Call me back if you can make it, but do it before eight o'clock." Another laugh. "It's dollar movie night. We're seeing an old Doris Day film. Love you! Bye."

Still smiling, he ambled into the kitchen to fix himself a sandwich. His coupon-clipping foster mom loved a good bargain. Always had. One of the first lessons she'd taught him was, don't squander your money or your talents. At the time, he didn't have any money and he doubted he had talent, so the words hadn't sunk in until at least a decade later.

Jace stared at his reflection in the dark window, his vision blurring as the film strip in his mind rolled back ten years, then twenty…then twenty-four. Images appeared. And suddenly he was twelve years old again and watching nervously for his mother to come back, his hands cupped on another dark window.

Jillie Rae had dropped them off early that morning, saying she was going job hunting and she'd see them around lunchtime. But it was nearly ten o'clock when the phone at old Mrs. Conrad's place finally rang. Scrambling from the glass, he and Ty had stood in the living room of her neat-as-a-pin trailer like proper soldiers, waiting for word that Jillie was on her way.

Mrs. Conrad's shocked voice cut like a laser through Jace's consciousness. "What do you mean, you're not coming back? I can't take care of these kids! I have a heart condition!" Then she'd become angry. "Jillie Rae, you get back here right now. Just clean up your act and catch the next bus home. You brought these children into the world, and they're your responsibility. You need to do right by them!"

Then Ty had started to cry, and Jace had held him and told him it would be okay. Jillie'd come for them. But after Ty finally fell asleep, curled against him on Mrs. Conrad's studio couch, Jace had cried, too, because he was afraid he'd lied. No matter what kind of mother she'd been, no matter that she sometimes passed herself off as their older sister and she wanted them to call her Jillie Rae, she was all they'd had and they'd loved her.

The next day, they'd met a woman from Children's Services and a few hours after that, they'd moved into the Parrish's home on Calendar Street. Betty and Carl had opened their arms to them, and in the process, saved their lives.

They'd never seen Jillie again.

The hum of an engine broke his thoughts. Feeling a quick shot of adrenaline, Jace strode to the front door and looked out. But it wasn't Abbie's SUV. It was Ty's dark gray Silverado. Moments later, his brother was stamping snow from his feet and coming inside.

"Hey," he called.

"Hey, yourself," Jace answered stepping back. "Thought you were hanging out at Candy's tonight. I was there for a few minutes around six, but I didn't see you."

"Yeah, I know. I got tied up."

Jace raised a dubious brow. "A little early in the evening for that sort of thing, isn't it?"

Blue eyes twinkling, Ty slipped off his gray vest and tossed it through the archway to land on Jace's brown leather sofa. "It's never too early. Unfortunately, this kind of tie-up wasn't that much fun."

"Oh? Where were you?"

"The hospital. I wanted to talk to Arnie."

The mood in the room sobered. "Think that was wise?" Jace asked.

"You phoned him," Ty pointed out.

"A phone call's not a visit. We're supposed to steer clear of Arnie. The bloodsucking lawyers are doing the talking."

"I know, but we've known Arnie for a long time, and I wanted to hear what he had to say." Ty inclined his head toward the kitchen. "Got any coffee made?"

Hoping Ty's visit hadn't done more harm than good, Jace started walking. "No, but it'll only take a minute to make some."

"Good. Because we need to talk, and I think better with a mug in my hand."

Minutes later they were standing across from each other at the kitchen bar, ignoring the leather stools, and listening to the spit and splash of coffee brewing on the adjacent countertop.

After height, similar facial structure and the requisite jeans and boots, people had to look hard to see that they were related. Ty's hair was as thick as Jace's, but it was medium brown, not black, and his eyes were the deep blue women loved. But then, women loved everything about his little brother, and Ty felt the same about them. Short, tall, blond, brunette, he enjoyed them all. But he'd never had a serious relationship in his life.

Then again, neither had he, Jace admitted. Not one that had been totally reciprocated. In that way, he and Ty were like their mother. All flings, no strings.

"I don't think this lawsuit is Arnie's idea," Ty began. "I think it's his wife's. Callie's a nice woman, but they've got four kids and I think she's worried that Arnie'll never work again."

Jace nodded gravely. He and Ty understood the need for security more than most people did. Financial *and* emotional. "She could be right." The tree that put Arnie in the hospital had done enough damage to his leg that it would be a minor miracle if he was able to walk again without a cane.

"I've been giving that some thought, though," Jace continued. "If he can't log anymore, we'll find something else for him."

"Not the sawmill. Callie'd never go for that, even with all the safeguards." Leaving the bar, Ty went to the refrigerator to rummage around. When he returned, he was balancing assorted packages of deli cold cuts, cheese and spicy mustard on his arm. "Want a sandwich?"

"No, you go ahead." He wasn't hungry anymore. Now, he just wanted this thing with Arnie Flagg settled in a way that benefited all of them, and he wanted Abbie Winslow to get the hell out of his mind. He could still see her staring through that open window, her hair lifting in the wind and her dark eyes serious.

Ty pulled a loaf of sliced rye from the bread drawer. "By the way, I passed a dark-colored Ford Expedition about a half mile up the road. Looked like our favorite banker's ride."

Jace shot a glance at him, wondering if Ty was fishing. "It was."

"You're kidding."

"No. I'm not."

Eyes brimming with interest, Ty pulled a plate from the cupboard. "So, what did Morgan want? Another opportunity to toss around a few insults? A pint of your blood?" He grinned suddenly. "Or did he just drop by to tell you to keep your nasty Rogan lips off his daughter?"

"None of the above," Jace returned dryly. "It wasn't him. It was *her.*"

Chapter 4

Several minutes later, Ty narrowed his bewildered gaze on Jace, took a bite from his sandwich then chewed for a moment. "She's working with you on the project? How did that happen?"

"She came to the meeting. I gave her something to do."

His brother stared as though he couldn't believe what he was hearing. That made them even. Jace couldn't believe he'd suggested it. Good God, he was mere days away from turning thirty-six. Most men his age had a working brain by now.

"Let me get this straight. You asked and she said yes? With all the bad blood between you, her and her dad?"

"Yep." But he'd never admit to Ty or anyone else that his reason for doing it was more than a little muddled in his mind.

Feeling a worm turn in his gut, Jace collected Ty's sandwich fixings and put them away.

"Why would she agree to something like that?"

"Beats me. Maybe because this was the most appropriate job for her if she wanted to help. Obviously, she won't be dishing out carrots at the dinner. She'll be back in L.A. before Easter."

Closing the refrigerator, he crossed to the counter beside the sink where the coffeemaker had finished brewing, and filled two mugs. He slid one over to Ty.

"Is this about sticking it to Morgan again? I thought you'd gotten past that."

"I have gotten past it." Raising his mug, Jace took a cautious sip. "I'm just filling a position that needs to be filled."

"Right. First the dance and the kiss at the country club, now this." He spoke again before Jace could comment, mild surprise entering his voice. "Or *is* it payback? She's the one who served you your nuts on a plate way back when. Don't tell me you're thinking about riding that train again."

Jace sent his perceptive little brother a firm look. "My interest in Abbie starts and ends with the project. All I'm looking for is a warm body to handle some publicity and contact last year's sponsors for donations. She's pretty, well-spoken and strong. She'll get us some money. Now, can we talk about something else?"

"Sure," Ty replied, sampling his own coffee. "You pick the topic. But we both know your pat answers about her warm body are major crapola. You're interested again."

"Ty?" Jace said coolly.

"Yeah?"

"Eat your sandwich."

An hour later, Jace walked Ty to his truck, then crossed the snow-covered gravel to his workshop and let himself inside. He flicked on the lights and the small electric space heater, then went to his workbench to finish sanding the drawer fronts on the small chest he was building for Betty. Okay, so Ty hadn't been too far off the mark. Part of him *was* interested again. But it was only his nocturnal caveman part—the part that wouldn't sleep again tonight. As for anything beyond that… He wasn't the same guy who'd let her use him back then.

Sex with him had been the quickest way to send a message to Morgan, and she'd done it. Jace slipped on his earmuffs and safety glasses and plugged in the sander. That night had been all about Abbie's emancipation. And he'd been the gullible fool who'd made it happen.

The clerk behind the counter motioned that one of the workstations had opened up, and Danny smiled at the too thin, fiftyish woman sitting across from him in the busy mall's Sweet Bytes Internet Café. Soft pop music played over the low conversation coming from the dozen or so tables. "You're up, Miss Murphy. Time to surf the information superhighway."

Smiling broadly, Janice Murphy retrieved her cane from the floor and winced as she got to her feet, a few biscotti crumbs falling from her cheap navy pantsuit. "Time to collect my e-mails, anyway," she replied.

Just then, the half-dressed brunette who'd been giving Danny the eye since she got there passed by, banging into the older woman and knocking the cane from her hand.

Shooting her a murderous look, Danny leapt up from the tiny table where they'd been sipping mocha lattes, then steadied his new friend and returned her cane. "Sorry about that," he muttered. "Someone should teach that girl some manners."

"It's all right, Anthony," the graying woman replied,

using Danny's new name. "It's crowded in here. I'm sure she didn't realize what she did."

Danny doubted that. The harlot—that's what his holier-than-thou father called women who looked like that—was too interested in showing off her boobs and spandex to care about anyone else. Too interested in teasing every guy in the place with a free show so she could steal their cash later.

Miss Murphy tried to put a dollar down on the table, but Danny stopped her. "Uh-uh," he said, giving it back. "You let me share your table. I'll get the tip."

Smiling again, she tucked the bill back into her pocket. But then her pale eyes filled with sympathy. "Anthony, I'd love to let you go ahead of me. I know you're eager to get busy. But I'm afraid I'll already have a dark walk to the bus stop."

"Don't even suggest it," Danny replied. Las Vegas was teeming with people who could prey on a woman alone. *Men, too,* he thought, glancing across the room again at the lipsticked and eye-shadowed harlot. This time, she intercepted his look and waved coyly. Dozens of tinkling silver trinkets waggled to him from her charm bracelet, and Danny wondered if they were like the notches on a gunslinger's gun. One charm for every man she'd bedded.

Danny brought his gaze back to the angel goodness in Miss Murphy's eyes. "Don't worry about me. Another workstation will open up soon, and I'll find her." He hid the quick tickle of excitement in his belly and dropped his voice forlornly. "I'll find her if it's the last thing I do."

She squeezed his arm. "I'll pray that you do, Anthony. I was young and in love once, too."

Taking his seat again, he watched her cane her way to the open station.

It was eight o'clock on Wednesday night, and as Danny finished his latte, he caught sight of his reflection in the café's etched glass wall. He looked good. Different. Besides the black dye job and amber glasses, sunless tanning lotion had darkened his skin to a shade more in line with his new name, and the eyebrow pencil had darkened his brows and deepened the creases beside his mouth.

He'd made his transformation in a cheesy motel room, but he had to watch his money. He'd cleaned out his savings after his acquittal—six thousand dollars. But after buying Eddie's old Cutlass and putting aside money for "favors," he needed the rest for travel expenses. Because he'd had one of his *feelings*. And when the feelings came upon him, he knew he could trust them.

An ugly guy at one of the six terminals stood, grabbed a few sheets from the print station, then went to the counter.

The clerk gave Danny the high sign. A minute later, his fingers were flying over the keyboard and his heart was pounding as he began his search. He knew there could be dozens of telephone calls in his future, but that was okay. Pretty Abbie had said she was originally from Pennsylvania. Somewhere in the Alleghenies. And where did pretty girls go when they got scared? He smiled inside.

Why, home, of course.

On Thursday night, Abbie drew a breath, grabbed her laptop from the passenger seat and slammed the door on her dad's Expedition. Then she crossed the snow-covered gravel to Jace's shoveled walk, the crisp air stinging her cheeks.

His log home was smaller than she'd originally thought, the wraparound porch and high peaked plate glass making it appear grander than it was. But it was still warm and welcoming. With his past, it didn't surprise her that he'd want a strong, sturdy home. In the glow of the spotlights, smoke curled from a broad fieldstone chimney, and once again, the drapes were open, framing his sparsely furnished living room.

Climbing the steps, she crossed to the front door and rang the bell, reliving last night's conversation with Miriam.

"I know your dad cares too much about appearances," she'd said, clearly disappointed. *"But blaming Jace for his mother's sins is so wrong. Still, it had to be hard for him to find his only child with* any *man, much less one he disapproved of."* Abbie had agreed, but that didn't make her father's humiliating words to Jace any easier to forget— or Miriam's next question any easier to answer.

"Were you in love with him?"

"I don't know. Maybe."

Or had it merely been a bone-melting combination of infatuation and curiosity? She'd been a virgin then, and just looking at him had made her knees weak.

"So, you never saw each other again after that summer?"

"Only from a distance," Abbie had replied, *"and I knew better than to approach him."* Her dad had preferred to visit her, so her trips home had been short, and few and far between. More than five years had passed since she'd last been home.

Thinking back, she knew part of the problem between her and Jace had been his fault for not returning her calls. But what should she have done? Her life was already mapped out, and changing it had been out of the question. She'd been enrolled in college with law school ahead of her, while Jace had no aspirations beyond cutting logs and collecting a paycheck. Besides, though they'd known each other for a year and had indulged in a few hungry kisses, they'd only been seeing each other for three weeks before they made love. That wasn't long enough to make a life change, no matter how much she cared for him. *And she had cared.* Cared enough to feel sick over what had happened for a very long time.

The door swung open, and Jace motioned her inside. "Sorry to keep you waiting," he said. "I was on the phone with my foster parents. They're wintering in Florida."

"How nice," she replied, glad for small talk. She stepped inside. "Have they been gone long?"

"Since Thanksgiving. They flew back for Christmas, though."

"That's good. The holidays seem to mean more when families get together."

"Yeah, I guess they do."

Jace turned from shutting the door to meet her eyes. And suddenly—with the closing of that door—conversation stopped and things got awkward. Despite his cavalier attitude as they'd talked in their cars, he was uneasy about tonight, too.

Recovering, Jace broke eye contact and returned to the subject at hand. "They'll be back for good next month. They'll want to get their garden ready to plant."

Hoping they were back on track, Abbie made a sound of agreement in her throat because she'd already used up her pat replies. She reached low to unzip her boots and slip them off, her brain and body both deciding that he looked too good for words.

He wore snug faded jeans and a navy blue Penn State sweatshirt with a tattered neckline. The sleeves were ripped off at the shoulders, showcasing the toned, muscular arms of a man who wasn't afraid of hard work. Her stomach lifted airily.

She should've expected this. If sitting across from him

in separate cars last night had affected her, being with him behind closed doors was bound to double her reaction. Especially with that kiss and intimate knowledge of each other crackling between them. "I brought my laptop along so I could make notes."

"You didn't have to. I've already printed the phone numbers and addresses of the people you'll want to contact." He nodded through the living room. "My office is this way."

Good. He wanted to get straight to work. They'd get their meeting over quickly, and she could leave.

Unzipping the brown suede jacket topping her dark jeans and yellow angora turtleneck, Abbie scanned the cathedral ceiling and loft as she followed behind him. Music from an oldies station flowed from somewhere in the house…Chad and Jeremy crooning about soft kisses on a summer's day.

Sighing, trying to quell the bittersweet memory the song evoked, she concentrated on Jace's home, on the warm brown logs on the exterior walls and the interior's creamy textured plaster. The walls were unadorned except for a large oil of a woodland scene above the brown leather sofa, and several black-and-white framed enlargements of old time loggers and sawmills on an adjacent wall. A color photo of his foster parents sat on one of the tables flanking the sofa, and the dark oak flooring was broken up by nubby alpaca area rugs.

It was a man's room, a man's home, and it suited him perfectly. "Nice place," she said.

"Thanks. I bought it from Jim Freemont the same day Ty and I bought the company. Nothing like going whole hog into debt."

The source of the music was clear when they crossed

the short hallway and entered his office. It was larger than she'd expected with an L-shaped desk, file cabinet, bookcase, floor lamp and a short, blue-and-gray patterned sofa. Abbie set her laptop on the floor and tugged her shaggy beige tunnel scarf from her neck. Gooseflesh ran the length of her when Jace moved behind her to take it and slip her jacket from her shoulders.

Tossing them on the sofa, he motioned her into the swivel chair near the desk's extended workspace and took the chair beside it. Pulling it close, he opened the first of two folders and got down to business, his voice as detached as any living person could make it.

He really did want to get this over with.

"This first sheet's a list of area radio and television stations that have helped us out in the past. The TV guys charge a fee to announce events on the community bulletin board—and we want that exposure—so that means you'll have to beg the merchants on the second sheet to donate some cash when you ask them to put posters up in their windows."

"Posters?"

"I'll get to that after we talk about newspapers. Ads can get expensive, so instead, you'll want to write two or three short articles—to be run at different times—mentioning the success of other dinners, asking for volunteers to cook, serve and clean up and tying this year's event to the food bank."

"Okay," she said, turning to meet his gaze, "but forgive me for asking—" She banged right into a look of unadulterated male lust. Fourteen years had passed, but their memories of loving each other in the dark had lingered, whether they liked it or not.

"Go on," he prompted, an ironic half smile softening his expression. "I'm a forgiving kind of guy."

No, he wasn't, and his smile said he knew it. But that was a conversation for another time. "All right. What will *you* be doing while I'm taking care of the writing, begging and poster placing?"

"I'll be finding a place to hold the dinner, handling the stuff in the second folder and going to work every day. Is that enough to satisfy you?"

"I'll let you know."

"I'll just bet you will."

But then they forgot to look away, the room began to warm and shrink around them and suddenly, there it was again...that feeling of being pleasantly smothered.

Thoroughly annoyed and physically pulling himself out of the moment, Jace opened the second folder. He removed a letter-sized announcement printed on card stock and searched for his sanity.

"This is last year's poster," he said, locking his gaze on the sheet and refusing to let his eyes drift again to the full mounds shaping her yellow sweater. At nineteen, her body had been slender and coltish, her breasts little more than soft swells around her nipples. Now they would fill his hands.

He slid the poster across to her. "I have the file for this one in my computer. If it's okay with you, I think we'll just update it and add some color and fancy fonts."

"It's okay with me," she said quietly, keeping her eyes averted.

"Then it's good for me, too," he returned brusquely.

By eight o'clock, Jace's nerves were stretched to the wire. He'd known the chemistry between them would show up the second she walked in. He just hadn't expected this constant battle between good sense and his libido. If the radio DJ hadn't played so many summer make-out tunes—or if her hair hadn't smelled so good and her mouth hadn't looked so inviting—maybe being alone with her wouldn't have been so difficult. Now…now he had to move around before she noticed how little control he had over the lump in his jeans.

Standing, he shoved a stack of card stock into his printer. "Come on. Let's get something to drink while those are printing."

"Good idea. I wouldn't mind having something."

Jace wouldn't either, but he'd bet the something in his mind was a far cry from anything she came up with.

When he'd filled their iced tea glasses and they'd taken seats at the bar, she told him she liked his kitchen.

"Thanks, but none of it was my doing. Before I moved in, Betty insisted on prettying up the place." Now a border of blue cornflowers stretched around the white walls, blue-and-white checked curtains hung on the windows and a wicker basket of fake flowers and greenery sat on a crocheted doily in the middle of his maple table.

"The house is small, but if I ever need more space, there's plenty of land for an addition. There's a narrow creek running through part of it."

"You're lucky. Land's a real luxury in L.A." Ice cubes chinked against the glass as she sipped and he had to look away from her mouth. "If I want to commune with nature, I have to go to a park."

"There are no trees where you live?" Perpetual sunshine without shade wouldn't work for him.

"A few palms and Joshuas in the courtyard—nothing like you have here. But life's a trade-off, isn't it?" she asked, her voice growing somber. "I don't own a snow shovel."

Jace stared thoughtfully for a moment, then slowly brought the tip of his tongue to his upper lip. He almost didn't ask the question rolling through his mind, then did. "Why do I get the feeling you're not all that happy in L.A.?"

Her brown eyes widened. "I'm happy."

"Are you?"

"Of course." But despite her words, there was something disturbing in her gaze when she spoke again. "Believe me, there are worse things in life than being treeless."

"Like what?"

She hesitated then, almost as though she'd realized she'd revealed a secret. And that piqued his interest. Especially when she set her glass on the bar, glanced at the small gold timepiece on her wrist and forced a smile. "I should be going."

"All right," Jace replied, still curious but deciding not to press. "I'll get your jacket." He didn't understand what had just happened, but suddenly he found himself wondering if her uneasiness was tied to her jumpy response when that champagne bottle had smashed. "We can finish tomorrow night if you're free."

"Sorry, tomorrow's my dad's wedding. I think he'd like me to be there." She spoke wryly as they reentered his office. "Care to join us?"

"Only in a body bag." He knew she wasn't serious, but it would be a cold day in hell when he set one foot on Morgan Winslow's property again.

Scooping up her things, he handed her the shaggy scarf and waited until she'd twirled it around her neck. Then, despite her wary look, he held her jacket while she slipped her arms into the sleeves. He felt her tremble when he settled it on her shoulders and freed her hair from her collar. Little bursts of heat tripped through his blood.

"Just give me a second to grab the finished posters and slip them into a folder," he said, stepping back. "You can start placing them at the local businesses anytime you're ready."

"Then I'll start tomorrow morning."

They didn't speak again until she was preparing to leave.

"Thanks for your help tonight," he said at the door. "If you're free on Saturday, we close at noon. We can probably finish up at the office. Would that work for you?"

"It should. Dad and Miriam are catching an early flight, so…yes."

"Then I'll see you around twelve."

She started to leave, then for some odd reason turned back. "You still do that," she said quietly.

Those traitorous little blips tripped through his veins again. "Do what?

"Touch the tip of your tongue to your lip when you're thinking about something." Then she said good-night, he told her to watch for deer on the roads and she escaped to her dad's SUV.

Jace watched grimly as she drove up the slight incline to the road, then waited until she'd made the right turn at the top of the drive and her red taillights disappeared before he closed the door. Calling himself a jerk for giving even minor importance to the comment she made, he and the unhappy little knot in his gut went back to the kitchen and his watery ice tea. He drained it, then set the glass in the sink and thought about dropping the remaining slivers of ice where they'd do the most good.

If this kept up…

Well, he knew a few women who never minded some no-strings fun.

* * *

You still touch your tongue to your lip when you're thinking about something.

Why had she said that? For the hundredth time, the question battered Abbie's mind, and she felt vulnerable for letting him know that she remembered. Where was her courtroom finesse when she needed it?

Her headlights illuminated the open black iron gate, and slowing the SUV, she coasted down the paved drive to the house and the three-stall garage. She clicked the remote, the door on the first bay opened and she drove inside. The garage boasted the same mottled white-and-gray dappled brick facade and black roof the house did, though her father's home was more of an estate with its European influence, dormers and regal landscaping. Successful stock trades and shrewd business decisions had made Morgan Winslow wealthy, and his home reflected that.

Parking, then following the cobblestone walk to the back entrance, Abbie thought again about that tongue-to-the-lip comment.

Strange. She couldn't think of one distinct mannerism that had been Collin's alone. He was handsome and charismatic, a gifted attorney and a witty, intelligent conversationalist. But she couldn't pinpoint a single gesture that summoned the same tenderness she felt when she thought of Jace. Swallowing, she let herself inside. How different he was now…and yet…not so different at all.

Laughter and conversation carried all the way to the enclosed back porch as Abbie paused to slip off her boots. Then she strode through the kitchen and dining room to the formal living room where Miriam was overseeing the last-minute decorating.

The sweeping room with its vaulted ceiling had been

designed with entertaining in mind, and her mother had
seen to it that it was furnished beautifully—even though
the family room, with its overstuffed furniture, had always
been more to her liking. Now, entering and seeing Miriam's glowing face as she and the decorator set crystal
vases in place for the cream, pink and peach roses the
florist would deliver tomorrow, Abbie was glad again that
her dad had Miriam in his life.

She couldn't deny feeling a pang of disloyalty over the
upcoming nuptials, but she knew her mom would've
approved. That made it easier to blink back a sting, cross
the oak flooring and exchange a hug with Miriam.

"The room looks great," Abbie murmured, kissing her
cheek. "It's going to be a beautiful wedding."

Beaming, Miriam glanced around the elegant room, her
gaze moving from the white brocade sofa and matching
love seats to the faux Louis fourteenth chairs, to the curio
cabinet filled with porcelain collectibles, cherry tables and
white brick fireplace. Clouds of voile and clusters of
greenery and silk roses were everywhere.

"It's not too much, is it?" she asked, as the decorator
draped the fireplace mantel with more gossamer bunting
and secured it with more greens and silk roses.

Abbie squeezed Miriam's hand. "It's perfect." On the
mirrored buffet, crystal and silver platters waited for the
canapés the caterer would bring, and creamy white candles
were everywhere.

With her smile fading a little, Miriam drew her aside.
"I…I want to tell you something, Abbie," she said hesitantly, and Abbie waited, somehow knowing what she
wanted to say. That was the kind of woman Miriam was.

"I never knew your mother," she began, "but everyone
who did agreed that Jennifer was one of the most loving

women they'd ever known. I want you to know that I'll never try to replace her in your heart—or in your dad's. We've talked a lot about the wonderful people we've lost, and he knows that a part of me will always belong to Evan. That's why we decided to be married here instead of in a church. We wanted to keep the memories of our first loves sacred and separate from the life we'll be starting tomorrow."

Emotion knotted Abbie's throat and she blinked back a new tear. "You're doing this for me."

Miriam smiled. "We're doing it for all of us. That doesn't mean that we love each other less—just differently than we loved before."

Abbie nodded, her heart brimming with gratitude. Then, slipping her arms around Miriam, she kissed her cheek again and whispered, "My mom would've loved you."

Later, upstairs, crying softly for no reason other than she'd needed to cry for a long time, Abbie's mind wandered from her mother's warmth and laughter to Miriam's tender understanding, to her father's subtle softening since Miriam had come into his life. Eventually, her mind moved on to the evening she'd spent with Jace, and she released a sigh as her spirits dipped.

He'd been friendly tonight—even smiled at his claim to be a forgiving kind of guy. But his guard would always be up where she was concerned. How could she get through to him? Make him believe she hadn't deliberately betrayed him? She'd never willingly betray *anyone*.

But then a chill moved through her and she corrected that statement. She had betrayed someone. Someone who hid his unstable personality and volatile temper behind a boyish smile and charming manners.

Someone who wanted her dead.

Chapter 5

Two hours later, Abbie sprang awake in bed, her nightie soaked with sweat, her heart racing wildly as she surveyed her unfamiliar—then recognizable—surroundings. Slowly, the terror that had awakened her began to ebb, and with shaky hands, she smoothed her damp hair back from her face.

She was all right. She was safe here in the bedroom her mother had decorated for her with all the love a mother could have shown a child. Safe here in Laurel Ridge, far from the deranged man she'd been running from in her dream. A cold chill racked through her as she sat there, and Abbie pulled her comforter up to her throat. It had all seemed so real…the slogging heaviness in her legs that had kept her mere inches from his reach, the cold eyes, the same maniacal laughter she'd heard on her cell phone.

Her mind filled again with bloody crime scene photos. Dear God, how could she have been taken in so completely? She prided herself on being able to read people, had always had surefire instincts about a potential client's guilt or innocence. Danny had fooled everyone but the prosecution—until his enormous pride couldn't deny her a peek at the truth, and smiling, he'd murmured a secret that had chilled her blood.

Abbie wasn't sure how long she sat there in bed, grieving for the justice pretty Maryanne Richards had never received. But when she looked at the clock again it was nearly midnight. Eight-fifty-five in L.A.

Crossing to her dresser, Abbie took her cell phone from the charger, then slipped back into bed and called Stuart. He answered on the second ring.

"Hi, it's Abbie," she said. She'd heard her dad go to his room around ten, so she doubted he'd overhear, but she kept her voice low anyway. "Any news?"

"Nothing that will help the police put him back behind bars, I'm afraid. He's having a high time eluding them, playing games. They see him only sporadically when he goes to his apartment for a change of clothes or to take his mail from the box. He's apparently staying somewhere else now."

"They need to follow him and *find out* what he's doing. He could be stalking another woman right now."

"They do follow him when they see him slip out. But he's aware of their presence and he knows how to lose them. The last time, he slipped into a club in the middle of a rave. It was utter mayhem. You know how those things can get."

"Not personally," she sighed, but yes, she knew. And if he could give police the slip now, he could do it when she returned to L.A. And he could get to her.

"Abbie, I realize this is difficult, but please try to put this out of your mind. I'll let you know if anything changes."

"I know," she murmured. But that dream had been so frighteningly real—as if it were an omen, a sign of things to come.

"Why are you up so late on the eve of your father's nuptials?"

There was no point in telling him that Danny was now even stalking her dreams. "Too much excitement, I guess. Either that, or my body's still trying to adjust to Eastern Standard Time."

"Well, you should be sleeping so you're well rested for the festivities."

"I know," she said again.

"Then stop thinking about Long and enjoy this time with your family. You're safe where you are, and obsessing about any of this won't do anyone any good. Leave it to the authorities," he added quietly. "You can't solve the woes of the world single-handedly."

"Don't I know it," she returned. But she'd certainly tried, for Maryanne Richards's sake. "Good night, Stuart. Sorry to bother you with this. My love to you and your family."

"Likewise, my girl. Sleep tight—and it's never a bother to speak with you. It's always a pleasure."

Abbie hit the End button, then dropped the cell phone beside her on the bed, not feeling safe at all, and knowing it would be hours before she slept. Then, oddly, after only a few minutes, she began to drift off. And in that drifting state between wakefulness and slumber, she found herself, not in the gazebo she'd dreamed of many times before, but in the loft of a lovely log home on a bed of soft green moss…safe in the powerful arms of a man with midnight hair and warm gray eyes.

* * *

At 10 a.m. on Friday, Jace strode through the reception area, desperately needing to bite someone's head off, but refusing to show it—and refusing to admit that Abbie was the reason for his lousy mood. The sun was shining, the sky was blue and there was a fair chance that spring would eventually show up. He had to center on that.

Ty followed him into the office. "Okay, who spit in your cornflakes this morning?"

Jace dropped into his seat to look over the latest kiln reports, then scanned a new order that had just come in. "What are you talking about?"

"I'm talking about two hours of James Dean in *Rebel Without a Cause*. What's up? Did we get another call from the bloodsucking lawyer?"

"No." And he'd thought he'd hidden his foul mood fairly well.

"Then what?"

Jace looked up. "I told you, nothing. Everything's fine. Now, if you don't mind, I'm busy."

"Okay," his brother replied, shrugging. "Be a pain in the ass if you want to."

Ty had barely entered the hall when he suddenly stopped, and came back in. "You saw Abbie last night."

"So?"

"So, obviously your problem's not the bloodsucking lawyer, it's the lip-sucking lawyer."

Jace motioned to the door. "Out. Now."

"You seeing her again?"

"You writin' a book?"

"Nope, just taking an interest in your love life, pathetic as it is."

Jace started an annoyed response, then quit. Ty would

find out when she showed up here tomorrow, anyhow. "Yes, I'm seeing her again. She's coming here tomorrow around noon. We didn't finish last night."

His brother's gaze twinkled. "Didn't finish? You need some little blue pills, buddy?"

"You know what I meant," he growled. "Now, scram so I can figure out how many tree huggers we'll have to offend to fill this order for Granthan."

"What do they want?"

"Cherry and oak—green."

"Pete just left to look at some timber up in Warren County. There's a lot of oak on the block. If it's good, we'll bid on it."

Ty grabbed a few caramels from the apothecary jar on the desk, dropped two in the pocket of his dark green shirt and unwrapped the other one. "Mind some advice from your little brother?"

"Yes."

Popping the candy into his mouth, he spoke around it. "You need to get laid. Maybe two or three times."

Jace sent him a bored look. "Ever think about taking care of your own busy love life and leaving mine to me?"

"Occasionally," he replied, grinning, "but that wouldn't irritate you nearly as much. See you later."

When Ty had gone, Jace tipped back in his chair and stared at the ceiling, feeling the low clenching in his gut just as vividly as he had last night. Ty was right. He did need to get laid. Get the kinks out. Find that smooth, mellow feeling again. It had been so long, he could barely recall what it felt like. Abbie was looking too good, moving too well and smelling like springtime in a warm, curvy bottle. But it wasn't going to happen with her. That bottle was heading back to L.A. in two weeks.

Tipping forward on his chair, Jace released a ragged breath, checked his Rolodex for a number and dragged his phone closer. She wasn't the woman he wanted, but she was nice and she wasn't into commitment. That made her perfect.

Frustrated, Danny left his car at the service station and sprinted across the highway to the small Oklahoma eatery with the striped awnings. The banners outside advertised Breakfast All Day for $2.99, and Friday Fish Fries for $6.99. It was just about noon, but he'd be having breakfast—not the fish. Now it was even more important that he watch his expenses because he'd be replacing the freakin' alternator in that rusted heap of scrap metal. But not until Monday. The dull-eyed mechanic at the garage swore he couldn't get to it any sooner—swore he had to order the part and he couldn't expect delivery until Monday around noon.

Danny's anger grew as he crossed the diner's dusty parking lot. He would lose almost three days! Three days he could've used to track her movements, learn her patterns, choose the best place for the *event*. He'd already chosen the day—and that would sweeten his pleasure, because it was a special date he'd already circled on the calendar inside his wallet.

He'd struck pay dirt almost immediately on Wednesday when he'd started making phone calls from his list of Winslows north of Interstate 80. An old lady from Erie, Pennsylvania, who didn't mind a late-night call knew of a distant cousin who had a lawyer daughter living in California. She'd sounded so eager to talk to someone, he'd had a hard time getting her off the phone.

"I don't know her name," she'd gone on in a voice

cracking with age, *"but his name is Morgan. Odd name for a man, don't you think? Sounds like a horse. I believe he lives somewhere southeast of here."* After that, finding the right address had been almost too easy.

He'd made a call to another friend back in L.A. then— a *loyal* friend. The cards were already stamped and sealed, and the envelopes were already decorated with creepy crayon flowers. All his buddy had to do was type in her name and address. *"Just don't forget to wear the gloves I gave you, okay?"* Danny had said. *"And get it in the mail right away."* Big, lumbering Donnie Fieldhouser had replied sweetly and dutifully, *"I will, Danny. I'll do it just like you told me."*

Now, striding into the restaurant, Danny glanced at the sign that said Please Seat Yourself and dropped into a padded red vinyl booth. He grabbed a laminated menu from behind the salt and pepper shakers and napkin holder. The place reeked of grease and fish, and country music nearly drowned out the chatter of people gulping down the Friday special.

Things started looking up when a young waitress with a sweet toothpaste-ad smile came over to take his order. She looked freshly scrubbed and country pure, and couldn't have been more than eighteen. Her sky-blue eyes and blond hair were a breath of fresh air after the vulgar Vegas whore from the Internet café.

A pleasant little shiver worked through him as he felt the spiky prickle of silver charms pressing through his jeans pocket and into his thigh. She'd crawled into his back seat so willingly, it really had been a crime. *Hasta la vista, Lorelei.*

"Afternoon," the girl said brightly, then took a pad and pen from her black apron. "Can I start you off with some coffee?"

"No, thanks," Danny replied, smiling back. His pulse did a hot little kick when he spied the religious medal hanging in the V of the white blouse she wore with her jeans. *V for virgin.* "I'd rather have a nice tall glass of cold milk, please."

Laughter tinkled through the girl's reply and her voice dropped to a stage whisper. "Good choice. I'm not a big fan of coffee, either—stains the teeth."

Oh, and he wouldn't want anything to ruin those teeth. They were perfect. Just like her hands.

She nodded at the menu he held. "Do you know what you want, or do you need a few more minutes to decide?"

Danny slipped off his dollar-store shades, his refocusing gaze drifting from her almost pretty face to the name tag pinned above her small, soft-looking left breast.

"No, I don't need more time, Misty," he said, smiling and feeling his heart beat fast as a tender storm swept through him and he realized that he loved her—*loved her blindly.* "I know exactly what I want."

The wedding had been truly lovely. A small string quartet had played from the wide landing on the staircase, the food was delicious and their guests had been warm, friendly and supportive of the marriage. But it was Saturday morning now, the newlyweds were on their way to Florida to meet their cruise ship, and Abbie was busy overseeing the cleanup.

She'd already greeted the caterer who'd come by to pick up his chafing dishes and platters, and helped Dorothy Carson straighten the house. Then, as the housekeeper was leaving, she'd given Dorothy her pick of the huge bouquets of roses. Abbie had decided to keep one of the arrangements because they really were beautiful, but would drop the others at the local nursing home where they'd be welcomed and enjoyed.

By eleven-thirty, she'd run all of her errands, including taping Friends Without Families posters to a few windows in town and picking up the mail at the post office.

Now, with the bundle beside her on the seat, she drove through the melting slush toward RL&L and her meeting with Jace.

It had been a strange, dream-filled, sleepless night. First, the terrifying nightmare…then the half dream of being in Jace's arms had morphed into the most erotic, skin-scorching sex she'd ever experienced, and shockingly, responded to.

Abbie rolled her eyes in utter bewilderment. That kind of thing didn't happen to her. She was sensible—had both feet firmly on the ground. Erotic dreams about ex-lovers were for women who needed more in their lives, and she was perfectly satisfied with hers.

Well, excluding the obvious.

And if she didn't have much of a social life, it was because she was too busy to have one. In L.A., someone always needed a lawyer, not just the high-profile clients whose cases made *Headline News* and *Court TV.* There were always real people with real problems, and that kept life hectic.

The Rogan Logging & Lumber sign appeared, seeming to spring out of the thick pines and hemlocks lining the road. Abbie made a left turn down the lane to the business.

The first fifty yards were paved, but most of the crisscrossing lanes were potholed and muddy from steady, heavy vehicle traffic. Riding the brake, taking it all in, she eased the Expedition over the ruts, past log piles that were sorted and tagged by species, past the sawmill, loading dock and huge warehouse holding the kilns...past the grading building.

She was approaching the office when the SUV banged into a deep pothole she'd overlooked, and her purse and mail bounced up and spilled to the floor.

Releasing her seat belt, Abbie parked in the area to the left of the log office where a few passenger cars, a dark gray Silverado and Jace's black Explorer stood. Then, flipping down the visor and glancing into the mirror, she finger combed her hair and tried to quell the rush of butterflies in her stomach.

"He's just a man," she scolded as she flipped the visor back up. "Just a man you used to know who doesn't even like you much." Bending, she grabbed her purse, then reached for the mail.

Shock frizzoned through her system.

With a startled cry, Abbie dropped the stack of letters. *She couldn't breathe, couldn't move.*

The sudden rap at her window made her whirl in terror.

Jace's face lined instantly, and he yanked the door open. "What's wrong?" he demanded.

Abbie scrambled out of the car and into his arms, had to fight back tears when he held her close. "He found me," she said in a low, shaky voice. "I thought I was safe, but, Jace, he found me."

She was still shaking five minutes later when Jace rolled his chair close to hers and pressed a mug of hot tea into her hands—tea he'd brought in from the reception area.

Now his gaze flicked over the red crewneck sweater she wore with her jeans. Her suede jacket and scarf hung on the coat tree to the right of the closed door.

"Are you sure you don't want your jacket?"

"I'm sure. I'll be okay."

"All right," he returned, worry still lining his rugged features and darkening his gray eyes. "Tell me what's going on." He nodded at the large envelope lying on his desk—the one with the primitive, drawn-in-Crayon flowers on it. "I have a fair idea why you wanted me to pick it up by the corner, but who sent it?"

"It's…it's a long story."

He glanced at the door leading to the outer office. "Ty's closing today, and no one's going to open that door but me, so we have plenty of time. Tell me."

Abbie studied the warm mug between her hands, swallowed, then nodded and started at the beginning. "Last month, I defended a young store clerk named Danny Long on a brutal rape-homicide charge."

She glanced up briefly and saw the uneasiness in Jace's gaze, but he didn't comment, and she went on.

"He and the young woman—Maryanne Richards—had been seeing each other for a while. He cried like a baby when he told me he'd been in love with her. She was a member of Danny's church in L.A. Danny swore he could never have hurt her—that he loved her blindly. That she was his dream, and he'd wanted to marry her someday."

Abbie raised her gaze to Jace's again. "The evidence against him was damning, but he was so devastated and sincere, I believed him. He had reasonable answers for every question the police threw at him. The medical examiner's time of death was plus or minus two hours, and Danny had alibis for much of that time. The presence of his DNA was easy to explain because they'd had an intimate relationship. Even the rage inflicted on that poor girl's body was easy to explain away because every character witness I called swore Danny wasn't capable of such a grisly act."

"She was beaten?"

Remembering the crime-scene photos, Abbie huddled her hands more tightly around her cup. "Savagely. But the police never found the murder weapon. The crime scene guys determined that it was a baseball bat, but the prosecution was never able to produce it. Most of her injuries were postmortem, and sexual in nature."

When Jace's questioning gaze searched hers, she murmured, "Her…pelvis was smashed. Yet every witness I put on the stand—women he worked with, his local minister, his employer, his landlady—all said he was every mother's dream. And every time one of the prosecution's expert witnesses offered testimony, I cross-examined them until they admitted that what they'd said wasn't absolute."

She began to shake harder, and Jace took his corduroy jacket from the back of his chair.

When he'd settled it on her shoulders and pulled it around her, she thanked him with a weak smile and continued.

"I put Danny on the stand, and he was brilliant. It was easy to read the expressions of the jury, eight of whom were women. They believed him, too. No one could be as torn up as he was and still be guilty. When it was the prosecution's turn to cross, Assistant District Attorney Garrett shoved the crime scene photos under Danny's nose, and he actually threw up."

Abbie met Jace's attentive gaze again. "Garrett questioned other women he'd dated, hoping to find a pattern of abuse, but there were only a few, and his relationships never lasted. Not until Maryanne. I suspect Danny lost interest with the others when he realized they were too experienced." She drew a breath. "Danny wanted a virgin."

"Then he did it?" Jace asked gravely.

Abbie nodded. "But no one could believe someone with Danny's boyish good looks and charm could leave a woman's brutally beaten body on a sandy beach…arranged in a humiliating position…and still sob his heart out on the stand."

Jace's voice went cold and shaky, and he glanced at the sealed envelope on his desk. "This is the bastard who sent you the card?"

She didn't have to nod. He knew the answer. "He fooled us all," she murmured. "Then one morning, the day before we were to make our closing arguments, he spazzed out on me—got all churned up and started crying again. I tried to reassure him that the trial had gone very well for us. I told him that I didn't think he'd have to pay for that sweet girl's death."

Abbie shook her head, still stunned that she hadn't seen his guilt until then. "That's when his eyes changed and he got this…this strange, feral smile on his face. Right in the middle of the most heart-wrenching display of grief and fear I'd ever witnessed, he stopped and *smiled.* Then he said, 'She wasn't that sweet, you know. Some other guy broke her in.' And I knew he'd done it."

A soft rap sounded at the door, and hesitantly, Ty poked his dark head inside. After nodding soberly to Abbie, his troubled gaze shifted to Jace. "Everyone's gone, so I'm taking off, too," he said. "I'll lock up. There's still coffee in the pot if you want some."

"Thanks."

"No problem." He hesitated again. "Call my cell if you need me for anything."

"I will," Jace returned. "Have a good weekend." Then the door closed, and he murmured his apologies. "Sorry about that."

"It's okay. What did you tell him?"

"Just that something had upset you and we needed some privacy." He nodded at the tea she'd barely touched. "There's a microwave across from Ida's desk. Can I warm that for you?"

Abbie nodded and stood. It was still drinkable, but she needed time to regroup before she continued. Before she admitted to him that she'd trashed every legal tenet she believed in, and she didn't know if she would ever get over the guilt. "Do you mind if I do it? I need to walk."

"Sure." Jace pushed to his feet, too, and as she glanced up into his solid gaze and towering confidence, she was reminded of her dream—the first part of it, when she'd felt so safe in his arms. And she was glad she was here with him now.

He motioned her ahead of him. "After you."

In the sunlit, pine-paneled reception area, she waited beside Ida's desk while her tea reheated and Jace poured himself a cup of coffee. "I'm guessing this guy's the reason you jumped out of your skin when that champagne bottle smashed the other night."

"Good guess."

"I'm also guessing he's not behind bars."

"No, and if anyone needs to be, he does. After I left the jail that day, I talked with a psychologist friend, Susan. She said he has to be totally around the bend."

The microwave beeped. A few moments later, they were back in his office and Jace was perched on the edge of his desk.

Abbie took a sip of her tea. "Without examining him, these are just suppositions on her part, but she thinks that Danny probably did love Maryanne, and that he'd built up a dream of her purity in his mind. He's the son of a fire-and-brimstone preacher who hammered the need for chastity into him from the time he was old enough to understand the word. Not that Danny's into hero worship. He loathes his father.

"Anyway," she said, returning to her story, "Susan said it's possible that when Danny fell in love with a girl who didn't live up to his expectations, he was so outraged to see his dreams die that he lashed out. She also said that Danny's tears and pain were probably real, but they were for himself—for what he'd lost—not for her."

"What happened after you spoke with your friend?"

Abbie set her tea on his desk before facing him again. "I wrestled with my conscience. I knew the reputation of the judge on the case, and I knew he wouldn't allow me to step down. The county had already spent too much time and money on the trial, and the court docket was full."

She glanced away. "I also knew that if Long was as screwed up as Susan and I thought, he could do it again. While I was preparing his defense, we had some long talks. He'd told me that there'd been another girl he'd loved, several years ago—a girl from his hometown. I told Danny that if the character witnesses I called weren't making an impression on the jury, I'd put her on the stand to establish that from an early age, he'd been respectful of women. But he didn't want the girl involved. He was so adamant about it, he wouldn't even tell me Prudence's last name."

"But you found out."

"On a hunch, I phoned his father. The relationship between them was extremely strained when I saw them together, and I wondered if Dr. Long had detected something disturbing about his son when he was growing up— but was too loyal to come forward. When I contacted him,

I learned that Prudence had been a member of his congre-
gation, but had suddenly stopped coming to services a few
years ago. Then, without my asking, he gave me her phone
number. When I asked if he planned to tell Danny about
our conversation, he said no."

"You took a real chance."

"I could've been disbarred." A terrible weight settled on
her chest as guilt returned. "I still might be. I'm bound by
law to give my client the best defense I'm able to give. And
I did my best to get him convicted."

"Then the girl told you something useful."

"It took a while because she was embarrassed, but yes.
She finally admitted that she and Danny had had sex once
when they were in high school, and she'd been the one
who'd initiated it."

Abbie slipped Jace's jacket from her shoulders and
handed it to him, then walked to the rear window
and peered through the open slats of the mini blinds. The
sun shone brightly, melting patches of snow…warming
the tiny birds pecking nervously at one of the redwood
feeders.

"When Danny realized there was no resistance when he
entered her, he went ballistic. He slapped her around
and demanded that she take off the gold cross and chain
she wore because she wasn't fit to wear it. Then he threw
her and her clothes out of his father's car. Susan said his
hormones were undoubtedly warring with his upbringing.
He wanted sex, but he wanted his partner to be pure. He
saw Prudence's sexual past as a betrayal."

Jace came over to stand beside her. She sensed his
hesitance, but then he covered her shoulders with
his hands. "And that's what you think happened with the
dead girl?"

"Maryanne. After I threw up, I drove eighty miles out of the city, bought a track phone and made an anonymous call to A.D.A. Garrett. I disguised my voice, but I think he knew who I was. When Prudence Reese showed up in the courtroom the next day, I made a mild objection to the state calling a 'surprise' witness, but Garrett justified it, and her testimony was admitted. Long knew I'd betrayed him. I saw it in his crazy eyes."

Abbie swallowed. "Her testimony wasn't flawless, but she was good. It took three days for the jury to come back—three long days for Danny to sweat. In the end, they found there was reasonable doubt and acquitted him. When the verdict was read, he laughed and threw his arms around me, which no one thought was odd. I was the only one who heard him whisper, 'I would've told on you if the verdict went the other way. Now it's time for *you* to sweat.' Then he winked and said, 'I'll be thinking about you.'"

Jace strode to his desk phone. "I'm calling the police."

"Wait!" Following, Abbie covered his hand on the receiver and met his eyes. "Not until we see what's inside. I could be wrong. But I'm betting it's a cheap musical greeting card and the sentiment says 'thinking of you'— or something close." She finished with a trembling breath. "That's what the first one said."

"There was a *first* card?"

"Yes."

Jace paused for a long, steely-eyed moment, then he took a slim metal letter opener from the drawer and cloaked his hand with a tissue. A moment later, the envelope with the Los Angeles postmark was back on the desk…and a pretty card with a sprig of violets was open and tinkling out a lilting melody beside it.

Abbie started to shake again when she read the message.

How's your deodorant holding up? I missed on purpose, you know.

Swearing softly, Jace slipped an arm around her again. "What does he mean, he missed on purpose?"

"He shot at me. At least, we assumed it was him. It was dark in the lot behind my apartment building. That's when the partners at my firm ordered me to come home early for my dad's wedding."

"Abbie, we need to get the cops involved. Now."

"Not the locals. Not yet. First I need to contact the LAPD. They'll want to see this card." After pulling her cell phone from her purse, she speed-dialed the precinct captain and raised the phone to her ear.

While it rang, she spoke to Jace again, her voice trembling. "I know the post office closes early on Saturday, so I can't overnight it. Where's the nearest FedEx, and how long are they open?"

Chapter 6

"You need to get out of your father's house right now," Jace said firmly as he followed Abbie out of the Laurel Ridge Police Station three hours later. "This jerk knows where you are."

The time and temperature marquis on the bank across the street said it was 2:27 p.m. and the temperature was fifty-one degrees. But Jace was so illogically churned up, it felt liked eighty. The more details he learned about the creep who was after Abbie, the more uncomfortable he got. And that made no sense. They'd been strangers for over a decade before she'd entered his life again. Everything he was feeling was too deep, too over-the-top. Too damn *emotional*.

They'd made it to FedEx before it closed, then they'd returned to town to speak with Chief of Police Glenn Frasier. Abbie'd been right: the LAPD wanted the card immediately for fingerprint, DNA and handwriting analysis.

The card had Glenn more than a little concerned, too. After hearing the story—minus Abbie's anonymous tip to the prosecution—he'd requested a description and mug shot from the LAPD on the outside chance that Long would suddenly decide to come East, then went a step further and put out a B.O.L.O.—Be On The Lookout—for Daniel Long Jr.

Jace opened the door of his black Explorer, waited for Abbie to shed her jacket and step inside, then closed the door and walked around to the driver's side. In a moment he was backing out of the parking space beside Frasier's office.

He watched as she stretched her seat belt across her red sweater and snapped it in place. Unbelievably, her face was composed and she now seemed to be taking it all in stride. That made him wonder if she dealt with this kind of thing often.

"Did you hear what I said to you?" he asked.

"Yes, but you're wrong. He knows where he *thinks* I am. He can't know for sure unless he has contacts here, which he doesn't."

"That card was postmarked three days ago. If he hopped a plane, he could already be holed up somewhere close. And if he's as wacky as you've said, I can't believe you haven't considered that he'd come after you."

"We know enough about him to know that he wouldn't fly. Also, the Department of Motor Vehicles says Long doesn't own a car."

"That still leaves buses and trains, and he doesn't have to *own* a car to *have* a car." Jace pushed harder. "You need to move into a motel or stay with friends for a while."

"No."

"Why not?"

She stared at him incredulously. "First of all, because

it's not necessary. I spoke to a friend two nights ago, and he told me that Danny's still there. Secondly," she went on, "I've been gone for years. Most of the friends I had in high school have relocated, or we've drifted apart. And I'm certainly not going to show up on the doorstep of a friend who stayed, and ask if I can use her spare room because I *might* be at risk." She spoke wryly. "As for motels, the only one in town has outside entrances to the rooms, and that's scarier than staying alone."

She slid her fingers back through her auburn hair, revealing the clean line of her jaw and her classic bone structure before letting it slide forward again. "I'll be okay. My dad has a state-of-the-art security system."

Jace stopped for the red light at Market and Main. "And you have a state-of-the-art nutcase after you who might not give a damn if he sets off a few bells and whistles."

She lowered her voice. "Jace, I appreciate your concern, but I'm not moving."

He didn't want her appreciation, he wanted her to exercise some caution. And suddenly he wondered why Morgan didn't feel the same way. "What does your dad say about all of this? Considering the way he ran roughshod over your life before you headed for the West Coast, it amazes me that he left you here alone."

"If he'd known about the threats, he probably wouldn't have."

Jace sent her a startled look. "You didn't tell him?"

"Of course not. He would've gotten all upset and postponed his honeymoon for no good reason. He and Miriam have been pouring over brochures and planning this cruise to the Bahamas for months. I'd never ruin this trip for them."

Grimly, Jace stared dead ahead through his windshield

at the Market & Main Diner while sporadic traffic rolled by. By the time the light changed, he'd made a decision.

Easing his boot off the brake, he made a left and pulled into the diner's parking lot.

"We're stopping here?" she asked, surprised. "I thought we were picking up my car."

"We will," he said. "In a few minutes." After releasing his seat belt, he reached over and released hers, his fingers brushing her hip and his face only inches away.

For the briefest moment, their gazes locked, and the light scent of her perfume filled Jace's nostrils. Then he felt a quick, hard thump low in his gut and her cheeks got a little flushed.

"Come on," he said, getting out, then coming around to the passenger's side to open her door. "You haven't eaten since breakfast."

Abbie's dark eyes met his warily, then she turned her body away and reached into the back seat for her purse. "Why do you care that I missed lunch?" she asked as she stepped out and he shut the door. "For that matter, why do you care where I stay?"

Damned if he knew. "Look," he grumbled, evading the question. "All I want to do is get something to eat and talk about this. If you'd rather pick up your car now, that's fine. Hop back inside. But if you're not in a hurry, you're welcome to join me."

The amusement in her dark gaze was unexpected. "You do go on and on about things, don't you?" she asked, then added, "Thank you. I'd like that. But I'm picking up the check."

Scowling, Jace touched his hand to the small of her back as they crossed the tarmac to the diner. She hadn't changed. She'd talked often about standing on her own two feet during the three weeks they'd seen each other. She didn't like people thinking of her as Morgan Winslow's pampered princess. Now, as she slung her bag over her shoulder and preceded him into the old-fashioned, railcar diner, he saw that she was still determined to make her own way.

That kind of thing could be a major drawback in some situations.

And suddenly Jace wondered why her marriage had ended.

They were midway through the Blue Plate Special when she jerked her head up in disbelief and repeated the statement he'd just made. He'd been thinking about it for the better part of a half hour, weighing the pros and cons and he'd finally voiced it. Although, if he was being honest, he and the cautious little voice in his head had reservations, too.

"Move in with you?"

"Just until Morgan gets back. Obviously, my place is smaller than your dad's, but you'd still have your own space. My office has a sofa bed in it, and you'd have the family bath to yourself. I use the master bath off my room in the loft."

She set her fork down. "Thank you, but no. This is carrying the Good Samaritan thing too far."

"Then check into a motel."

"I'm not moving into the Stay-at-Your-Own-Risk Inn."

"And I don't want you there. But there are at least five or six places within a twenty mile radius, and one of them even has a pool."

"I have a place to stay, and it has a pool, too."

Jace remembered that pool. One summer night they'd

planned to take a dip in it, but they'd dipped into each other instead. "This one's indoors."

Abbie sighed. "Jace, I can't move in with you."

"Why not? Believe me, your father won't keel over if you spend some safe time at my house. You can only lose your virginity once."

She sent him a long, was-that-really-necessary? look, then answered quietly, "This has nothing to do with my father. It has to do with the two of us living under one roof. We have an intimate past, and whether I want to or not, when I'm around you, I think about it. You think about it, too."

Jace sent her a bored look to mask the lift in his belly. "What makes you think so?"

"It's my job to read people, and I do it very well."

"Oh, yeah," he returned dryly, "you were right on the money with Danny Long."

That stopped her cold, and the composure on her face gave way to the fear he'd seen earlier. She drew a shaky breath.

"Look," she began, then glanced around the relatively empty diner to be sure she wasn't overheard. "I'm not being stupid about my safety. If I thought I was in any immediate danger, I'd find another place to stay so fast, it would make your head spin. But my dad's home is secure. I grew up there. I'm comfortable there. There's a gate across the driveway leading down to the house, and—"

"And anyone can park and walk around it," Jace reminded her. He pushed his plate away, and decided to be honest with her about the sexy stuff. "As for the chemistry, yeah, I think about it. That's only natural, isn't it? That doesn't mean I plan to do anything about it. I'm not interested in going down that road again."

If his words stung, it wasn't apparent because she kept

her voice subdued. "Good, because neither am I. I'm still passing on your offer." Lifting her water glass, she took a sip, blotted her lips with her napkin then glanced at his pushed-aside plate. "If you're finished, maybe we should pick up my car now."

That night as Abbie stepped out of the shower and finished drying her hair, the darkness, isolation and sounds she'd never paid attention to before issued from every corner of the house. To her annoyance, she found herself reacting to every creak and wind gust. She checked the doors and windows, and satisfied herself that the security system was in place and working. And all the while, she kept hearing Jace's words over the distant yipping of the coyotes on the far hill.

And you have a state-of-the-art nutcase after you who might not give a damn if he sets off a few bells and whistles.

Striding into the kitchen, she fixed herself a cup of hot tea, carried it up to her room, climbed into bed and stacked her pillows behind her. Then she reached for the TV's remote and clicked through the channels. Old movies...reality shows...tired sitcoms with annoying laugh tracks...sports...the All News channel...

Abbie halted abruptly when she saw the bright red Breaking News banner running across the bottom of the screen. A mobile team was broadcasting from outside a cute country restaurant along Interstate 40, and the blond female reporter speaking into the microphone looked somber.

Abbie turned up the volume. A moment later, the tiny hairs on her arms rose and a sickening feeling of déjà vu washed through her.

"The naked body of missing seventeen-year-old honor

student Misty Gardener was found this afternoon, stran-
gled and savagely beaten to death in the woods behind this
Oklahoma eatery where she'd waited tables part-time.
Local and state police are investigating, but as yet have no
motive for the killing. Channel Eight has learned, however,
that two days earlier, another woman's body was found just
outside of Las Vegas along this same Interstate. Since the
MOs bear striking similarities, investigators from both
states are sharing information, trying to determine if the
murders are connected."

The brunette anchorwoman in the studio spoke tenta-
tively. "Are the police thinking serial killer here, Josie?
And have they mentioned what those similarities are?"

"No, to both questions, Pamela, but we've learned that
in both instances, the women's more brutal injuries were
postmortem and sexual in nature—though there's no word
yet whether either of the victims was sexually assaulted.
We hope to have more for you later."

Abbie drew a shuddering breath and her heart pounded.
It was just coincidence! Terrible as it was, young women
lost their lives every day to violent encounters. That didn't
mean Danny was behind them. Still, what little information the reporter had shared was enough to take her breath.
Deep in her mind, the lilting, wandering melody of yesterday's greeting card played over Jace's troubled voice.
This jerk knows where you are.

Did he know she was here? *Did he know for sure?* Or
had he simply found her father's address, and assumed
she was here?

Something banged against her window.

Abbie jerked bolt upright and she listened for it
again…listened hard. Then she heard the scratch of a pine
bough against the glass and realized that the bang she'd

heard was probably just the same windblown limb her father had been talking about trimming for ages.

Probably.

Maybe.

On the hill, the coyotes began yipping and howling in earnest again, the sound echoing eerily in the darkness.

Abbie grabbed the phone's handset from her nightstand and started to dial. She had to know if Danny had been seen more recently than the other night!

She stopped after tapping in the area code. She couldn't call Stuart every time she got frightened. There was nothing he could do for her from twenty-five-hundred miles away, and there was no point in getting a sixty-eight-year-old man upset. Besides, he would've called her if anything about Danny's status had changed. That is…if he knew something had changed.

Dialing a second L.A. number from memory, she phoned the LAPD and asked for Detective Rush or Detective Powell. Five minutes later she was thanking Powell and hanging up. He'd been kind as he'd assured her there was no reason to believe Danny had anything to do with either crime—that it was a coincidence, or even a copycat crime. The kid had been spotted going into his apartment the night the Las Vegas woman was killed.

So why did she still have that niggling feeling that all was not well? That the crimes had something to do with her?

Hating the way her hands shook, Abbie snared the phone book from her nightstand drawer, found Jace's number and dialed. She drew a few calming breaths. She'd just say she called to thank him for the lunch he hadn't let her buy, maybe talk about the Friends dinner for a few minutes. And strangely, she began to feel a little more secure just listening to the phone ring because there was a strong man on the other end of the line who still worried about her. But then, to her dismay, his answering machine clicked on and his recorded voice said to leave a message and he'd get back to her as soon as he could. She didn't leave a message.

Swallowing, she left her bed briefly to grab her pepper spray from her purse, returned and laid it on the bed beside her phone. She pulled her puffy comforter up to her neck, suddenly chilled to the bone. Then, eyes glued to the TV screen, she watched and waited for an update on the murders.

She was bleary-eyed and her muscles ached on Sunday morning when the sun finally pushed its way through the fine cracks between the curtains and blinds. Dragging herself out of bed, Abbie crossed the pretty violet-and-white-voile room and twisted the wand on the blind to let in more light.

Last night's terror came screaming back when sunlight glinted off a vehicle half-hidden in a break of the trees near the locked gate.

Racing to her father's room, Abbie grabbed his binoculars from a closet, then returned to rattle the field glasses between the slats of the blinds. She quickly adjusted them. Then, feeling her heart slide back down where it belonged, she exhaled in relief, set the binoculars aside and dressed.

Minutes later, she'd made the fifty-yard walk to the top of the driveway. The lean, dark-haired man sitting behind the wheel of the SUV was wearing a brown leather bomber jacket and a grim look. After briefly turning the key, her bodyguard lowered his window, then shut the car off again. Abbie caught a whiff of coffee, saw a Thermos bottle on the passenger's seat and a sleeping bag in the back.

"Good morning," he said.

"Good morning to you," she replied, her emotions still running the gamut from heartfelt gratitude to guilt. His gray gaze looked like a before ad for eye drops. "I take it you were in the neighborhood?"

"Just out communing with nature."

Abbie shook her head. No wonder she hadn't been able to reach him. He'd been here, watching over her. *Why* he'd done it was a mystery. "Jace, you shouldn't have done this. It was cold last night." The sun was up and spring was only two weeks away, but it was still barely forty degrees. "You couldn't have been comfortable."

"I wouldn't have had to if you'd shown some sense and stayed at my place or found somewhere else to go." He paused. "Did you sleep well?"

She cracked a bleak smile. "Not really."

"Bad dreams?"

"No, bad television. Come inside where it's warm and I'll tell you about it. I'll fix us some breakfast."

Sarcasm edged his voice. "No, thanks."

"Jace, don't be like that. My dad's miles away."

"Yeah? Where have I heard that before?"

A flush crept into her cheeks. "Please," she coaxed.

"No way. But if you'd like to hop in, I'll let you buy me breakfast at the diner."

She could do that. Especially since he'd treated her again yesterday. "Just give me a minute to grab my wallet and pull a brush through my hair."

"Take all the time you need," he said. "Afterward, I'll drive you back here so you can pack your bags."

"Jace—"

He cut off what he assumed would be her refusal, his serious gaze boring into hers. "Abbie, I'm offering my spare room—one last time—with no expectations and no strings attached. If this jerk shows up looking for you—and you have to admit that after getting that card yesterday, it's a possibility—he won't think to look at my place. He *might* try hotels if he's convinced that you're in the area. But you need to know something. I'm not sleeping in my car again tonight."

Abbie nodded. She'd hoped that her fears would leave when the sun came up, but despite Powell's assurance that Danny hadn't left L.A., she still had doubts.

He looked startled. "Was that a yes?"

"Yes. Thank you." In the back of her mind, she knew living with him was asking for trouble. They both had crystal-clear memories of their one night together. Wrapped in a world of their own, there'd been tenderness and shivery touches…warm deep sighs and hot sexy kisses that could've melted steel. The two of them were a tinderbox waiting for a spark, and every time they were together, the air crackled with electricity. It was here, even now, pulsing below their conversation.

"Good," he said, his tone suddenly a little subdued. It was almost as though he'd peered into her thoughts and come away with the same doubts.

"Does this mean all's forgiven?" she asked quietly.

He had no trouble answering. "It means I'm offering you a place to stay during the night when you're the most defenseless."

Abbie held back a sigh. So, that part of it hadn't changed; he still believed she'd used him, but he was willing to help her. Then she remembered how he'd kept Ty close after their mother had left them. He was a caretaker. He didn't look like one, and he had enough sexy alpha blood running through his veins to make the idea totally preposterous. But beneath his rough-cut exterior, he cared about the unfortunates of the world. And for the moment, he'd decided she was one of them.

He locked his gaze on hers, thoughts moving crisply through his gray eyes as he returned to her earlier reply. "Go. Brush your hair, grab your wallet and do whatever else you need to do. Then let's talk about the bad TV that—apparently—convinced you to accept my help."

By the time they'd entered the Market & Main Diner twenty minutes later, she'd told him everything—all about the disturbing newscast, Powell's assurance that all was well, Danny's call to her cell, and finally her own uneasiness. "It's like…a rash on the back of my neck."

Gravely exchanging a look with her, Jace guided her to the same black-and-white vinyl booth they'd used yesterday. He knew that back-of-the-neck feeling, and he knew that sometimes you could trust it. Growing up in Jillie Rae's trailer—even after he and Ty had moved in with the Parrishes—he'd felt the stares, sensed the pointed fingers of classmates. Jillie'd had the reputation of bedding any man with a wallet, and everybody in town knew it. He'd finally decided to grow a thicker skin and say to hell with all of them. He knew who he was, and he had his own set of values. But that realization had only come after half a dozen all-out brawls.

The Formica table was already set with cups and napkin-wrapped silverware, and the aromas of coffee, bacon and home-fried potatoes seasoned the air.

Forcing a smile, Abbie changed the subject as they slid into their seats. Jace was glad. He wanted her to eat something, and he couldn't see how she could with those kinds of pictures in her head.

"Looks like the sunrise service just got out."

"Yep, looks like." All decked out in their Sunday best, the after-church crowd had the lunch counter and most of the front booths taken.

Jace watched her. She'd already flipped her coffee cup over on the saucer and reached for the menu tucked behind the napkin dispenser. Even without makeup, with her hair pulled back in a loose ponytail and little wisps around her face, she made every other woman in the place look like they'd tried hard and failed.

He was about to ask if she was hungry when he spotted someone he knew and his own appetite took a nosedive.

Frowning and feeling some reluctance, yet knowing he had to take the opportunity, he touched Abbie's hand. A little spark tickled the hairs on his arm, reminding him again that living with her was going to present a whole new batch of problems. "Excuse me for a minute? I need to talk to someone. If the waitress asks for our drink orders before I get back, I'll have coffee and orange juice." Then, thanking her, he crossed the room to the booth where Arnie Flagg's wife sat alone.

"Hi, Callie," he said respectfully. "How are you? You holding up okay?"

Callie Flagg glanced up from her coffee and Danish, and her sober face lined. She was in her early forties with short brown hair and pretty blue eyes, but they were eyes that had lost their sparkle. "How am I? I'm worried, Jace."

"I'm worried, too," he replied. "But I'm not worried about Arnie not having a job to come back to. I'm worried about losing a couple of good friends."

She ignored his statement, but her briefly averted gaze told him she'd heard and understood. "He'll never work in the woods again. His leg will never hold him."

"We don't know that yet, Callie. According to—" He sighed. "According to our attorney, the surgery went well."

"He's in pain," she said angrily, as if Jace were directly responsible. "A lot of pain. And there's no assurance that the bone graft will take, or that he won't develop an infection that could take the leg *and* his life." She stopped herself, seemed to find some calm from within, then spoke in a more even voice. "I'm sorry. I'm too emotional, and I shouldn't be talking to you about any of this."

Jace's spirits sank. If she cried, he didn't know what he'd do. "I know, and I don't want to upset you any more than I already have. I just came over to tell you that Ty and I will make a place for Arnie whenever he's ready to come back. If he wants to come back."

"I don't want him in the sawmill."

"Neither do we." Every job in the mill was dangerous, and they didn't want a man who wasn't sure-footed operating any of the machinery. "There are always jobs in the drying end of the business—overseeing temperatures in the kilns, sticking, waxing… I know he doesn't have any experience there but he's a smart guy. He'd learn quickly."

She didn't reply, but she didn't get up and leave, either, and that gave Jace hope. "Ty and I want the best for him. Will you tell him what we've talked about? In the meantime, if there's anything we can do for you and the kids while he's laid up, give us a call." But he knew she wouldn't, because the lawyer who was camped on her doorstep would advise against it.

When he got back to the table, Abbie's tentative look told him she'd watched his discussion with Callie and was wondering. Mustering a weary smile, he sat down and decided to spill his guts. "Remember the phone call from the personal injury lawyer I got the day you were there?"

"Your company was facing a lawsuit."

Settling in, thinking that there didn't seem to be any pleasant breakfast topics for them today, Jace said wryly, "Well, the problem's like that imaginary rash at the back of your neck. It's not going away."

It was strange, how their talkative, almost friendly mood changed the second they carried her things into his house an hour and a half later. The house seemed too small, they seemed too aware of each other and suddenly the bone-deep realization that they'd be eating, bathing and sleeping under the same roof hit them both like a thunderbolt. At least, it hit Abbie that way. Sure, she'd thought about it before. But the realization of actually doing it left her with a breathless, cautious feeling.

"I wish you'd just take the loft," he said when she'd refused. "You'd have more privacy up there."

That might be, but she wouldn't kick him out of his own bed. "No, you've already gone above and beyond the call of duty. The sofa will be fine."

"All right," he said, carrying her bags into his office and setting them down next to a closet. "Then you can put your things in here." He opened the door, shoved three garment bags and a few jackets to the rear of the rod. "If you need more room, I can take these upstairs."

Abbie set her bag of laundry on the floor. "No need. I didn't bring many clothes with me." She wasn't sure what she'd do with her socks, sweaters and underwear, but she'd lived out of suitcases when she was in college. She could do it again. She shifted her gaze from the closet to him, and caught him studying the front of her sweater. Unexpectedly, her breasts went weighty and full. Heat flooded her cheeks, and he looked away.

"Do you have a washer and dryer?" she asked.

"In the utility room off the kitchen," he returned brusquely. "I'll get the rest of your things from your car."

When he came back inside and set her laptop on his computer desk, he nodded toward the doorway again. "I'll just grab a chest of drawers for your other things. There's a small one out in my workshop. It's not stained and finished yet, but it's clean and you can line the drawers with shelf paper."

He did carpentry work, too? Abbie watched him stride across the short hall to the great room, her gaze lingering on his broad shoulders in his hunter green shirt…his muscular thighs in his faded jeans. "Jace?"

He turned in the archway.

"Thank you," she said softly. "Really. I won't be a bother, I promise."

"I know," he returned. But the skeptical look in his gray eyes said that was wishful thinking—on both of their parts.

Thankfully, the afternoon flew by.

While Jace was outside collecting maple sap and storing it in his shed to be boiled later, Abbie arranged her things in her new room and made phone calls. She would've liked to have joined him because her curiosity was piqued, but she sensed he needed time alone. Whether he'd invited it or not, his space had been invaded, and the dynamic in his home had changed.

The first call she made was to her father and Miriam, who were getting settled in their stateroom. "I just called to wish the two of you *bon voyage*," she'd said lightly, "and to tell you that if you need to reach me and I don't answer at the house, call my cell phone. You have the number. I'm thinking about joining the Y and signing up for aerobic classes—maybe doing some swimming. I'm just not good at sitting around keeping the home fires burning."

That hadn't been a lie because she actually had considered joining the local gym, even if it was only temporarily. Her dad had applauded her energies. Then Miriam had called out that they were about to set sail, and they'd said a hurried goodbye.

The second call she made was to her dad's housekeeper, Dorothy Carson, who was pleased to have the next two weeks off to fuss over her grandkids, and still collect a paycheck. "But I'll give the place a good going-over a day or so before your dad and his new bride come home," she'd replied happily. "Even though you won't be using the house, dust does collect."

Dorothy hadn't asked which "friend" Abbie would be staying with, but Abbie knew all she'd have to do was put her ear to the ground and she'd soon know the answer. Everyone would. Juicy gossip swept through Laurel Ridge faster than a flu epidemic.

Her last call was to Stuart. If anything new materialized, she wanted to know about it, and if for some reason he couldn't reach her cell phone, he needed to know where she was staying. She gave him Jace's phone number.

A skitter of awareness moved through her when Jace walked by her open door as she was ending her call, but he didn't stop to talk, and she decided he was handling the initial awkwardness in his own way. Just as she was. The difference was he seemed to have found a way to approach it in an almost businesslike way. She envied him that talent. For better or for worse, emotion ruled her world.

The wonderful smells of food cooking woke her just before five o'clock, and Abbie sat up on the sofa, startled that the sun was gone, and darkness was on its way. She *never* napped…yet she had, probably because she hadn't slept more than two hours last night. Unsure of how much freedom she should enjoy, she'd been reading in her new room and had dozed off. Now she was ravenous.

Jace looked up from sliding steaks under the broiler as she walked into the dusky kitchen. "Hi," he said, his uncomfortable look telling her that he wasn't handling their proximity as well as she'd thought. Then he shut the oven door and turned off the small TV on the nearby counter, and she realized his uneasiness had nothing to do with their living arrangements. It had been tuned to the All News channel. "I was just coming in to wake you. How was your nap?"

"Longer than any nap I can remember," she answered guardedly, praying that he wasn't sparing her more grisly news. "I hope my mouth wasn't open."

"Might've been," he said with a smile. "I didn't look that close." Opening a cupboard, he took a bottle of steak sauce from a shelf. "The baked potatoes are almost done, and our salads are in the refrigerator. How do you like your steak?"

"Medium," she replied. "And please turn the TV back on. I've been wondering what's going on, too."

His rugged features sobered. "You're sure?"

"I'm sure. Is there anything new?"

He shook his head. "Nothing more than what you told me this morning."

Maybe that was a good thing. "Can I set the table? Or dress the salads?"

"Do whatever makes you comfortable."

Moving, she decided, watching the play of taut, toned muscles beneath his shirt. Moving made her comfortable.

Lights made her even more comfortable, and she flicked on a couple of switches. Then she went to the cupboard he indicated, handed him two matching dinner plates from the stack of assorted patterns and got busy.

Thirty minutes later, Jace was clearing the table and Abbie had started the dishes when CNN broke in with an update on what they were referring to as the I-40 Murders.

Exchanging a tense look with Jace, praying that there'd been an arrest, Abbie inhaled, wiped her hands and moved closer to the set.

Chapter 7

The pretty anchorwoman gazed into the camera and spoke. "Though the police are still reluctant to say the Las Vegas and Oklahoma killings are related, they have confirmed that both women died shortly after having sexual intercourse and the killers' signatures were the same. However," she continued, "on condition of anonymity, a source close to the Las Vegas Medical Examiner's office has revealed that there's little doubt that the murders were committed by the same individual. Both bodies showed traces of the powder found on surgical gloves, the strangulation bruises were identical in size and the same type of weapon was used in the postmortem beatings. The source also said that the second murder was more brutal, indicating that the killer's rage had escalated."

Abbie went weak, and the soul-deep guilt she felt for

breaking her code of ethics paled compared to the remorse she felt for defending and freeing a monster.

Danny's mocking phone call, last night's terror and the fear that she shared the blame for these new deaths all coalesced in her mind and her eyes filled with tears.

Jace saw them before she could blink them back.

He only hesitated for a second. Then he held her close. "Don't cry," he said, dropping his voice. "You're safe here."

But her throat was a rock, and she couldn't tell him that guilt, not fear, was the reason for her tears. Abbie slid her arms around his waist. He was big and solid, and considering their past, she knew he was only soothing her out of obligation. But she held on tightly anyway and took what he was willing to give because her heart was in shreds.

"Abbie, you can't know that this has anything to do with you. Your detective friend said Long hasn't left L.A."

She wanted to believe that more than anything. But that sensation at the back of her neck wouldn't allow it. There were just too many similarities between the recent murders and Maryanne Richards's death. "It's him," she said, her voice breaking. "I know it's him. And those women are dead because I got him off."

"Don't talk like that. You had an obligation to defend him and you did your job. You're too smart to be thinking this way. Put the blame where it belongs."

"I am," she whispered.

Sighing, Jace brought her with him as he eased back against the kitchen counter, stroked her hair. His compassion for her was getting all mixed up with the primal feelings he'd been fighting all day. Standing here with her legs tucked between the spread of his, absorbing her warmth and her weight, was like a time travel moment. Suddenly it was that college summer again, and he was tugging her back toward the Ferris wheel at the county fair. He saw the high color in her cheeks, saw her shake her head no and insist that the wheel was too high and too fast. He'd teased her until she'd finally agreed to face her fears.

She'd clung to him like dew to clover that night, sweet and scared and vulnerable at first, then finally, laughing and excited. That night there'd been no hint of the tough L.A. lawyer she would become...just the girl he'd wanted for his own since she'd walked up to him needing help with her term paper. He'd felt strong and protective, and so turned-on, if it hadn't been for shirttails, the whole world would've known he was irreversibly hot for Abbie Winslow.

Now, unable to stop the beginnings of arousal and acutely aware that the temperature in the kitchen was rising, Jace eased her away a few inches and met her watery brown eyes. He wiped her tears with his thumbs. "Let's go for a ride." He needed to break this up before his emotions got out of hand. Because suddenly he realized that something in him had been waiting for the opportunity to hold her again, and that wasn't good. He was losing his objectivity, remembering too much of the good stuff and shoving the bad to the back of his mind.

"Where?"

"Just into town to the Quikky Stopp. I have to fill my gas tank. If you smile for me, I'll buy you a cup of fake cappuccino."

"I don't need cappuccino," she said, tears in her voice. "I need absolution, Jace. I need to feel good about myself again, and I need to get rid of this clawing anxiety that won't let me sleep and keeps my nerve endings vibrating like tuning forks! I need—" She stopped abruptly, then flushed deeply and glanced away.

And everything in Jace said, "Uh-oh," because he was intimately acquainted with that clawing feeling, too.

The dizzying scent of pheromones filled the air, filled his nostrils, filled his mind. He didn't know if she was aware of it, but as she'd spoken her hands had slid down from his shoulders to his forearms, and he swallowed, watching her thumbs move aimlessly over the hair below his turned-back cuffs.

"How can I help?" It was getting hard to breathe naturally, and his kitchen was shrinking to the size of a postage stamp.

She shook her head as though she didn't know. But she knew. *They both did.*

Jungle drums pounded in Jace's head, and he lowered his gaze to the fluttering pulse at the base of her throat. Then he returned to the fire in her brown eyes. If he'd had doubts before, he now knew for sure that her thoughts were swimming in dangerous waters, too.

That's when the heat took over. That's when he lost every speck of discipline he had, and brought his mouth down on hers.

They dove hard and hungry into the kiss, snatching the moment as though there would never be another like it. He filled his fists with her hair, shoved his tongue inside her warm wet mouth, stopped to breathe and dove in again.

Time fell away. Common sense followed. They tried to deepen kisses that couldn't go any deeper, tried to grip and touch and explore all at the same time. Their lower bodies began to move, began to remember, began that sexy undulating dance that had driven him to the brink fourteen years ago.

Jace's heart raced. He was in that time machine again, back on the Ferris wheel, back in the gazebo, imagining her long smooth legs wrapping his hips. He thrust his tongue into her mouth again, and a shudder racked through him when she began to suck.

A thought echoed back to him, hazy at first, then shattering the moment.

He was back on that Ferris wheel…*back in the gazebo. And that was nowhere any man with an ounce of pride ever wanted to go again.*

Gasping, he broke from the kiss, struggled to bring himself out of the moment. *Where was his mind?* They had almost two weeks to go, and with a start like this there was nowhere to go but forward. Neither of them wanted that.

By the time her stricken, what-have-we-done look met his, he knew Abbie had come to the same conclusion. "It's okay," he said, everything he owned still thumping like a drum. "It was only a kiss."

Shaking her head, she combed her hair back from her face and whispered, "No, it wasn't. That was foreplay. Thank you for stopping."

Somehow, "you're welcome" didn't feel like the right reply. "If I hadn't, you would have."

But she didn't look all that certain, and the mindless lump in his jeans got hopeful again. Jace's gaze drifted down to her mouth. It was red and puffy, and his end-of-day stubble had left a mark on her chin. He blew out a breath, searched for conversation that would bring them back to the moment before they'd lost their minds. "Do you want to talk about the newscast?"

Her voice sounded small. "No. I'm afraid if we do any more talking tonight…"

He finished her thought silently. *They'd end up on the kitchen table.*

"I'll just finish the dishes," she murmured, going to the sink.

"I'll get them."

"No. You cooked." Sliding her hands into the sudsy water, she rattled some silverware around, then turned on the tap, rinsed them and put them in the drainer. "When I'm through here, I think I'll phone Powell again."

"Yeah, that's a good idea," he replied lamely. Then, glancing toward the down vest he'd shrugged off, he said, "I think I'll head out to the Quikky Stopp, anyway—fill my tank." Abstinence throbbed sick and heavy in his gut. He needed to get some air. "Sure you don't want a cappuccino?"

"Positive." She spared him an uncomfortable glance, and he knew that he wasn't the only one who needed some time to regroup.

"Okay," he said through a breath. "Then I'll see you in little while."

She nodded. Then she went back to rattling dishes around and he headed for the door, leaving the vest right where it was.

An hour later, Jace lay in the darkness, listening to the wind soughing through the tall pines and hemlocks surrounding the house, every nerve and muscle in his body attuned to her movements downstairs in his office. He knew she was trying to be quiet. But he had good ears and a fertile imagination he couldn't turn off. She'd showered a few minutes ago, and now he could hear the low hum of her hair dryer. The steamy fragrance of peaches and something flowery had drifted up to the loft the moment she'd opened the bathroom door.

Swearing softly, he flipped his pillow over to the cool side and tried to ignore the renewed activity spiking south of his navel. He could still taste her, still feel the way she'd fit so perfectly in the saddle of his hips.

The phone on his nightstand rang. Jace snatched up the handset quickly, checked the caller ID, then pressed the Connect button and sighed. He'd called Ty earlier to tell him Abbie was moving in for a few days, but he'd kept it short, saying only that the problem she'd had on Saturday was still ongoing. His brother had asked a lot of questions, but with Abbie napping only a few dozen yards away, Jace had left most of them unanswered. "What?"

"Just calling to ask if you need the number of a good psychiatrist," Ty said casually. "I found a few that look promising in the Yellow Pages."

"Very funny."

"Is it? What's going on with you?"

"I'm trying to sleep," Jace grumbled, "but nosy people keep bothering me. Now, if you're done with your comedy-club routine, I'll tell you what you want to know. But it's just between the three of us, for now."

A few minutes later, after sharing the abridged version of Abbie's story, Jace returned the handset to the night-stand. During the conversation, he'd gravitated to the side of the bed and he sat there now, staring down at the oak flooring. Even though Ty was worried that Abbie's presence would put Jace in jeopardy, he'd admitted that he'd do the same. So now Abbie had another ally—two tough guys who were willing to keep her safe if the need arose.

Would it? Was that sensation at the back of her neck reliable? Or was she too filled with guilt and fear, and tied too tightly to the murder in L.A., to see things clearly? She'd spoken to Powell tonight. But even after he'd reminded her again that both greeting cards had been post-marked in Los Angeles, and a stakeout team had seen Long in his apartment on the night of the Vegas murder, she still doubted Powell's off-the-cuff theory. She'd admitted that someone else could have copycatted the L.A. killing because the gruesome details of the Richards girl's death had been in the papers and on the news. But she still looked far from convinced when she hung up.

Jace wasn't sure what to believe, but he was uneasy enough over Abbie's intuitive feelings to give them at least *some* credence. That brought him back to something he'd though about before, but would never say to her.

Why would a guy with limited means come all the way across the country for revenge—killing as he went and risking an arrest that would keep him from Abbie, his main goal—when all he had to do was sit tight and wait for her to come back to L.A.? Her apartment was there. Her life, job and friends were there.

All Long had to do was be patient, and Abbie would come to him.

The image that materialized next made Jace's blood run cold. Jerking to his feet, he walked to his window, stared out at his backyard pavilion, and gave himself a firm talking-to.

What happened or didn't happen in L.A. wasn't any of his business—*she* was none of his business. He'd committed himself to keeping her safe while she was here…but whatever happened when she went back to L.A. was out of his control.

The wind was still kicking up, bending the tall hemlocks and whistling under the eaves…bringing warmer, more welcome temperatures. But, in the way one thought tumbles into another, a different kind of wind snagged his attention, and Jace drew a shuddering breath. Her hairdryer was still humming, still blowing through all that dark, silky hair…still blowing her scent straight up the stairs and into his nostrils.

And suddenly Danny Long and any danger Jace might be facing vanished from his mind, replaced by the powerful urge to haul her into his arms again and finish what they'd started in the kitchen.

The Oklahoma sun was high in the sky on Monday afternoon when Danny left the service station and roared onto Interstate 40. Glancing into his rearview mirror, he noted the cop cars still haunting Misty-the-waitress's restaurant. The news vans had moved on, though, probably speeding off to the next big story.

Maybe he'd give them one. But not until he'd changed routes—turned north on I-44, then to I-70.

Danny scowled. Interstate 40 Murders? What genius had come up with that one? He deserved something more creative, something cool like the Zodiac Killer or the Hillside Strangler. His mood sobered. But then...he hadn't killed those women for some deviant rush like those criminals had. He'd done it because, as his father said, evil needed to be dealt with. The women were evil, and they'd deserved to die.

Danny rolled his eyes sarcastically as organ music filled his head and his father's charismatic voice thundered over it. *When the just allow wickedness to thrive, they too are destined for hellfire! But no one will burn hotter than the betrayers and the fornicators!*

Betrayers and fornicators. He'd heard those words almost every day after his mother had turned in her choir robe and tambourine and run off with one of the faithful. So basically, his father had given him permission to kill. He liked that idea. All of the pleasure, none of the blame.

Quickly, Danny retracted his thought, silently denying that he liked the way his skin tingled when he approached one of them, denied that he'd killed for the pure breath-lessness of the moment. He was merely ridding the world of evil. Each time he'd swung the tire iron, he'd grown more powerful and confident, and he'd performed a little better. But he could improve. He knew it! He just needed more practice. Because *her* death had to perfect. It had to be better than Maryanne's. Better than Lorelei-the-painted-whore's. Better than Misty-the-waitress's. She'd hidden her sins behind a white blouse and an innocent smile, but when he'd peeked inside that parked car and saw her whoring with her rutting boyfriend, he'd known what he had to do, and he'd done it.

He flipped down the visor on the windshield, the sun hurting his head and eyes, making it hard to think.

Until he'd logged onto the Internet last night at the motel's dinky little business center, the Winslow bitch's location had been one of his never-fail hunches. Then he'd checked to see if her town had a Web site and struck gold when he'd clicked on the link for their daily newspaper. In their pride and stu-pidity, the *Laurel Ridge Herald* had run photos of the town's Mardi Gras benefit. Only one snapshot had filled him with loathing and nervous excitement at the same time. There she was on the screen, whoring with some guy in a tux.

That's when he'd known it was time to execute the next step in his plan—keep her confused and uncertain about his location. All it had taken was another phone call.

Cranking up the radio, Danny put the pedal to the metal, then focused happily on the DJ's latest selection. "Please, Mr. Postman"? He nearly split himself laughing.

It was fate! Everything he did, saw and heard was a reminder of his quest! Humming along, he hoped his letters were being delivered, like the song went. And the sooner they were delivered, the better.

He wanted her to sweat the way he had while he waited for the jury to come back. Between her and his blabber-mouth father, they'd nearly put him on death row. She *never* would've found Prudence without the preacher's help.

Danny's heart beat fast, feeling the added weight of Misty's warm gold medal against his chest. *Fornicators and betrayers.* He chuckled, bloody images filling his brain.

Maybe when Abbie was dead, he'd kill his old man, too.

On Tuesday morning at nine o'clock, Ida popped into the office with the morning trivia question. "Got a good one for you today, honey."

Jace looked up from the figures he'd been trying to make sense of and summoned a smile. After nearly swallowing Abbie whole on Sunday, Monday had been an exercise in gut-wrenching frustration. Last night as they'd discussed the articles and public service announcements she'd written for the two area newspapers and the local TV station, they'd kept their twitching libidos under wraps. But there'd still been enough electricity between them to light his house for a month. One more sleepless night and he'd be a raving lunatic. "Okay, shoot."

"On what continent did dinosaurs first appear?"

Rising, Jace walked around his desk and grabbed his navy quilted vest from the coat tree. "I don't know. Asia?"

"Wrong," she declared smugly. "During the early Triassic period, all the continents were joined into one great big lump called Pangaea."

Grinning, Jace zipped his vest. "Stumped me again."

"You'll do better tomorrow. Where are you off to?"

"I need to toss some wood in the back of Ty's truck. It's sap cookin' time."

"Wonderful! When?"

"Tomorrow, probably. Interested?"

"Only in the finished product. I'll leave the work to you boys, and just enjoy the syrup."

Grinning, Jace tugged a lock of her gray hair and followed her out. "We'll make sure you get some, Curly."

Forty minutes later, after collecting scrap wood and seeing off a load of lumber headed for Indiana, Jace came back inside. The day had warmed, and shrugging off his vest, he returned to the back office to check the latest kiln data.

Ida followed him in, mischief in her blue eyes. "Got another trivia question for you. Why would that pretty Abbie Winslow be calling you from *your* house?"

Instantly anxious and damning caller ID, Jace faked a smile. "No idea. Maybe she broke in." Then he waved Ida out of the office, grabbed the receiver and depressed the flashing light on his phone. "Yeah, Abbie. What's up?"

Her trembling voice started his nerves twitching again. "I just picked up my dad's mail at the post office. I got another card. Another L.A. postmark."

"I'll be right there."

"No, stay. We both have work to do. It's already on its way to L.A."

"Did you open it?"

"No, I—I didn't want to hear the music again."

Adrenaline pumped through him. An L.A. postmark seemed to say that the bastard *was* still in California and posed no immediate threat to her. But there was also the chance that Long just wanted her to think that. "I'll pick you up in a few minutes. Throw the files and whatever else you need in a bag. You can finish your work here. And Abbie?" he added, suddenly uneasy with her daily checks on Morgan's house.

"Yes?"

"Do *not* take your dad's mail out to the house alone. From now on, we'll do it together."

That evening, Abbie's gaze moved nervously as she and Jace finished gathering the day's sap and carried the plastic pails to the tree-shaded shed for storage. Dried maple leaves whispered along the gravel and crunched beneath their feet as they approached. Spring was coming. Hard red buds were popping out on a few of the trees, the afternoon sky was a clearer blue and the days were getting longer.

Less darkness, more light. Fewer shadows where a man could conceal himself.

Jace unlatched the door, and she glanced at him as they carried the pails inside. She felt edgy, but he seemed worse. At least Danny's latest card had given them something more to focus on than that kiss.

"Feels colder in here than it does outside."

"Has to be cold," he said, emptying their buckets into a plastic trash can. "Sap's like milk. If it gets too warm, it spoils."

"How much more do you need?"

He replaced the lid and led her outside. "Depends on how much syrup we want." Handing her the empty buckets, he relatched the log shed, reclaimed the buckets and started toward the house. The sun was beginning to set and it flashed golden red on the house's warm brown logs and plate glass. "A quart of syrup takes ten gallons of sap."

"Will you do that soon?"

"Tomorrow, after closing." He nodded toward the stone-and-timber picnic pavilion below the house. "We cook down there. Ty and Pete—our forester—will probably get things started."

When they entered the kitchen, Jace shrugged off his vest, hung it on a hook then went straight to the sink to rinse the buckets. His burgundy shirt was tucked into his jeans, and his sleeves were rolled back over his muscular forearms. Abbie felt a tingle remembering the downy feel of hair beneath her fingertips last night. Remembering the touch, smell and taste of him.

"Something wrong?" he asked, looking over at her.

Shaking her head, she turned away to slip off her suede jacket. She'd just taken her cell phone from her pocket when it rang. Quickly checking the ID window, she flipped it open.

"Hi," she said lightly. "How are things in the City of Angels?"

Stuart's tone was serious, yet calm. "Not very angelic, I'm afraid. I have news, Abbie."

Abbie sank onto one of the maple chairs, aware that Jace had stopped rinsing the buckets and was alertly standing by. "What kind of news?"

"The lab work is back. He was careful not to leave his prints on the card he sent you, but he licked the envelope. His DNA is all over it."

"That means—"

"That means there's enough evidence to hold him. For a while. Hopefully, once they grab him, they can build a stronger case for stalking."

"Then he's not in custody?"

"No. Powell and Rush went to his apartment a while ago, but he was gone. And before your mind starts spinning off in the wrong direction," he added quickly, "I must remind you that he's still visiting his apartment sporadically. He will be picked up."

Abbie's reply came through a relieved breath. "Good. I guess."

She didn't have to explain. Stuart understood her fear.

"No matter what happens afterward, you'll be *alive*," he returned solemnly. "That's the important thing."

Would she? How alive would she be if she could never practice law again? What kind of life was that? Not much of one.

When they'd discussed the latest card and Powell's theory on the new murders, and said goodbye, Jace came up behind her and settled his hands on her shoulders.

"You okay?" he asked. "You're shaking."

"It was cold in the shed."

"That's not why you're shaking." After a pause, he continued a little stiffly. "The man on the phone. Was that your ex-husband?"

Despite her distress, Abbie couldn't stop an amused smile. "No, Collin and I don't speak. Stuart's the senior law partner at my firm. For the time being, he's my eyes and ears in L.A."

"Well, whatever he said has you worried again." Moving to the front of the chair, he drew her to her feet. As usual, his touch sent a thrill through her, and Abbie wondered if he knew that Stuart's call was only part of her problem. "Come on. I'll make a fire and get us something hot to drink."

"You're hovering."

"So sue me."

The brown leather sofa in the living room sat at an angle near the polished fieldstone fireplace. Leading her to it, he sat her down, grabbed the cream-colored afghan from the back and tucked it around her.

He didn't speak again until he was crouched beside the hearth, arranging the logs and tinder. Snug denim strained over his lean hips and powerful thighs as he worked. "So, what did your boss say?"

"The lab found Danny's DNA on the envelope. They know he sent it—or at the very least, licked it."

The dry tinder caught quickly. "And?"

Abbie pulled the afghan more tightly around her, uncertainty creeping in again. "As soon as he surfaces—*if* he surfaces—they'll pick him up. Stuart's going to call when it's a done deal."

Grim-faced, Jace looked askance at her. "You're still convinced that he's headed east."

A few moments ago, she was ready to believe everything Stuart had said. At least she'd wanted to. Now...

Abbie massaged the tension over her eyes. "I don't know what I believe anymore. Danny's been seen going in and out of his apartment from time to time, so he must be in the city. And it's natural for him to want to evade police because they've been dogging his every move for a month and he and his lawyer are tired of it. A few nights ago, he flipped off the surveillance team parked down the street from his apartment."

"Nice."

Abbie nodded, something about the hand gesture bothering her. After a thoughtful moment, she realized what it was. "He's changing. I don't think he would've done that before. He has this warped code of respect. On the one hand—if my friend Susan is right—he felt justified in committing murder, yet until the end of the trial, he stood when I came into a room, called me Miss Winslow and never raised his voice. The character witnesses I spoke to said similar things. He's charming and helpful."

"And nuts?"

"Probably," she replied. "The bottom line is, Stuart wants me to believe Danny's still in L.A., Powell insists there's a copycat killer out there ripping off Danny's MO and logic tells me to accept that." She sent him a woeful look. "Maybe I'm the one who needs a shrink."

Standing and dusting his hands on his jeans, Jace ambled to the sofa and sat, then threaded his warm fingers through hers. Though she tried to ignore it, Abbie felt the tender connection.

"You don't need a shrink. You've got a good head on your shoulders."

She blew out a breath. "Right."

"I mean it."

Abbie's gaze dipped to their interlocking hands, then met the concern in his eyes again. He might never forgive her for the past, but he didn't let old hurts stand in the way of compassion.

"Thank you, but I suspect even you have moments when you wonder if all of my synapses are firing."

"Are you forgetting I'm the one who insisted that you move out of Morgan's place?"

"No, but that was before Powell came up with the copycat thing, and the stakeout guys said Danny was nowhere near Vegas when Lorelei Jardin was killed."

The fire cast his rugged features in shadow as the flames leapt and flickered, but it couldn't disguise the truth in his gray eyes. "Yes, I have doubts."

Hurt, nodding slowly, Abbie slid the afghan off her shoulders and stood. Only a second behind her, Jace stood, too. She'd hoped he'd tell her that he believed everything she said and felt, but to his credit, he wouldn't lie.

"I wasn't finished, Abbie."

"You don't have to finish. You think I'm delusional, too. Maybe it would be better if I went back to my dad's."

She tried to move past him, but he caught her waist and brought her back to him, his touch rippling through her.

"As I was saying, yes, I have doubts. But if you're afraid and you feel as strongly as you do about this, I will absolutely try to keep an open mind." He coaxed her closer, and those ripples intensified. "The last thing I want is for you to move out."

"Just in case?"

He nodded gravely. "Just in case. Now, let's talk about something else."

"There is nothing else. If my mind isn't on Danny, it's on what will happen if Danny's picked up. The second they arrest him, he'll tell everyone what I did, Reverend Long will confirm it and I'll never practice law again."

"You did what needed to be done."

Unexpectedly, tears stung her eyes, but she would *not* cry. A couple of nights ago her tears had led them in the wrong direction; they didn't need that kind of awkwardness again.

"Unfortunately, an ethics board won't see it that way. I did a terrible thing. I betrayed my oath, and there are rules. When they're not followed, there are consequences."

Jace remained silent, hesitant to say anything that would minimize the seriousness of her situation. Instead, he brushed a few strands of hair back from her face. It took all of his restraint not to do more. Their little mistake in the kitchen had pumped up the volume on his neglected libido, and his head was full of rumpled sheets and banging headboards. "Let's get that cocoa—or better yet, let's make popcorn and watch some TV."

"Okay," she murmured. Turning away, she picked up the remote. "I'll put CNN on, maybe there's more news on the—"

In a flash, restrained libido became blunt irritation. *"No."* He said it more sharply than he'd intended, but this was not going to happen. He plucked the remote from her hand and tossed it on the sofa. "No CNN. You've been living and breathing murder and gore for days, now dammit, give yourself a break. Why do you want pictures like that crawling around in your head?"

Abbie's dark eyes flashed. "You're censoring my television programs?"

"Only that one. It's been on almost nonstop since you got here."

"All right," she said crisply, marching away. "Your house is full of TV sets. I'll watch it in my room."

Three long strides put him in front of her, blocking her path to the hall. His penetrating gaze held hers and she glared right back.

Then without warning, the snap and sizzle they'd been dealing with since Sunday night exploded in their faces.

Chapter 8

They came together in a frantic rush, their kisses hot from the start and growing hotter with every shuddering breath they took. Jace plunged his tongue deeply into her mouth, felt his blood rush to the business end of his body.

Abbie tore her lips from his, her words a fast, breathy tremble. She wanted this but— "Jace, we got past a kiss, but this—this is different. What happens afterward?"

"I don't know," he gasped, then said, "We—we ignore it, pretend it never happened."

"Impossible," she blurted breathlessly.

He nuzzled her ear, then blazed a trail of kisses down to her jaw and throat. "Nothing's impossible if we want it badly enough. We take what's here tonight, get rid of the craziness and finally get a decent night's sleep." He slid his mouth down to the scooped neckline of her sweater, and Abbie closed her eyes as his warm breath spilled over the high swells of her breasts. "God, Abbie," he rasped, "you're so beautiful and I need you so much. Yes or no?"

The need to be his again surged full force and she knew she couldn't step away from this. Not from the wild, reckless pounding in her temples, and not from the desperate need to leave the wolf at the door. It had been years since she'd felt this kind of heart-hammering, mindless passion. *Fourteen* years.

"Yes."

Jace pulled her sweater over her head and dropped it to the floor. Then with bumping hands, he unhooked the front catch on her bra and slipped her straps off, while she fumbled with his buttons and tugged his shirttails from his jeans. Seconds later, his shirt, jeans, socks and briefs were on the floor, too. He reclaimed her mouth, and flames licked over Abbie's raw nerve endings.

She drove her hands into his hair and pulled him closer, opened wider for his thrusting tongue. She felt her breasts go heavy and full in his hands.

From the moment she'd stepped into his arms at the country club, she'd wondered what it would be like to love him again. Wondered if the years had changed him. They had, and it was all for the good.

Breaking from the kiss, Jace unsnapped her jeans and tugged her zipper down—helped her yank and wriggle until her jeans and socks were on the pile, too. Then, shuddering, unashamed of their nakedness or the boldness of their touches, they kissed and stroked, letting their hands relearn their hard swells and tender hollows.

Jace dropped to his knees to kiss her ribs, her fluttering stomach, dispose of her lacy panties. He brought her down on the hardwood with him—then seemed to realize he'd missed his target and scooted them over to the long alpaca rug.

It was as though they both wanted this so desperately, they needed to hurry before either of them had a chance to change their mind.

Blood thudded in Jace's temples as he covered her with his body—thudded a dozen other places, too. Somewhere in the back of his mind a voice was saying, *She just wants to forget for a while. This means nothing to her.* But he didn't care. Once he'd wanted her forever, but tonight, he was in it for the here and now. They both were. And the release he'd fantasized about since he saw her in that backless dress at the Mardi Gras party was only moments away.

Braced on his elbows, he felt her hands slide down the slope of his back to his hips, felt her reach for him. And a second later he was sheathed in her warmth and moving, moving. Her breathing changed almost immediately. When he felt her contract around him and tuck her face into his neck, he knew she was on her way.

He tried to wait. Tried to give her more time. But she felt too good, and suddenly that slamming fierceness claimed him. With a breathy catch in his throat, Jace turned her face up to his again. Then he sealed his mouth to hers and gave himself permission to feel.

It happened so fast for both of them, it was as though a dam had burst, sweeping them high on rushing waters then plunging them into suffocating sensation. They gripped each other hard, rode the wave to the end…then slowly and tiredly, found purchase again.

For a while, tiny aftershocks pinged through her, and a languorous peace turned Abbie's bones to butter. But as those feelings slowly ebbed and her legs and arms became her own again, the reservations she'd cast aside settled in.

She stopped stroking the thick hair at his nape, stopped scattering kisses over his shoulder and collarbone…became aware of the soft rug against her shoulder blades and bottom. The sounds she'd blotted out were back now—the wind against the window. The ticking of the woodsman's clock on the wall.

"Jace?"

He lifted his head, and in the flickering light, his warm, groggy gaze stroked hers. "What?"

Suddenly feeling vulnerable and uneasy, she wondered what he thought of her now—wondered if he thought she did this sort of thing often. Dear God, they hadn't even taken the time to find a bed or make it back to the couch. "We need to get dressed."

His breath stirred the hair at her temple, his voice amused. "Why? Are you expecting company?"

"Please," she whispered. "I need to get up."

Brow lining, Jace raised his head to search her troubled gaze, then touched his index finger to her lips to silence the thoughts he saw in her eyes. "Shh," he said softly. Then he took his finger away and replaced it with his lips.

Even though she returned his kiss, Abbie's heart dipped a little. He really did want to stick his head in the sand and pretend that one taste would be enough. But no matter what he wanted, she needed at least *some* acknowledgement of what "hadn't" just happened between them.

"And after tonight?" she whispered when he met her eyes again. "No expectations? Jace, I…I don't want to be a convenience while I'm here."

His gaze cooled for just an instant, but then he seemed to understand. Nodding, he repeated her words as though he were making a pledge. "No expectations."

Several minutes later, as Abbie adjusted the spigots in

the shower and stepped inside, she felt their wordless parting even more deeply. She'd wanted to tell him she'd had a wonderful time—that *he'd* been wonderful. And she'd wanted to tell him that the pleasure he'd given her had eclipsed anything she'd ever felt with Collin. She wanted to tell him, too, that she didn't sleep around and that she'd never made love on a floor before, and was almost embarrassed by her behavior. Almost. But he hadn't wanted to hear those things, maybe because if she opened up, he'd have to, too, and he didn't want that kind of bond with her.

Swallowing, she squeezed peach body wash on a puffy net, then smoothed it over her shoulders, the rushing water making it foam. She could still feel…everything.

But now it was time to stop feeling and find her common sense again, remember that this—this thing they had for each other—was only physical. It had no substance, no future, and *could not* happen again. She'd been lucky this time, she realized. It was a safe time in her cycle and there was very little chance of her getting pregnant.

Still her thoughts roamed like lost waifs, wondering what would've happened fourteen years ago if she'd stayed—not returned to college. Would they be together now? Married, with babies?

Probably not. He'd never said it outright, but she suspected that he wasn't the marrying or the family kind. He obviously wasn't seeing anyone on a steady basis. No phone calls had come in, and no explanations had been made for her living here with him. Besides, if he had a steady, what "hadn't happened" between them tonight wouldn't have. He was far too honest to cheat.

And they were both far too smart to think this selective amnesia plan of his would work.

* * *

Anything that could've gone wrong did go wrong the next day. A fully loaded rig heading for a customer in Ohio had broken down on Interstate 80, slowing a special delivery; a saw had gone to hell and logs being cut for a new sale had shown signs of mineral discoloration. Naturally, the weather man had chosen this day in mid-March to send north central Pennsylvania late-June temperatures.

If that wasn't enough, Abbie had been on his mind all day.

When he walked into the quiet office just after quitting time, his nerves were shot. Dear God, what if she was pregnant? He couldn't begin to imagine how much a baby could change his life. What did he know about raising a kid? There hadn't been a whole lot of role models waltzing through Jillie Rae's trailer when he was young. Carl Parrish had stepped in when he was twelve, but it wasn't the same as having a father figure from birth.

Then there was the other thing. The disturbing thing he hoped he'd never have to deal with.

As he approached the men's restroom near the back office, the door to the women's opened and Abbie came out, smoothing lotion on her hands. The smell of peaches filled the hallway.

"Hard day?" she said, the previous night's uneasiness still in her eyes.

"Not one of my best." Suggesting that they pretend nothing happened between them had been sheer lunacy. Every time he looked at her, he remembered everything they'd done and wanted more. "Just give me a minute to wash up, then I'll drive you to your dad's house so you can drop off his mail and do the daily walk-through before we head to my place."

Leaving the door open, he strode inside, turned on the spigot and soaped his hands. "Ty called a few minutes ago. He and Pete started cooking the sap around noon, so we won't be up all night. It takes quite a while."

The phone rang.

"Ida's gone home," Abbie said from the hall. "Do you want me to answer that?"

Jace sent her a sidelong glance. "No, let the machine get it. If it's important, I'll take it. If not, we're closed."

The flirty feminine voice that breached the silence had Jace quickly reaching for the paper towels, and sidestepping Abbie to get to his office.

"Jace, it's Carol. I just got in and saw your business number on my caller ID. I was out of town on a buying trip. Why didn't you leave a mess—"

Jace snapped up the phone. "Carol," he said, dropping the paper towels on his desk. "Hi."

"So you *are* there. I tried you at home first, but there was no answer. What's up?"

What *had* been up was a gut-gnawing need for female attention, but he'd broken the connection after only a few rings because he knew calling her had been a mistake. He hadn't wanted Carol; he'd wanted a woman he'd had no business touching. He swore silently, once again damning caller ID when Abbie walked into the reception area.

They had no claims on each other, and last night "hadn't happened." So why did he feel like he'd broken a damn vow or something?

But Carol was waiting for an answer, and he came up with a half truth. "It wasn't important, Carol. Just a spur of the moment thing. I need a gift for my foster mom sometime before Easter, and I wondered if you carried porcelain teapots at your shop. She collects them."

"Oh." She sounded disappointed. "I'm sure I have a few. Any special pattern? I could look around, maybe box a few up for you to choose from."

Jace declined her offer. He needed to get back to Abbie. "Thanks, but there's no rush. I have four weeks yet. I'll just drop by sometime."

"Great," she said, her voice upbeat again. "My door's always open."

"Thanks," he returned, knowing it wasn't open only for him. Carol Sheridan was a pretty, fun, no-strings woman who enjoyed dating and paled at the idea of commitment. Still, there'd been times when he'd thought she might change her mind if he pushed for more. "See you sometime before Easter." Then he hung up and walked out to the reception area where Abbie was straightening the sitting area and coffee station in the corner near the door.

As he approached her, he tried to hide his discomfort behind a carefree tone. "All set?"

"Sure." She looked up from arranging packets of sweeteners and stir sticks in the basket, then sent him a seemingly unconcerned smile and preceded him to the door. "You feel uncomfortable about that phone call."

Instantly irritated, he said, "No, I don't."

"Yes, you do, and there's no reason to be. You don't have to feel guilty if you're seeing someone."

Silently counting to ten, he set the locks and they walked to his Explorer. "I *don't* feel guilty, and I'm *not* interested in Carol."

"She's interested in you."

Jace felt a nerve leap in his jaw. "And I suppose you got that from the six words she said on the machine."

"No, I got that from the way she purred your name."

"Could we not talk about this anymore?"

"All right, but if you want to see her—or anyone else, for that matter—just do it. What 'didn't happen' between us last night didn't put a ring on either of our fingers."

He nearly said, "damn straight," but he knew commenting would only prolong the discussion, and he wanted it—and the knot in his stomach—to go away. Squeezing the remote on his key chain, he sprung the door locks, opened the passenger's door for her, then shut it when she was settled in her seat.

The Fates hated him, he decided. After a hellish day, he should've been looking at a great night. But it didn't look like that was going to happen.

It was nearly midnight when they finished cooking down the sap, and thirteen sealed jelly-size jars of maple syrup were lined up on the picnic table under the pavilion. The temperature had only fallen into the fifties, and the sweet aroma of hot maple syrup still hung in the air. Abbie moved to Jace's side as he placed the jars in a cardboard box to make them easier to carry. Ty and their staff forester had each taken a jar home, and there was a partially filled margarine container in Jace's refrigerator that he and Abbie would sample soon.

At the edge of the pavilion, a few coals still glowed between the stacked concrete blocks holding the long grates they'd used to cook on. The pots they'd used had already been washed and put away for another year.

"You didn't get as many jars as you thought," Abbie said.

"No, but there'll be enough for us, Ida, and a few pancake breakfasts over at Betty and Carl's when they get back from Florida."

She nodded. She'd been glad for Ty and Pete's presence tonight. Being busy with other people had helped them get past that phone call, and the disturbing jealousy that had been so hard for her to hide. She *had* hidden it, though, despite the fact that there was no logical reason for it.

She was just lonely, that's all, she told herself. And it didn't help that whether he was boiling sap or trouble-shooting problems at the mill, Jace was a walking, talking remedy for what ailed her.

"Did you enjoy yourself tonight?"

"Yes," Abbie answered, reining in her thoughts. "It was fun. Not at all what I expected."

"Oh? What did you expect?"

"I'm not sure. Work, maybe."

But what they'd had was an intimate little party in the woods. And oddly, the thick stand of pines, maples and beech trees hadn't given her pause tonight. She'd felt safe. The big coffeepot had been going all night, and they'd grilled hamburgers and hot dogs on one end while shallow pans of sap bubbled on the remainder of the grates. Pete had seen that country music kept playing and they never ran out of donuts. And Ty…Ty was friendly and fun as she'd held the cheesecloth filter and he'd poured the thickened syrup through it into the clean containers.

Now it was time to go in.

Taking the blue-and-white flecked metal coffeepot from the grate, Abbie added it to the box containing their mugs and the remaining donuts, then picked up the carton.

"I guess there is some work involved," Jace said belatedly as they carried the cartons to the house. "But I look forward to it every year. I'm not sure why."

Abbie knew why. It was a down-home, wholesome tradition—a family event that spoke of love, roots and camaraderie, and paved the way to warm buttery syrup breakfasts at Betty and Carl Parrish's house. It was the kind of life he'd never known growing up in Jillie Rae's trailer and deep inside of him, Abbie knew he needed it. As for her own needs… She kept walking along beside him. There was no place for them here.

She'd barely fallen asleep an hour later when something woke her. Uneasy, she sat up and listened hard. The scraping sound came again. Her pulse sped up as bloody crime scene photos and cold blue eyes fired her imagination.

Bolting from the sofa bed and leaving the lights off, she left the room and hurried through the hall to the great room. Jace was just descending the steps from the loft, bathed in moonlight pouring through the long plate-glass walls.

Bare-chested and wearing loose gray string-tied sweat-pants, he spoke quietly. "I know. I heard it, too."

After a quick glance at her short dorm shirt, he shifted his gaze to her face again. "It's probably nothing—just an animal. Stay away from the window. I'll get a flashlight."

She was about to say, *What if it isn't an animal?* when she saw the automatic handgun he held. It only startled her for a moment. Hunting and fishing were big here, and most local businessmen were granted protection permits to carry concealed weapons, her father included. Laurel Ridge didn't have L.A.'s crime rate, but there'd been a few attempted robberies as the day's business receipts were taken to the bank.

When Jace returned from the kitchen with a flashlight, he was wearing the boots he routinely left by the back door. "Stay here," he said. "I really don't think it's anything, but if there's trouble, call 911."

Then he grabbed a jacket from the closet in the hall, pulled it on and shoved the flashlight into one of the pockets. He stepped outside. Moments later, spotlights blazed around the house's perimeter, and shortly after that, he came back inside, chuckling.

He set the gun and flashlight on the end table in the great room. "Grab your jacket and put something on your feet. You need to see this."

"What's out there?"

"Bears. Two of them. I guess hibernation's over. They're in the pavilion, knocking the grill around and licking up syrup spills."

Sending him a wary look, Abbie took her jacket from the entryway closet and wiggled into her sneakers. "Okay, but I'm not leaving your porch."

"Chicken."

"And not ashamed of it. How did they find it so fast?"

He tapped his nose, then opened the door for her. "Black bears have an amazing sense of smell."

They were amazing, period, Abbie decided, smiling as Jace turned off the spotlights close to the house, and let those near the pavilion burn. The bears couldn't have cared less. As she and Jace stood watching from the far end of his porch, the furry interlopers continued to lick and bang around on the grates, hoping to find more sweets.

"I haven't seen anything like this in a long time," she murmured. A breeze kicked up, and she pulled the sides of her jacket together. "One spring when I was little my mom and I picked wild strawberries—you know, for short-cake and homemade jam."

"No, I don't know. But go on."

No matter how casually he'd said the words, Abbie sensed his underlying hurt, and once again she felt a stab of remorse for the child he'd been. "When we were finished cleaning the berries, we tossed the leaves and stems into the wastebasket, but of course, they ended up in the trash can outside."

"And the bears did, too," Jace guessed.

"Did they ever. I was scared, my mom was thrilled and my dad was furious because they made such a mess."

After pausing for a moment, she glanced over her shoulder at Jace and spoke hesitantly. "I guess there was no homemade jam or strawberry shortcake at your house."

He slipped his arms around her to shelter her from the wind. Or maybe…maybe he just needed to hold someone. His low voice burred near her ear. "Nope. Not until Ty and I moved in with the Parrishes. Jillie wasn't much for cooking. She could handle the easy stuff—macaroni and cheese, hot dogs, French fries in the oven—basically, anything we could make ourselves, and generally did. But the closest we got to homemade strawberry shortcake was store-brand jelly on our toast."

Abbie squeezed his big hands. "I'm sorry."

He squeezed hers back. "No need to be sorry. I didn't tell you that because I was looking for sympathy. It's just the way it was."

"Even so, it had to be hard, living that way."

"Not as hard as it was *not* living that way."

A lump rose in her throat. He couldn't say the words, but his meaning was clear. He'd loved and missed his mother. That was something the two of them had in common. But unlike Jace, she'd been born to money and their cupboards had always been filled with good things to eat. She turned in the circle of his arms. "Jace, I wish…" She faltered. "I wish your life had been different."

Shrugging, he met her gaze in the white moonlight.

"So do I, but who knows? Maybe it was a blessing in disguise. Everything in life shapes us. You had a controlling father, and that made you work hard for your independence. In my case, Jillie—and a couple of other people—gave me the incentive I needed to get where I am today. Now I can buy as much homemade strawberry shortcake as I want."

Once again, he'd spoken carelessly, but thinking of him *buying* homemade things—and knowing she and her father were the other people he referred to—tightened her throat even more. No matter how many times she apologized, nothing would heal the soul-deep cuts of that night.

Easing up on tiptoe, she kissed him softly. It was remorse for something she couldn't fix, but it was also a plea to forgive and move on.

"I don't want your pity," he said.

"It wasn't pity."

He searched her eyes. "Then why?"

"Because you showed me the bears," she whispered. "And because you're a good man, and I wanted to kiss you."

He didn't nod. He didn't smile. He didn't even tighten his arms around her. He merely lowered his head, gently kissed her back, and Abbie felt a chunk of her heart tear away.

They stood there for a time when it ended, feeling the March air cool their lips and ruffle their hair, last night's memories curling in their bellies and imaginations. Then Jace's gaze dropped to her mouth again.

Somewhere far away a voice whispered that this was another mistake Abbie would regret. But it drifted off like morning fog the second his lips found hers again.

Chapter 9

Jace unzipped her jacket and smoothed his hands down her sides, then moved lower to find the hem of her dorm shirt. Slipping beneath it, he gently cupped her bottom and coaxed her to him.

Then soft gray cotton stoked silk and lace until the thudding between them became too much, and with enormous difficulty, Abbie broke from the kiss. They were headed for trouble again. What was it about this man that made her forget every promise she'd made to herself?

Exhaling, Jace touched his forehead to hers. "Maybe coming out here wasn't such a good idea."

"Maybe not," she repeated. But that hadn't made it any easier to stop when all she'd wanted was to keep feeling, keep tasting. How naive they'd been to think they could settle for only one bite of the apple.

A crash, bang and ting of metal shocked the night's stillness.

Springing apart, they looked toward the pavilion as the bears ran from the heavy grates and the toppled concrete blocks. A shower of sparks burst from the few remaining coals as the second grate fell.

Exhaling, Jace brought his gaze back to her. "I think that was a sign." With obvious reluctance, he pulled her jacket closed, then sent her a bleak look and nodded toward the front door. "We'd better get some sleep. It's late, and I have to be at the mill early tomorrow."

Abbie nodded, grateful for bears—and Jace's good sense.

Last night she'd said she didn't want to be a convenience. Tonight, she'd nearly offered herself to him on his front porch.

She was dead to the world the next morning when Jace called her name from the doorway. It took her several blinks to see that he was dressed and ready for work.

Pulling herself up on her elbows, she spoke groggily. "What time is it?"

He smiled. "Daytime. Stay here and get some sleep. I'll lock up and call you later."

She didn't have the strength to argue. Between the syrup-licking bears they'd watched from the porch, and the thoughts she hadn't been able to ignore when they'd returned to their own beds, she couldn't have had more than a few hours' sleep. "Have a good morning."

"You, too."

The next sound she heard was his car starting.

Sighing, Abbie eased back on her pillow and brushed her hair from her eyes.

It would be so easy to fall for him again. And not just

because her blood caught fire whenever he got within twenty feet of her. He was everything Collin hadn't been.

Jace was kinder, more attuned to people's needs. Collin would've made her feel guilty for sleeping in. And when it came to lending a hand or throwing money at a problem, Collin would always choose the latter.

He certainly wouldn't have given up a half hour's sleep to watch foraging bears lick syrup off a grill grate. No, Collin's joy came from sampling a good bottle of wine or going to a Los Angeles Lakers game. The things Jace cared about were simpler, more solid, more straightforward.

Better.

Just after midnight, Danny flicked on the light and carried his things inside the small motel room, then tossed everything on the red plaid bedspread and locked the door. He was bleary-eyed and dizzy after driving for so many hours, but he'd had to put some distance between him and the dead girls in Springfield and St. Louis. St. Louis had been a near-masterpiece, even though the bartender at the roadhouse almost caught him when he stepped into the alley to throw out some trash. He couldn't believe he hadn't heard that door open.

Danny paused uncertainly for a moment, his mind suddenly fuzzy on the event. Then he remembered the roaring in his ears. That's why he hadn't heard the guy. Funny. Since Springfield, the noise had gotten a lot louder.

Calculating the hours between Eastern Standard and Pacific Time, he flopped down on the bed beside his duffel, bag of snack food and the open Pennsylvania map. Then he pulled his track phone from his pocket. He was beat, but he had to talk to Eddie—make sure the druggie was still wearing that red baseball cap and showing up at

Danny's apartment. Make sure he got the hundred bucks Danny'd put in the mail a few days ago.

Three minutes later, Danny was in a rage listening to Eddie's rat-faced girlfriend Leticia sobbing out a story Danny didn't want to hear.

"He got some bad stuff," she wailed. "He got this money in the mail, and he wanted to celebrate last night, but I didn't want to on account of I had to work at the Cheese Barn, and he just…died." She sobbed again, then sniffed and said, "Who is this, anyway?"

Danny cut the connection. He got up and paced, felt sweat bead his upper lip and worry make it hard to breathe. This wasn't good. Not good at all. But…maybe it would be okay. He still had Donnie helping him fool the cops into believing he was in L.A.

Quickly tapping in a second number, he sank back down on the bed and listened as a different track phone rang, this one in Donnie Fieldhouser's third-floor walk-up. Donnie wouldn't be gone after ten o'clock L.A. time on a Thursday night—or any other night, for that matter. Donnie was a loner.

Not many of the employees at the market where they'd worked had bothered with the big awkward kid, but Danny had always liked him. Donnie was one of the innocents. He was slow, but he was bright enough to live on his own and pack groceries without crushing the bread. He'd also been the only one who'd spoken to Danny after the trial when he'd come in to pick up his last paycheck—and his lousy pink slip. Despite his acquittal, Old Man Gannon had decided Danny wasn't good for business.

On the fifth ring, Donnie picked up the phone Danny had given him. "Hello," he mumbled sleepily, "this is Donald Fieldhouser speaking."

Danny felt a softening in his chest. "Hey, Dastardly Don, how're they hangin'?"

Donnie's embarrassed laughter carried across the miles. "Izzat you, Danny?"

"You know it. It's Dandy Dan, the shorter half of the Dandy Dan and Dastardly Don Super Stud Lady Killer Society. Who else calls you on this phone?"

Donnie seemed to grow uneasy—didn't laugh the way he usually did when Danny talked about their "secret club."

"Hey, Danny," he said morosely, "that don't seem funny anymore, you know, because of Maryanne."

Danny was instantly and sincerely apologetic. "You're right, big guy. We should change the name of our club."

"I think we should, too, Danny. Maybe we could call ourselves the—"

"But right now," Danny cut in, "I need to ask you something. Did you do what I told you to do in the letter I sent?"

Excitement returned to his voice. "Yeah, I did, Danny."

"Good. Tell me exactly what you did."

"I took the hundred dollar bill to Mazie at the store and told her I needed a hundred dollars worth of quarters for the arcade, just like you said. Then she called the manager, and Mr. Gannon sneered at me and said, 'Donnie, where would you get a hundred dollar bill?' And I said, 'Danny gave it to me for the arcade because we're friends.'"

"Great." Danny's pulse quickened. "Now think hard. Did you say I *gave* it to you or I *sent* it to you?"

"I said *gave,* just like you told me. And when Mr. Gannon asked me where I was when you gave me the money, I told him I couldn't remember—someplace near my house. Then he called the cops, just like you said, and they asked me the same thing. But I told them I couldn't remember, too. Did I do good, Danny? Did I help you?"

"You sure did, buddy. Thank you."

"When are you really going to come and see me, Danny?"

"Soon, Donnie. As soon as I clear my name. Some people still think I hurt Maryanne."

"Yeah, I know," he replied sadly. He switched gears suddenly. "I still got the card in the plastic bag."

Danny exhaled a soft breath. "Good, because that's the other reason I called. I want you to mail it tonight. After everybody has gone to sleep, I want you to sneak out of your apartment and walk as far as you can, then put the card in a mailbox, okay? But don't touch it. Just shake it out of the plastic bag into the box. You know that Miss Winslow is a lawyer, right? And all the lawyers in the country have their mail checked for fingerprints *every day*—even their junk mail. It's a big law."

"It is?"

"Yeah, and I don't want Miss Winslow to think you sent her the surprise birthday card. I just want her to know it came from me, and how grateful I am because she got me off."

"Okay, Danny, I'll do it tonight."

"Super." Danny smiled, feeling better, his gaze straying outside his window where the distant light from the Bradford Airport swiped the night sky. "So, did you blow them away at the arcade, buddy? Did you show 'em who the king was?"

"Not so much," Donnie mumbled. "But I still got thirty dollars left."

"That's okay," Danny returned. "If you promise to keep being my friend and not tell anybody about the card, I'll send you some more money in a little while. Remember what I always used to tell you?"

"Practice makes perfect?"

"You bet." Danny felt his blood warm, felt it swell as he stroked the chains he wore beneath his hoodie, cupped the bumpy trophies taped to his chest. "The more we practice…the better we get at what we do." Dragging the map onto his lap, he located the tiny blue letters that spelled out Laurel Ridge, then twisted his fingernail into the paper until he'd bored a hole through it. "You take care, buddy. I'll talk to you soon."

Danny set the map and phone aside, then slowly eased back on a pillow, feeling his dizziness return. He heard that roaring again—distant this time, but Danny knew it was practicing for the big event.

He'd stay here a day or two—had to stay, in fact. He needed time for the card to be delivered and handed over to the police, then time for them to convince her she was safe. After that…justice. Last night he'd visited another Internet coffee shop and checked out her hometown newspaper again. *She was alone in the house.* Her rich daddy was on his honeymoon cruise.

Suddenly Danny gritted his teeth in anger, felt the fire of righteousness flame in his belly. He would get her! He would get her good for betraying him!

But for now… He felt himself fade as his mood swung the other way again and his eyes drifted closed. For now, he needed to sleep.

On Saturday afternoon, Jace was in his carpentry shop working off some tension after walking in on Abbie's Pilates session when he noticed the red light above his cordless wall phone flashing. Shutting off the noisy router and removing his ear protection, he dusted his hands on his jeans and walked to the still-ringing phone. The light stopped blinking when he picked up the handset. "This is Jace."

The voice on the line was older, male and a little hesitant. "My name is Stuart McMillain, and I'm trying to reach Abbie Winslow. Perhaps I've misdialed."

Surprised that she'd given her boss his number, Jace replied, "No, this is the right number. She's in the house. I'll get her for you."

"Thank you, but apparently she's indisposed because she didn't answer her cell phone. I'll just leave a message for her, Mister...?"

"Rogan. I'm a friend."

"Good. She can use a few of those. Please ask her to phone me when she has a moment. I'll be at my home."

Jace couldn't help himself. He was concerned and he wanted to know what was going on. "Mr. McMillain, I know all about her trouble in L.A. Is there anything you can tell *me?*"

When he hesitated, Jace pushed harder. "Look, if she's staying here, she obviously trusts me. Now, if you have information I need to keep her safe, you need to tell me that right now."

A smile crept into the older man's voice. "Are you a tough guy, Mr. Rogan?"

"When I need to be. What's going on?"

When Jace walked into Abbie's quarters a few minutes later, she was still wearing black spandex tights and a long pink tied-at-the-hip tank top. But instead of doing those slow bends and stretches that had driven him out of the house twenty minutes ago, she was doing some sort of...weird martial arts exercises? Short wisps of hair fuzzed around her face and headset, and exertion had her classic features damp and glowing.

He sighed, seeing the TV tuned to the All News channel again, and realized what had sparked the new exercises. He waved a hand to get her attention. She was upset again.

With an embarrassed look, Abbie slipped off her headset, the springy plastic band circling her neck and trapping her long auburn ponytail. The pumping beat coming from the black foam earpieces ceased when she turned off the tiny CD player clipped to her waistband.

"What's with the kung fu moves?"

She averted her gaze. "There've been more murders. Missouri this time. And it's not kung fu. They're self-defense moves I saw in a Sandra Bullock film once. I thought I'd give them a try." Briefly, her gaze slid to the TV set, then back to him. "Apparently, if a mugger approaches from behind, the best thing to do is elbow him in solar plexus, stamp on his instep, smash his nose with the heel of your hand and jam a knee into his groin."

Jace winced.

"Yeah," she murmured. "That Sandra knows her stuff." Then she seemed to realize he'd come in for a reason. "What's up?"

"Your friend Stuart phoned. He wants you to call him back, but—"

She was off like a shot to grab her cell from the charger on the desk.

"*But,*" he repeated, stopping her with a hand on her shoulder. "He also gave me a message to give you."

Abbie set the phone down, her dark gaze sharp and searching. "What did he say?"

"He said the cops spoke to an employee at the market where Long used to work. The kid told them that Long is definitely in Los Angeles. Not in Las Vegas, not in Oklahoma—" He nodded at the TV set. "And not crossing the country to get to you."

"This employee *saw* Danny?"

"Apparently. He handed the kid a hundred bucks to play arcade games."

"A hundred dollars for video games?" she repeated incredulously. Brows furrowing, she moved to the sofa to pick up a white towel, then daubed her face, thoughts moving through her troubled eyes like a computer compiling data.

"Okay," she said after a time. "Okay. He can be generous when he cares about someone. And he's obviously able to hide his manic tendencies when it suits him." She drew a breath and nodded. "Okay. Okay, good."

"You still have doubts."

"Only until he's behind bars."

Jace had doubts of his own. Then again, maybe he just wanted to have doubts. He'd gotten used to having her around—just for company—and if she wasn't at risk, there was no reason for her to stay. Stuart McMillain's closing words came back to him, strangely unsettling. *We're all hoping this terrible business is settled soon so she can come back home. We miss her.*

Abbie picked up her phone again. "I should probably call Stuart back."

Jace nodded. The other thing she should probably do was change into something that didn't shut down his lungs. "He said to call him at home. I'll be in my shop if you need me."

"What are you building?"

Nothing complicated, that was for sure. "Just a tabletop for now. I'll be back in a little while."

Except his feet wouldn't move away from all that black

spandex, and he fumbled for a reason to look at her a little longer. Or maybe what he wanted was her assurance that she wasn't going to pack up and move back to her dad's place. "Want to grab dinner at a seafood place tonight?"

Abbie met his eyes. Did that mean he wasn't planning to throw her out? And if not, why *wouldn't* he want her to leave? It had been three days since their tumble into lunacy on the porch, and absolutely none of the stress and dicey awareness had faded. They'd even drawn a few curious looks at last night's food bank meeting, but no one had commented on their living arrangements—probably because Jace would've shut them down if they'd pried.

"I'd like that," she said finally. "I didn't realize there *was* a seafood place in town."

"There isn't. This one's a few miles north, but their Saturday buffet's pretty good. They start serving around five."

"Okay, what time should I be ready, and what's the dress code?"

He gave her outfit a long, slow once-over. "Anything but what you're wearing will be fine. If you show up in that getup, every man in the joint will go up in flames."

When he was gone, Abbie let her eyes drift shut, told her heartbeat to settle down and reminded herself that this was a temporary arrangement. Then she took off her headset and CD player, laid them on the desk and picked up her phone.

"Abbie," Stuart answered heartily after more than a half dozen rings. "Sorry for the delay. I was helping Margaret with the shrimp for this evening's barbecue."

"No problem," she replied, envying Stuart's forty-year-marriage to his college sweetheart. Envying their contented life when hers was such a mess. She mustered a smile. "Jace said you phoned. I understand it's time to put my doubts to rest."

* * *

Dinner at The Sassy Seas had been delicious, Abbie thought the next day as she shifted clothes from the washer to the dryer and set the timer. But all the scallops, crab legs and drawn butter had destroyed any benefits she might've gained from her workout. Today, she vowed to eat sensibly. If this kept up, she'd be on cholesterol medication by the time she returned to L.A.

The kitchen door opened and closed, and Abbie froze for a moment. Jace had been in his shop most of the morning, sawing and routing and sanding, and basically keeping a boatload of distance between them. Their daylight drive to the restaurant had been fairly stress free. But on the dark trip home, tension had turned up like that proverbial bad penny, and the copper had been red hot. And neither of them had broached the subject of her leaving.

His low grumble came from the doorway between the kitchen and utility room as she tossed a load of jeans into the washer. "I told you I'd take care of those. You're not here to do my laundry."

"I'm not doing *your* laundry, I'm doing *our* laundry."

"Dammit, Abbie—"

A horn blared and honked and beeped all the way down the driveway, snagging their attention before they could get into a verbal tug of war.

He glanced out the window—and his impatience vanished. "It's Ty," he said, his voice warming. "And he's not alone." He took her hand. "Come on. You're finished for the day, Cinderella. There's someone I want you to meet."

Moments later, he was helping his foster mother down from the cab of Ty's truck and chuckling. "Look what the wind blew in."

Laughing, the short, sandy-haired woman in the jeans, pink shirt and denim jacket eased up on tiptoe to give Jace a hug and a big noisy kiss on the cheek. "Happy birthday, Jacey."

"Thanks," he said, grinning and returning the kiss.

Today is his birthday?

Ty came over to shake Jace's hand. "Happy birthday, big brother, but if you don't mind, I'll pass on the kiss. We brought Chinese for lunch and birthday cake for dessert." Reaching into the bed of the truck, he produced a huge carton and a bakery box. "We grabbed four different entrées so we could have a buffet." He handed the carton to Jace and grinned. "I'll take care of the cake."

"Ma," Ty said before Jace could introduce her, "this is Abbie Winslow. Abbie, Betty Parrish—or Ma, or Mother Teresa. She answers to whatever you call her."

Laughing again, the petite woman with the sunny Florida tan shook Abbie's hand. "Just plain Betty will be fine. Nice to meet you, Abbie—but I believe I do know you. You went to school with Ty."

"Same grade, but always different rooms. And it's nice to meet you, too."

Releasing Abbie's hand, Betty glanced at Jace, at Abbie, then back at Jace again, a smile crinkling the skin beside her blue eyes. "Well, now. Things seem to be looking up around here. When did all this happen?"

With a good-natured sigh, Jace nodded her toward the house and fell into step beside her. "Now, don't get nuts and start hunting up a preacher. Abbie's just a friend. She'll be flying back to L.A. in a week or so."

And though everything he'd said was true, Abbie's heart sank like a stone.

Chapter 10

After they'd eaten and embarrassed Jace by singing "Happy Birthday," talk had turned to family business, and Abbie had felt like a fifth wheel. As soon as they'd cleared the table, she'd excused herself to take a walk and make a few phone calls, one of them to her dad's housekeeper.

When she returned a half hour later, Ty's truck was gone, and Betty was in the laundry room folding the clothes that had come out of the dryer. "The boys had to run to the mill to check out a problem with one of the squirrel cages," she said, smiling. "They shouldn't be long."

Feeling self-conscious because there was a stack of her underwear on the narrow table, Abbie walked to the bar to help Betty fold. "Squirrel cages?"

Betty grinned. "Fans that circulate the air inside the kilns." She finished folding a pair of Jace's briefs and added them to the pile. "Actually, I'm glad you came back before they did because I wanted to talk to you alone."

Hearing the slightly serious shift in her voice, Abbie assessed her warily. "What about?"

"Jace, of course. And forgive me if I get straight to the point. I need to say this before the boys get back."

Abbie waited.

"Jace was always a great kid," she began. "Bright, polite and respectful. But it took him a long time to warm up to us when he came to live with Carl and me. Ty was another story. He was four years younger and desperately needed someone to cling to—well, someone besides Jace. The two of them were practically joined at the hip for years before Jace let Ty try his own wings."

She folded the last pair of socks. "You've probably noticed that Ty calls me Ma, and Jace calls me Betty."

Not sure what this had to do with her, Abbie nodded.

"Well, despite the bad choices Jillie Rae made, Jace worshipped her. I doubt he could ever see anyone as a mother *except* Jillie. Jace was devastated when she left them—no matter how unselfish her reasons might have been." Scooping up the stacks, she set them in the blue plastic basket. "And now you're wondering why I'm telling you this."

Abbie smiled. "It crossed my mind."

"I'm telling you because I saw you and Jace come out of the house hand-in-hand, and noticed how he deferred to you during lunch. It was subtle...but I think something nice might be happening between you."

Claiming the basket, Abbie spoke breezily. "There is— friendship. Jace told you that."

"But I sensed something more, and I just wanted you to know that he's slow to trust, even today. So if I'm right, be patient, give him time to let it grow." Her smile warmed.

"That's why I always make a big fuss over the boys' birthdays, even if it means flying in from Florida. I want them to know that they're loved, and more importantly, that all women don't walk away."

Abbie averted her gaze, feeling a pang of guilt and wondering if Jace had seen her actions after their night in the gazebo as desertion, too. Had he seen her as another woman who walked away?

"He's a good guy," Betty went on, "but he's driven to succeed and he works too hard. He'd never admit it because he hates sympathy, but I know he feels he has something to prove to the people of this town. That said, it was nice to see my workaholic foster son at home, enjoying the day."

Abbie's attention sharpened. "Jace is a workaholic?"

"He was when I left for Florida. And the fact that you didn't know that says he hasn't been burying himself in logs and lumber since the two of you hooked up."

"Betty, we haven't hooked up, we're just—"

"Friends, I know. But there's a reason he's sticking close to home, and I believe that reason is you."

Yes, it was, Abbie admitted silently, but not for the reasons Betty thought. Jace had merely been in protective mode, keeping her safe the way he'd kept Ty safe as a child.

Engine sounds, followed by reflected sunlight flashing through the window and lighting the beige wall broadened Betty's smile. "Well, how do you like that for timing? They're back." She touched Abbie's arm. "Are you angry with me for sticking my nose in your business?"

Abbie smiled wanly and carried the basket into the kitchen. "Of course not. But there was no need. As Jace mentioned earlier, I'll be returning to Los Angeles soon."

Jace and Ty were talking as they came inside, saying

something about checking the kilns again later. But apparently the problem had been solved because they were smiling. Jace's smile dimmed the moment he met her eyes.

Crossing to Abbie, he took the basket and spoke in an undertone. "Something wrong?"

"Nope," she answered flippantly, but underneath, part of her grieved for things that couldn't be. "Betty and I just folded the laundry. Now give it back so I can put it away. I'll only be a minute."

"I'll take care of my own—"

Her low murmur cut him off. "Jace, Betty will be leaving tomorrow, and business has already taken time from your visit with her. Let me do this."

His strong features softened. "Now I owe you."

"No, I'm the one who's indebted," she returned, experiencing some of those feelings Betty had sensed. She took the basket back. "I'll put your things on your bed." Then she hurried into the great room and climbed the stairs to the loft.

She'd never been in his room before, respecting his space, as he respected hers. But as was apparent from the floor of the great room, his bedroom was open except for the varnished twig fencing and rails that ran across the front of it. It was beautifully, primitively male.

Heat coiled in her stomach as she crossed the oak floor. His king-size bed featured a sturdy curved headboard of carved pine logs, and his chest of drawers, dresser and armoire were varnished distressed pine. Intuitively, she knew he'd built every piece of furniture because in style and substance, they were similar to the chest he'd offered her last week.

Quickly taking his things from the basket, she placed them on the hunter-green rib-cord spread—the only color in the room except for the matching curtains on the wide window facing the back of the house. Then she headed for her own room. Jace's room plucked at her nerve endings. Not because she was treading on forbidden ground, but because after their romp on his living room floor two nights ago and those midnight kisses on the porch, she *wanted* to tread.

She wanted his touch. She wanted his mouth, she wanted all of him. She wanted to crawl into his big beautiful pine bed and shiver and reel, and feel the total completion she'd read about in novels, but had never experienced. The completion she'd never felt with Collin—or with Jace, either time. Yes, she'd felt all the shudders and tingles a woman was supposed to feel when she was well-loved. But that heart-deep feeling of oneness had eluded her even when she and Jace had come together the second time. Maybe because they'd been rushed and were concentrating on the physical. Still, there was something simmering just below the sexual satisfaction—a promise of something wonderful and deeply important. But…it wasn't for her.

An hour later, after kisses, hugs and see-you-soons were accomplished, Abbie and Jace waved from the porch as Ty's Silverado crested the driveway, then disappeared. Betty had wanted to spend the rest of the day and night at her own home and visit with neighbors before catching her return flight out of Bradford the next evening. Ty and Jace had coaxed her to stay a little longer, but she'd laughingly insisted that Carl fell out of bed without someone to hold on to, and that she needed to get back. Hearing the affection in her voice, Abbie realized how lucky Ty and Jace had been to land in loving arms when Jillie Rae left them. She knew that not all foster children were that fortunate.

Jace turned to her. The mid-March day was still sunny,

the last of the snow running in narrow rivulets across his gravel driveway. "So, what do you want to do for the rest of the afternoon?"

Abbie jerked a look at him, remembering what he'd said about returning to the mill, and trying—for her own sake—not to place too much importance on his question. "Aren't you going back to work?"

"Nope. John'll call if there's a problem." He paused, then scanned her pale yellow sweater and jeans. "Grab a jacket and slip your boots on."

"Where are we going?"

"Someplace where it's wetter and cooler," he said, his gray eyes teasing.

"Okay," she laughed, ready for an adventure. "I'll be right back."

She was just pulling her jacket on when Jace rushed inside. "Wait for me on the porch while I get my field glasses. They're early this year."

"Who's early this year?" she called back.

Minutes later, sharing his binoculars, they watched a springtime courtship in the sky over his yard, enjoying the steep aerial climbs and death-defying downward plunges of coupling marsh hawks.

After several repetitions, Jace chuckled softly. "Gives new meaning to falling in love, doesn't it?"

Smiling, Abbie returned the binoculars. "Lucky for them, they can pull out of the dive before they hit the ground. People aren't that fortunate."

He assessed her curiously. "Talking about anyone in particular?"

"Yes. Me."

He didn't ask her to elaborate until they'd walked down the damp, leaf-strewn path behind his home, following the small creek that sprang up a hundred yards from the pavilion. The air was cool and damp, and lingering patches of snow lay in the hollows below the bare maples and shaggy hemlocks. Abbie heard the rush of water somewhere nearby.

"So, why didn't you pull out of the dive before you hit the ground?"

"Had my head in the clouds. I thought I was in love."

"Oh?"

She nodded. "Looking back, it was more like admiration and infatuation. Collin was—and still is—one of the most talented lawyers in L.A. So when he asked me to marry him, I said yes. I was twenty-eight and I had this weird idea that it was *time* for me to marry and start a family. But…we both had busy practices and didn't take the time to make the marriage work."

"Were you together long?"

"Two years." She picked her way over a mushy stretch of the path, then glanced at him. Her pulse did a silly little skip. Here in the woods with the blue sky skimming the tree tops and the rustle of spring awakenings around them, Jace was in his element. Dressed in jeans, boots, a dark gray flannel shirt and his down vest, he couldn't have looked more blatantly male if he'd tried.

"So what happened?" he asked.

"Besides apathy, you mean? He changed his mind about wanting children. I tried to change it back, but in the end he decided we didn't have enough in common and bailed out."

"Not every man wants kids."

Abbie stopped briefly. "You?"

"Yep. I have no desire to replicate myself."

"But why?"

"I just don't."

A sinking feeling took some of the day's joy away, but his life was his own, and she had to respect that—even if she didn't understand it. She changed the subject.

"How about you?" she asked. "Have you ever been married?"

"Nope."

"Ever come close?"

"Once."

The sound of rushing water was louder now, and taking her hand, Jace guided her down a steep incline.

"And?" she prompted.

"And it didn't work out."

When he didn't offer more, she backed away from the topic. That didn't stop her from wondering *why* he hadn't made it to the altar. And what woman in her right mind would let a man like Jace get away?

She answered her own question. She had. And suddenly, she knew that might've been the biggest mistake she'd ever made. She was part of a prestigious firm—for the moment, anyway—but Stuart had been right when he'd implied that there was more to life than practicing law.

When they reached the bottom where the creek fanned out then rushed down through rocks and fallen timber, Jace smiled and gestured at their surroundings. "We're here."

Awestruck, Abbie took in the massive black rock formation and the waters spilling forty feet down to the sun-struck pool at its base. "How beautiful," she murmured. "I wouldn't have guessed there was a waterfall this high in the area."

"The terrain's deceptive."

It certainly was. Until now, she hadn't realized that his

home was situated on a hill. "Did you know it was here when you bought the house?"

"Sure. It was one of the selling points."

"And you bought it so you could fish whenever you wanted."

"No, I bought it so I could *look* whenever I wanted."

A warm glow suffused her, and again, Abbie glimpsed the man he was inside. Water rushed and babbled in the stillness, and her heart beat fast when he shifted his gaze from the waterfall to her. She took in the thick shag of black hair grazing his forehead and brushing his collar…dropped her gaze to the faint beard shadow that never quite left his strong jaw…settled on the sensual curve of his mouth. And that tummy-dropping, Ferris wheel-falling feeling struck her full force when she saw the desire in his eyes.

"We have to stop this," she said, feeling her pulse race as he walked to her.

"I agree," he murmured. "Let's do that. Tomorrow."

The long, wet kisses and intimate touching were so intoxicating, by the time an unnatural sound filtered through the white-noise rush of the waterfall and their heavy breathing, Jace's hand was under her sweater and unsnapping her bra. Abbie tore her lips from his. "That's my cell phone."

"Let it ring," Jace said hoarsely, then covered her mouth with his again.

Abbie's heart pounded. She wanted to let it ring. With everything in her, she wanted to. But only a handful of people had her cell number and they didn't call unless it was important. She broke from the kiss again. "Just let me check the number."

Releasing a blast of air, Jace slid his hand from under her sweater. But he didn't step away and for that, Abbie was thankful. Quickly pulling the phone from her pocket, she checked the ID window, then begged him with a look. "It's Stuart again."

Jace nodded. "Take the call." Then he did step away.

"Stuart," she said in a breathy rush when she'd flipped her phone open. "Good afternoon."

"It's good morning here," he said, his voice strong and sure. "I was just about to leave you a message. I have more news, and it seems to confirm the claim of that young man who worked with Long."

"Then he did see Danny in the street?" Though she'd ordered herself to put that back-of-the-neck feeling to rest, she still hadn't been one hundred percent successful.

"Yes. I didn't mention it, but there was another questionable envelope in the stack with your home mail yesterday, and I turned it over to the detectives. Powell just phoned. There were no prints, but again, the saliva on the envelope was Long's."

It bothered her for a moment that he was hiding his prints but leaving his saliva. Then she considered that he might not have been able to resist licking the envelope. "Was there a message in the card?"

When he hesitated, she knew there was. "Stuart, what did it say?"

"It said, 'Patiently Waiting.'"

Chills raised the hairs on her arms.

"Abbie, he's simply casting out nets—trying to find you, or hoping these cards are forwarded. Remember, he's all about power. He gained power by killing that young woman, exerted power over the public by shocking them with his butchery and now he's using that power on you—making you worry even when he can't get to you. Don't let him."

Good advice, but impossible to follow. She'd been so wired for so long that, even when Danny's threats were absent on a conscious level, subconsciously he was always with her. "I take it he hasn't been back to his apartment yet."

"No, but as soon as he does, he'll be charged." His voice grew tentative. "Of course, this means it would be best if you stayed where you are until that happens. We want you to be safe when you come back."

Abbie looked over at Jace, drawn to his rugged profile, and the broad shoulders that had taken on her problems. Drawn to the caring he hid behind his tough-guy image. "Actually," she murmured, "I think I'd like to stay on a while longer if you can spare me at the firm."

Stuart's voice gentled. "I hear something in your voice, my girl. Have you found someone?"

"No," she replied, almost afraid to say the words. "I think I've refound someone."

Danny hung back from the checkout lines, scanning the frazzled store clerks as they scanned and beeped their little hearts out. The store was a big one—one of those places that advertised one-stop shopping and had twenty cash registers going on a busy night. He liked these stores. They were always hectic, and the checkout people were so anxious to clear customers from their lines, they didn't have time to notice or care what anyone bought.

He pushed his cart into a line, then—just in case—he added a few tabloids to disguise his purchases.

He felt a burst of anger when he noticed a juicy celebrity rape case splashed on one of the covers.

They'd tried to hang a rape on him, too, but it hadn't been rape. Rape was sinful. But after finding out she was used goods, sex was the perfect way to get her lying down on that beach. It was one thing for a woman to flaunt her sins like that Vegas whore. No guy would expect much. But a pretty girl pretending to be pure was deceitful and vicious and cruel and *wrong!*

Aware that he was grinding his teeth, Danny relaxed and pushed his cart forward in line. Then he unloaded his purchases and opened his wallet as the pregnant girl with the nasty blue eye shadow shoved his things through the scanner.

Scissors. Beep.

Dark blue vinyl tape, black spray paint. Beep, beep.

Penn State sweatshirt, tabloids, potato chips. Beep, beep, beep, beep, beep.

Baseball bat. *Beep.*

That night as Jace sat at the computer in his office scanning his e-mails and deleting spam, his nerves were so strung out he could barely function. Touching her, kissing her at the waterfall had him wanting her all the more, and from the way she'd responded he knew the feeling was mutual. But after McMillain's call, there was no going back to that moment. Worse, in the back of his mind a clock was ticking.

His peripheral vision picked up movement to his right, and Jace glanced up.

"Hi," she said from the doorway.

"Hi." She was all dark eyes, model's cheekbones and Pantene hair after her shower.

"Sorry to bother you, but I just put the kettle on for tea and thought I'd ask if you wanted something from the kitchen."

"No, thanks." Nothing in his kitchen was going to fix what ailed him tonight—unless it was her. "I'll just finish up and give you back your room."

"There's no rush. This is your space, not mine. And actually…that's what I came in here to say." She continued in a cautious voice. "I'm moving back to my dad's place."

Everything in Jace went stone still. *That's why that clock was ticking.* McMillain's latest assurance that Long was still in L.A. had finally convinced her. But her tone had said something else, too—something they'd both known for days. Things were getting too complicated between them.

"After all," she went on, "the danger's over—here in Laurel Ridge, anyway. And the honeymooners will be home soon. Dad phoned from Freeport a little while ago."

Shutting down the computer, Jace locked his gaze on her, a niggling concern bugging him again. And this one had nothing to do with her leaving.

Even though another card had been delivered to Abbie's L.A. apartment, and someone who knew Long had supposedly spoken to him, no one else had seen him. If Long was as manipulative as Abbie said, this could all be a cleverly choreographed distraction to make her drop her guard. Jace held back a sigh. Or was he, once again, just looking for an excuse to keep her with him a while longer?

"Okay, your dad's coming home soon. Why not stay until then? You're comfortable here, aren't you?"

"Yes, but you've been running yourself ragged, looking out for me, taking me to the post office, driving me to my dad's house for a daily walk-through. It's time I gave you back your life." She hesitated. "Betty said you're a workaholic. You haven't been doing much of that since I arrived."

"And you think I'm missing it?"

"Aren't you?"

"Not so far."

She didn't reply, just stood there looking too good and too sweet and too important for his peace of mind.

Jace pushed to his feet. "Maybe I do want something from the kitchen. I think there's ice cream in the freezer. Do you like choc—"

"Oh, Lord, no more sugar," she breathed. "I have to stop eating like this. Cake, ice cream, fried foods. No wonder I can't sleep."

"Okay," he replied, though he doubted that her diet alone was keeping her up nights. "I'll pass, too. I guess we have been hitting the sweets pretty hard."

That wasn't the half of it, Abbie thought as he followed her to the kitchen. They'd been hitting everything hard—especially each other—and they needed to stop.

Still, her interest in his love life overrode good sense as Jace poured ice water for himself and she waited for the teakettle to whistle. His being with someone else stung her in a way that Collin's past never had. But as darkness shaded the windows, and that unyielding awareness continued to dog them, she still wanted to know.

"We never finished our conversation this afternoon," she said, breaking the silence.

"What conversation?"

"You were about to tell me why you never made it to the altar."

Snapping the top on the pitcher, he walked back to the refrigerator. "No, I wasn't."

"Is it a deep, dark secret?"

"It's not deep or dark." He slid the pitcher on the shelf and closed the door. "It's just not important."

"Then tell me what happened. You owe me a story."

Clearly annoyed that she kept on pushing, he stared pointedly.

"Come on, Rogan," she said, refusing to back down. "I showed you mine. Now you show me yours."

Chapter 11

"You've already seen mine."

"You know what I mean. Was it Carol? The woman who phoned your office?"

Muttering something about being on a damn witness stand, Jace carried his ice water to the bar where Abbie stood, then set it beside her cup.

"No, she was just someone who couldn't handle the long hours I worked while Ty and I were building our business. She skipped out. End of story." He sipped from his glass. "Other than that, I've never found anyone crazy enough to *want* the Rogan name."

His off-the-cuff statement hit her in a tender place, and Abbie added one more woman to the list of those who'd walked away from him. No wonder Betty had said he was slow to trust. "I can understand why she didn't like the long hours. No woman wants to come in second in any man's life."

"In time, I would've made sure that she came first. But she couldn't see that I needed to build something that—" He looked reluctant to finish, then finally said, "Something that would give people more to talk about than the revolving door on a run-down trailer."

"Did you tell her that?"

"Why would I? If she'd been the right woman, she would've seen it on her own."

The teakettle shrilled.

Abbie took her cup to the countertop beside the range, then shut off the burner, poured hot water over her tea bag and let it steep. "Did you love her?" she asked quietly.

"I cared. I don't know if I loved her."

But if the woman would've eventually been first in his life, didn't that mean he *must* have loved her? "Do you still think about her?"

Impatient now, Jace walked over, took her by the shoulders and turned her to face him. "No," he said firmly. "I don't think about her. I don't dream about her, and I don't want her. What man with a pulse could want any other woman when he was standing next to you?"

Abbie held her breath, feeling the tumbling energy in the air intensify. She'd felt it all evening, the surreal feeling of walking on eggshells and waiting for him to reach for her. But even as her pulse quickened, she knew if they made love again, restraint would go right out the window. They would fall into each other's arms every time a light bulb flickered or a bird flew by. And making love had to mean *something* or it wasn't worth *anything*. She needed more from him than an admission of physical needs.

She kept her voice low. "That's a very flattering thing to say to a woman who's not wearing makeup."

"No, it's a dangerous thing to say. But I needed to say

it." He traced her cheek with his index finger, stroked downward to her lips. "As for makeup," he added, dropping his voice, too. "You don't need it. I like seeing exactly who you are. Come upstairs with me."

Abbie's heart thudded in her chest. Before, hormones and erratic pulses had taken them where they wanted to go. Now, with his frank invitation, he wanted her to choose.

"If I did… If I went upstairs with you…what would it mean?"

A dozen thoughts moved through his compelling gaze, but he didn't appear to like any of them. "Why does it have to mean something? Isn't it enough that we both want it?"

Slowly, regretfully, she shook her head.

"It was enough for you a few nights ago."

Abbie felt her jaw sag. Then she got hurt and angry, and jerked out of his hold. "Maybe you should call Carol. I think she has exactly what you're looking for."

Swearing softly, Jace reached for her again but she shrugged him away. "Look, that didn't come out right. It's not what I meant."

Really? Or had he said precisely what he was feeling. Either way, the words were out, and it was too late to take them back.

Abbie strode out of the kitchen and into the entry-way— kept moving through the great room, even though he called her name.

He caught up with her at the doorway to his office and snared her hand. "Dammit, Abbie, what do you want from me? A promise to phone or e-mail you every day after you go back to L.A.? Maybe send flowers or a poem once in a while?"

Her tears were close, but she refused to let them fall.

"If you're finished with the work you were doing on your computer, I'd like to turn in."

"Let's talk about this."

"Not tonight."

"*Yes,* tonight. Neither of us will sleep with this hanging over our heads. Maybe you could start by calling me a jerk, and we can go from there."

"All right, you're a jerk. Now it's my turn to ask. What do *you* want from *me?*"

For a long moment, he just stared down at her. Then he sagged back against the doorway, his expression grave. "Beyond friendship and sex? I don't know. You've got a life somewhere else, Abbie. When I think of you, I only think in terms of what's going on in the moment. Anything more than that…" He paused. "You're not being honest with yourself if you think either of us wants more."

It was a struggle, but she kept her face composed. She wouldn't humiliate herself by admitting that maybe she did.

"You said the law is your life," Jace went on. "Well, my business is mine. Betty was right. I am a workaholic. I'm just on hiatus right now. There's always something that needs to be done, and no one takes as much care with the job as the man who has the most to lose." An ironic look touched his features. "Know what? With the exception of your father's nasty tirade, we could've had this same discussion fourteen years ago."

Abbie pressed her back to the right side of the doorway as reality slipped in. Yes, they could have. Back then, their lives had been on different tracks, too—tracks that would never have met again if not for the Mardi Gras celebration and Jace's lingering bitterness toward her father.

"Your work is *it?* You honestly have no desire at all to have a family?"

He shook his head, and like cautious bookends, they held each other's gazes, their futures dangling in the narrow space between them. "None."

"How sad," she said quietly. "I can't think of anyone more suited to raising kids. Ty was so…so *broken* after your mother left. He never would've made it if it hadn't been for you. That's what parents do. They offer love and support, and you've been doing it for years."

"That has nothing to do with bringing my own flesh and blood into the world."

Abbie studied him quizzically, centering on the words *own, flesh* and *blood*. It was on the tip of her tongue to ask what was wrong with his flesh and blood when she realized that she already knew.

"You don't want to pass along bloodlines you're unsure of."

He didn't nod, but his assent was in his eyes. "Jillie was a runaway who never told us where she was from, or who her people were. As for my father—and I assume I had one since everyone on the planet does in one form or another—I don't have a clue. Butcher, baker, candlestick maker. Tom, Dick or Harry. Could've been anyone. The point is, I'll never know. What do you say to a kid when he comes home from school and asks who his grandparents are? Or what they did for a living? What do you say when he asks where his ancestors came from, or if he has a predisposition to certain illnesses? Do I tell him that I have no idea because his grandmother was a hooker who slept with half the county, and I can't ask her for the answers because I don't know if she's living or dead?"

Deeply moved, Abbie softened her voice. "I'm not sure. But your child would have a mother with parents and grandparents. And he'd have Betty and Carl. I've never met

Carl, but I like Betty, and I doubt she would've picked a jerk for a husband."

"No, apparently being a jerk is my gift." He paused to search her eyes. "Are we okay now?"

Were they okay? That depended on his definition of the word. Her anger was gone, but the truth now had a strong foothold and she felt bruised inside. She sent him a wobbly smile. "Do you still want to have sex with me?"

"With every breath in my body."

She felt the same. But there was no future with him, and she needed to stop this before she lost all respect for herself. "Sorry. No."

"Okay."

She felt a bittersweet ache in her chest when he pushed away from the doorway.

"Will you be here in the morning?" he asked.

"Yes."

"Are you staying until Morgan comes back?"

Dropping her gaze, Abbie studied her linked fingers. "I'm not sure that's a good idea."

Releasing a lung-clearing sigh, Jace nodded and straightened. "All right. Sleep tight. I'll see you in the morning."

Stepping out of the shower, Jace toweled off, then strode naked across the loft to his bed, yanked back the covers and flopped down on the cool sheet. Anyone who thought a cold shower was a quick fix for racing thoughts and a throbbing libido had never met Abbie. Not that he was masochistic enough to put himself through that. Not with winter rearing its ugly head again.

He flicked the button on his nightstand's alarm clock, then shut off the lamp. What had she expected? Some grand gesture? Temporary lies? That wasn't the way he operated.

The one time he'd nearly said the words, Morgan had shown up and blown that thought out of his head. *That* was the memory he had to keep in mind, not the others that kept slipping in. The last time he'd let himself care, she'd walked. And with a fancy L.A. law practice, she'd walk again.

Eyes accustomed to the darkness now, Jace watched the bobbing shadows on the wall, trees bending as winter returned just in time for the first day of spring.

Just in time for Abbie's return to Daddy's house.

He swore softly. He had to change her mind, convince her to stay until Morgan got back. Otherwise he'd be sipping coffee in his damn car all night again.

Rolling to his feet, he turned the lamp back on and paged through the phone book. He was surprised a minute later when Glenn Frasier picked up at the Laurel Ridge Police Station.

"Thought you worked days," Jace said when he'd identified himself.

"I'm on until eleven tonight," Frasier returned. "Got trouble at your place?"

"No—and believe me, I don't mean to hound you. I just called to see if you or your guys have noticed any strange vehicles in the area lately."

"All the time, especially on the weekend. But most of them are camera-toting tourists looking for the best place to spot elk—and they're all in a hurry. The bulls'll be losing their horns soon."

Jace waited through his pause.

"But no, we haven't seen anything with California plates, or anyone answering Daniel Long's description. If we had, I would've contacted you. Last I heard, the L.A. cops thought he was back in the city."

"I heard that, too," Jace replied. "I'm just on edge tonight. Abbie will probably move back to her dad's house tomorrow, and she'll be alone for a few days. I'd appreciate it if—"

"No problem. We'll keep cruising by the house until Morgan gets back."

"Thanks, Glenn."

"Sure thing. That's why you folks pay me the big bucks. Take care, now."

"You, too."

Jace hung up, dreading the morning, tension constricting his chest. He could hear her downstairs, opening and closing drawers, moving around. He didn't need X-ray vision to know she was packing.

Maybe Jillie'd had the right idea after all.

Twenty minute love was a lot simpler than the hell people put themselves through for relationships that never worked out anyhow.

When he came downstairs the next morning at seven-fifteen, Abbie was in the kitchen making coffee. Jace looked around for packed luggage, or any other sign that said she was preparing to leave. But there was none in sight.

"Good morning," he said.

"Morning," she replied quietly. "Did you sleep well?"

"Not really."

"Me neither."

Crossing the silent kitchen, he pulled two mugs from the cupboard and waited for the proverbial other shoe to fall. Had she changed her mind? Or was she planning to cut out after he left for work to avoid an uncomfortable goodbye?

She was dressed in belted tan chinos and a long-sleeved brown knit top, but she wasn't wearing makeup. Not that that meant she was staying.

There's only one way to find out, he thought, even though the acids in his stomach told him to play it by ear. "What are your plans today?"

She turned from pulling the orange juice out of the refrigerator and carried it to the bar. "I'm not sure. I thought I'd stick around here for a while, then drive over to my dad's place and meet Dorothy."

That jarred him. "Dorothy?"

"Dad's housekeeper. I phoned her yesterday afternoon to tell her dad and Miriam would be back on Friday. She's coming by to run the vacuum cleaner and freshen up the house. I told her I'd do it, but she insisted." She paused. "I'll help out, anyway."

Acids rolled again. So was she moving to her dad's place or not? Coming back here later or not?

Suddenly angry, Jace shoved his mug back in the cupboard. "On second thought," he said evenly, "I think I'll pass on the juice and coffee this morning. I'll grab a cup at the office."

Pulling on his boots and taking his down vest from the hook behind the door, he shrugged it on. "Give me a call later if you want," he muttered. Then he walked out and closed the door behind him.

With a bone-weary look toward Heaven, Abbie put the orange juice back. She didn't want juice or coffee, either. Last night she'd known exactly what she needed to do. She needed to leave so she could feel strong on her own again. She'd been focused.

Then Jace had walked into the kitchen, her focus had vanished and her heart had started to ache and want again.

Frustrated with herself, she shut off the coffeemaker, dumped the coffee and the grounds then rinsed the carafe.

She would launder the sleeper-sofa's bedding, finish dressing, then leave a note and carry her bags to the car.

She would get out while the getting was good.

That thought lasted until she turned the key in the ignition and backed her dad's SUV out of Jace's garage. Then she knew she couldn't do it—not that way. If she did, she'd be no better than Jillie Rae, who'd left without having the courage to tell him she wouldn't be back. He'd deserved better twenty-four years ago, and he deserved better today.

It was tension on top of chaos when she entered the RL&L office at 9:45 a.m. after picking up the day's mail. Ty was on the phone and searching through Ida's desk for something he apparently couldn't find, Fran was yanking open drawers in the nearby filing cabinets and Ida was nowhere around. The bookkeeper didn't look well. In fact, Abbie's dad had a saying for people who looked as sick as Fran did. He said they looked green around the gills.

"Fran, what's wrong?"

"Ida called in sick today, and none of us knows her job well enough to limp through." She snatched a file from a folder and handed it to Ty, who murmured his thanks.

"You don't feel well, either, do you?"

Ty said goodbye, hung up and spoke. "No, she doesn't. She's sick as a dog." He turned to Fran and released a sigh. "Okay, that fire's out. Why don't you head for home and get some rest?"

The dark-haired woman shook her head. "Can't. I have to do payroll today, and cut a few checks for vendors."

"I'll take care of the vendors, and payroll can wait until tomorrow."

"I could be dead tomorrow. I'll leave as soon as I take care of payroll." Swallowing hard and going even paler, she nodded toward her office. "And I'd better do it right now."

Ty waited until she was gone, swore under his breath, then apologized. "Sorry. It's been a day and a half already. Ida better live to be a hundred and fifty or we're all in deep spit."

Abruptly, his face brightened. "Abbie. How'd you like to man the phones and take messages today? Or do you have plans?"

Who was pulling her strings today? Angels or demons? She nearly told him she *did* have plans, but her conscience intervened. "No. Nothing I can't put off. I just came by to see Jace."

"He was in the grading building a few minutes ag—"

The phone rang.

Grimacing, Ty punched the lighted button on the phone and picked up the receiver. "Rogan Logging & Lumber, can you hold?" Pressing the button again, he hung up.

"How about it? Can you stay for a few hours? Pete took a bid out to the Forestry Service a little while ago, but he had a few stops to make afterward. He should be able to take over for you by one o'clock at the latest."

Knowing she had no choice after everything Jace had done for her, Abbie slipped off her jacket and Ty gratefully abandoned Ida's seat. "Sure. Just show me which buttons to push."

Despite his frantic mood, he grinned. "After seeing my brother's face this morning, I get the feeling you already know." Then he got on with the instructions and headed toward the door. "If you want to page Jace, just punch the green button and yell. He'll hear you if he's not in the sawmill."

Abbie nodded, but doubted she'd do that. He'd have to come into the office eventually. That was soon enough.

"Oh—and help yourself to tea, coffee or the soft drinks in Fran's office. You know the drill. Pop's free to employees."

So that's what she was, Abbie thought, depressing the lighted button when the phone rang again. An employee. That was quite a departure from being a lawyer. Or a lover.

Danny concentrated hard as he sat on the motel bed and cut two pieces of blue vinyl tape from the roll, then expertly turned an *E* into a *B* on the Pennsylvania license plate he'd lifted yesterday. He'd lucked out and found a car up on blocks shortly after crossing the Ohio-Pennsylvania border—one with a fitted cover over it. It was a convertible—shiny and ready for summer, not winter slush—and he'd known the plate wouldn't be missed for a while.

Holding up his handiwork, he smiled at the results, then pulled the hood up on his new sweatshirt and hurried into the early Monday morning snow flurries to replace the plate. There was a half-frozen mud hole in the parking lot, and he dug some dirt from it—smeared it around just enough to dull the tape's shine. A moment later, he was driving out of the lot. He'd paid cash upfront, so there was no need to stop at the office. It was time to head south.

Time for a little game of cat and mouse before he got down to the satisfying business of beating his lying bitch of an ex-lawyer to a bloody pulp.

"Ty shouldn't have asked you to stay."

Abbie glanced up at Jace, her annoyance matching his as he walked her toward her dad's SUV. Snow flurries tossed and blew around them, while a white smudge of a sun shone dully through the cloud cover, and noisy log trucks rolled past on their way to the yard.

"Well, he did ask, I said yes, and now that Pete's back, my shift is over. Why are you in such a foul mood? And why is helping you such a big sin?"

"Because you had things to do."

"They weren't as important as manning your phones. In fact, I think Dorothy was relieved that I didn't come over. She likes doing things her own way."

"Don't we all."

They were nearing her car, now. Abbie hit the remote on her keychain, popping the door locks on her dad's Expedition.

She saw a nerve leap in Jace's jaw when he glanced inside the vehicle. But he didn't mention the luggage on the back seat, which made her think he'd noticed it earlier.

Two hours ago, right after she'd paged the lift driver to the yard, Jace had called her from the grading building to ask what she was doing there. He'd been so grumpy, she'd hung up on him. She hadn't seen or heard from him again until Pete walked in five minutes ago, and she'd walked out.

She nodded at her luggage. "That's why I came by this morning. I wanted to tell you that I was leaving."

"Then you're definitely heading back to your dad's place?"

"Yes."

"All right. I'll follow you out there—carry your things inside and make sure everything's secure."

For a moment she was amazed and a little flattered because until now, he'd refused to go any farther than the driveway when she dropped off the mail. But on the way, she began to wonder if he'd offered to do it because he cared…or for another reason.

He'd shown less antagonism when she'd mentioned her dad lately, but she knew there was no forgiveness in Jace for that long-ago night. Two weeks ago, he'd kissed her on a dance floor just to cause trouble.

Glancing into her rearview mirror, she turned onto the curved road leading to the bridge near her dad's place.

Was walking through her dad's home another thumb-in-your-eye gesture? Could he be that petty?

She approached the pale concrete bridge, slowed down and prepared to cross it.

Suddenly Abbie's eyes widened and chills covered every inch of her. Pulling off to the side of the road, she stopped her car and leapt out, then turned to watch Jace swerve in behind her. He was at her side in an instant. "What's wrong?"

Then she watched his gaze go dark as he read the black spray-painted graffiti on the bridge abutment.

I'M HERE.

Chapter 12

"Okay," Jace said calmly. "Let's put this in perspective. It could be nothing more than the work of kids with too much time on their hands."

"Yes, it could," she agreed, hating the tremble in her voice and feeling anger slowly replace her fears. "But why that particular message? Why not Bob Loves Laurie, Eat Spit And Die or the ever popular F-You?"

"I don't know." Giving her a quick squeeze, he said, "Wait here," and strode back to his Explorer. He returned in a moment, hitting a key on his cell phone.

After a few rings, he said, "Officer Harris, it's Jace Rogan. I spoke to Chief Frasier last night about Abbie Winslow returning to her dad's place today. Did he pass the message along? Good. I just called to tell you that someone decorated the bridge near Morgan's house with graffiti. It's not overtly threatening, and it might not be anything important, but it wasn't here yesterday. Any traffic signs or billboards getting the same treatment?"

When Abbie sent him a questioning look, Jace shook his head. He listened for another moment, his brow furrowing. "I'm not sure," he finally said, locking his gaze on hers. "I'd rather she stayed with me, just to be on the safe side, but I won't push. See you soon." Jace broke the connection. "He's on his way."

Nodding, Abbie shoved her hands into her pockets and paced, anger and frustration energizing her. "It could be kids," she said again. "But I can't shake the feeling that I was meant to see that." Halting abruptly, she drew a breath. "Okay. I'll come back to your house. For tonight."

The lines of tension on his face deepened. "Only tonight?"

She was finally fed up with all of it. "Yes. I'm through running and worrying and feeling helpless. I'd move into Dad's place right now if I didn't need time for a crash course."

"A crash course in what?"

"You have a handgun. Teach me to use it."

"Have you lost your mind?"

"No," she said crisply. "I think I've just found it. Pennsylvania law isn't that different from California law. If he breaks into my father's house and tries to hurt me, I'm entitled to hurt him back. I'm sick to death of feeling powerless, and I'm tired of letting you coddle me while I run around with my hands in the air like a dimwitted teenager from a slasher film."

His face froze in unyielding lines. "Know what? That's tough. I'm not putting a gun in the hand of someone who doesn't know the first thing about firearms. Good God, if the worst happened and Long did show up, he could take it away and use it on you. You live in L.A.! Don't tell me you've never heard of that happening."

"Yes, I've heard of that happening. But at the risk of shocking you, from where I'm standing right now, a bullet would be quicker and a lot more humane than being beaten to death by a bat-swinging psycho."

Jace stilled, a storm raging in his eyes. Then he slowly raised a cautioning finger. "Let's just shelve this discussion right now. Do you feel well enough to drive? I told Harris we'd meet him at your dad's place."

"Yes, I feel well enough to drive. Haven't you heard anything I've said? Was I too subtle?"

Exhaling an exasperated breath, he strode to her idling car and pulled the door open wider. "Abbie, there's nothing subtle—or clear-headed—about you right now. Get in. I'll follow you."

When she'd slid behind the wheel, she looked at him again. "Are you going to lend me your gun?"

"No way in hell," he said, and slammed the door.

Quickly lowering her window she jerked her head outside and shouted as he returned to his SUV. "Then maybe I'll just *borrow* it!"

"You do that," he shouted back. "Then maybe I'll just report it stolen, Frasier will tuck your sweet little ass in a jail cell and all of our worries will be over. Actually, I might do it anyway!"

Releasing a frustrated curse, Abbie dropped the Expedition into gear and sailed across the bridge. She searched the barren trees fronting the road and the thicker evergreens deep in the woods.

Was he hiding in there? she wondered, her anger continuing to build. Was he smiling at her powerlessness, waggling his paint can and promising more with his crazy blue eyes? Or was the graffiti just the work of kids, after all? Well, she was through cowering in a corner. If he came for her, he was in for the fight of his life.

She felt another jolt when she approached the gated driveway and saw two sets of tire tracks in the dusting of snow. One set continued past the locked gate. The other stopped in front of it, then backed out onto the road again.

Pulling to the side of the lane, she parked and got out, leaving her door open again. "Two sets of footprints," she said when Jace joined her.

The small scuffling prints near the padlock were undoubtedly Dorothy's. The larger boot prints circumventing the gate and continuing down the long drive—then returning—weren't.

Abbie watched Jace take it all in.

"Obviously, whoever was here is gone now, and he made no attempt to walk in the woods or hide his tracks. It was probably just someone making a delivery or one of the utility companies reading a meter. But," he continued, snagging her hand. "As long as Harris isn't here yet, let's see where the tracks lead."

Two hours later, Jace snatched the paper plate they'd used as a target from the hay bales he'd stacked, then walked the ten yards back to where Abbie waited in the pavilion. He was still dead set against it, but teaching her to shoot was the only damn way he'd been able to get her back to his place. That didn't mean he planned to hand over his gun—or let her move back into her dad's house. He was less certain of his motives for keeping her with him—less certain about a lot of things.

She slipped off his earmuffs and safety glasses—set them beside the gun on the picnic table as he flashed the paper plate.

"One hit in twelve tries," he said grimly. "You're getting worse. You can't hold the gun steady, you flinch when you fire and sometimes you shut your eyes. You're more of a threat to yourself than he is."

She lifted her chin. "We still have a few minutes before we leave for the airport. I want to try again."

Feeling a headache build, Jace shoved a new clip in the automatic and waited for her to put the glasses and muffs back on. Then he stepped behind her and handed her the gun. "All right, once more—but that's it. Then we leave to meet Ty and Betty at the airport."

As he watched her squeeze off a few more rounds, he wondered for the billionth time if any of this was necessary. As he'd guessed, the boot tracks had led straight to Morgan's electric meter, and the inspection of the house and surrounding area by Harris had produced nothing useful.

The patrolman's search of the bridge area hadn't produced a paint can or other evidence, either, so with no reason to suspect anything but vandalism, Harris had left, and Jace and Abbie had returned to RL&L to bring Ty up to date. Ty had been the bearer of bad news, too. But when he'd said that Ida wouldn't be in to work tomorrow, either, Jace had had mixed feelings. He didn't want their little fireball to be sick, but being short-handed meant that Abbie would once again be manning the phones, and under his watchful eye. But did she need to be watched? Were her back-of-the-neck feelings reliable?

All he knew was she was determined to meet Long head-on—either here or back in L.A.—and she wasn't prepared. That worried him.

Taking off the muffs, she nodded at the torn holes in the plate. "That was better, right?"

"Yeah, you're a pro," he muttered, because he just wanted to end this. Betty's commuter left for Pittsburgh at 6:10 p.m., and if they didn't leave soon, they wouldn't have time to visit over coffee before she boarded.

"Dammit, Jace, don't patronize me. This is too important."

He gave her a piercing look. "That's right. It is. And that's exactly why you're not taking this gun to your dad's place or anywhere else."

She tore the safety glasses from her face. "Fine. I'll just stand around and wait for him to bludgeon me to death. Because whether you believe it or not, that's his plan. He wants me dead, but he wants it up close and personal—just like the Vegas, Oklahoma and Missouri murders that are taking up so much of the nightly news!"

Jace's stomach pitched, and his gaze dropped to the open collar of her jacket where a small gold cross on a chain lay against her black knit top. It had been a loving keep-you-safe-in-the-big-world gift from her mother on her eighth grade graduation, and she'd taken it from her old jewelry box during Harris's inspection of the house. Pretty. But it wouldn't keep her safe from a psycho bent on revenge. Not here, and not in L.A.

"Come on," he said grimly, recalling her pseudo-aerobic self-defense session. She was lithe and moved well, and he'd seen strength and balance in her arms and legs as she'd gone through her Sandra Bullock routine. "Let's meet Ty and Betty, then we'll get back to this."

Three hours later, Abbie stood across from Jace in the great room. She'd changed into sweatpants and sneakers while he'd found a roll of Christmas wrap in a storage closet, stuffed the tube with paper toweling and sealed the whole thing with duct tape. He gripped it, bat-like, as she faced him, the alpaca area rugs forming a mat of sorts around them.

"Okay," he said, his gray eyes serious, "we've talked about it, now let's try it. Stay focused. If he comes after you, you need to disarm him. He won't expect you to fight, so remember, yell loud and move fast. You'll have surprise on your side."

Abbie nodded, her heart pounding just looking at the silvery makeshift bat.

"When I start my swing, move into the arc of the bat and bring your forearms down on my arms in a stiff double karate chop. Do it hard and fast. Make me drop my weapon."

"Got it."

"Good. If I don't drop it, you're going to wrap your left arm around my right one and keep it close to your body so I can't pull back and swing again. Then throw your right elbow or fist into the side of my head to stun me."

Abbie nodded. She wouldn't be able to reach Jace's temple with her elbow, but Danny was shorter and a lot lighter. She would absolutely take him out. "Okay, then it's knee, knee, knee, and keep kneeing you until you're down, then run."

He sent her a dry look. "For that part, I'd prefer that you didn't take me too literally."

He swung unexpectedly. With a *thwack,* cardboard and duct tape connected with Abbie's upper arm. It didn't hurt, but the sound and slap startled and annoyed her.

"Wait a minute! I wasn't ready!"

"Lesson two," he said gravely. "He's not going to give you time to think. You need to react. You saw me pull back, but you stood there and did nothing."

He swung again, and still startled by the first hit, she let him hit her again.

"Dammit, Jace!" she shouted. "I didn't even have time to bring my arms up!"

"Then you need to change your mindset, don't you? I'm not me, I'm him, and I want to kill you. You need to commit 110 percent to this, or you're going to be dead."

He swung. Abbie moved into the arc, chopped her forearms on his before the bat could connect—trapped his arm and clamped it to her body, then jammed her elbow up to his neck. She stopped just short of inducing pain and smiled up at him. "Want me to keep going?"

His gray eyes twinkled in approval. "Yes, but do it gently."

She brought her knee up, bumped him, bumped him again, and, laughing, he went down on the rugs, pulling her with him. "Very good for your first try, Madame Ninja."

"Yeah?"

"Yeah." Smiling, he tugged her ponytail as she lay there on top of him, then he moved his gaze over her face. "But when you chop, chop harder. You're not swatting flies, you're trying to disable someone." He sobered then. "And if he keeps coming, remember the first thing I told you. Palm, knee, knee. Drive your palm into his face. Hit him with enough force to drive his nose straight through the back of his head. After you've hit him, go for his face, his eyes. Use your fingernails."

Abbie blew out a soft breath. She wasn't sure she could do that to anyone.

"I know," he murmured. "It's not pretty, it's down and dirty. But you only get one shot as a woman. If you don't get the job done, you're going to be raped or you're going to die. Maybe both."

Nodding, Abbie stared down at him, feeling her anxieties mount and—at the same time—an awareness of his warm, muscular body beneath her. And suddenly one emotion overpowered the other and coalesced into a breathless sensation. It was danger and pleasure all wrapped up in one, a buzzing, caffeine-like high that sent a Make Love, Not War message.

It was contagious.

She watched Jace's eyes turn dark, noticed a subtle catch in his breathing. Then things started happening south of his belt buckle, and scowling, he rolled her off of him. "Ready to try it again?" he asked. "Down and dirty, no holds barred?"

"You sure?" she replied, dredging up a grin. "I took it pretty easy on the family jewels a minute ago."

He chuckled, and she loved the low, husky sound of it. Loved the strength in his hand as he rose and pulled her to her feet. "Actually, those little bumps felt pretty good. But yeah, let's keep the contact on the gentle side."

That night, once again, coyotes howled and yipped, keeping Abbie awake as they played to a bright white full moon. Lying in the frosty half-dark, she fingered the small gold cross at her throat, every rustle of wind against the house or unfamiliar noise making her pulse race. She glanced up at the ceiling, picturing the loft bedroom several inches above it. And she admitted that her pulse was racing for another reason.

He was probably asleep, she thought, missing his closeness and his touch—missing *him,* and wishing their street-fighting session could've gone on a little longer. But there would be no more sessions tonight. No more lying on top of him and feeling his body respond to hers.

Swallowing, Abbie left the bed, slipped on her short silky green robe and quietly left the room. She was waiting for milk to heat when Jace ambled into the kitchen.

"Can't sleep?"

In the meager light from the range hood, Abbie took in his formidable height and broad shoulders—followed the soft tapering pattern of his chest hair down to where it disappeared behind the drawstring on his sweatpants.

"Nope. Sorry if I woke you."

"You didn't. I was awake, too."

She tipped the saucepan a little to keep the milk from scalding, then turned back to him. "Want a cup? It's supposed to help with insomnia."

"No thanks." But he did grab a mug for her from the cabinet over the sink. "Why can't you sleep?"

Sending him a small smile, she turned off the burner. "A lot of reasons," she said, filling her cup. "Coyotes. Bad memories." *Wanting you.* "I was impossible this afternoon, and I'm sorry."

"No problem. It all worked out for the best. It gave us something to do, and it got you back here." He hesitated. "Are you still planning to move back to your dad's place?"

Leaning against the sink, she shook her head. "No. I've had my psychotic episode for the month. If you still want me to, I'll stay here until dad and Miriam get back on Friday."

She took a sip, then set the mug on the counter and dropped her gaze to their bare feet. "That's another thing I've been worried about. If Long's not picked up by the time they get back—here or in L.A.—I'm not sure they should stay at the house, either. In fact, maybe they shouldn't be around me." Pausing, she continued on a lower, more serious note. "Maybe you shouldn't, either."

"I'm not afraid."

"You should be," she said soberly. "You didn't see what he did to that girl."

Jace ambled a little closer and tipped her face up to his. "Any man who beats a woman is a coward. This freak would run from a fair fight with a man."

"Is that so, Dr. Freud?"

"Absolutely." His gaze stroked hers for a while longer, his caring shining through and fanning the tender, soul-deep feelings inside her. Then, as though he suspected they might lose their heads again, he stepped away. "How's the milk?"

"Awful," she replied. "Needs chocolate."

He took a sip from her cup and made a face. And there was something very sexy about drinking from the same cup in a silent kitchen in the dim light of the range hood.

"You're right." He went to the refrigerator and grabbed the chocolate syrup.

"That's not going to help my insomnia. Chocolate's full of caffeine."

"I think you should chance it anyway," he teased as he squeezed some into her cup. "If the chocolate makes it worse, we'll just have to move on to nature's remedy. Hot, sweaty sex."

Abbie held a breath as he took a spoon from a drawer and gave the milk a quick stir, then put the mug in her hands. She knew he wasn't serious, but after their sparring round this afternoon, his words landed with a thump behind her navel.

A rattling bang outside startled them both as she raised the mug to her lips.

Before the fine hairs on Abbie's nape could finish standing on end, Jace was moving toward the door. He'd left the spotlights burning around the outbuildings, and quickly opening the kitchen door, he stepped onto the porch and scanned the area.

Abbie followed him out, her breath fogging. "Bears again?" she asked nervously.

Tension edged his low voice. "No. The door to my workshop's open." Gently shoving her back inside, he slipped into his boots, grabbed his down vest and pulled it on. "Lock the door and stay by the phone."

"I'm going with you."

"No, you're not."

"Take your gun."

He tapped his vest pocket. "Got it."

When he pulled the door shut behind him, she locked up, cupped her hand against the glass on the door and peered out, the wall phone only an arm's length away. Nerves thrumming, she watched him disappear inside the shop, then flood the shed with light. A moment later, it went dark again, and in the glow of the spotlights, he latched the door and retraced his steps.

"It was nothing. No tracks but mine out there. I was in a hurry when I put the safety glasses and earmuffs away earlier, and apparently I didn't latch the door tightly."

Still, his expression disturbed her. It was a mixture of believing it had happened that way...and uneasiness because there was no way he could know for sure.

Again, Abbie loathed the uncertainty of her situation. She loathed it even more when, as they reluctantly returned to their own rooms, Jace paused to double-check the locks on the doors and windows.

"It's just a precaution," he said.

But seeds of doubt had found a frighteningly fertile field in Abbie's mind.

* * *

Danny shook hard from the cold as he crouched deep inside the thick stand of fir trees. He was afraid to rub his arms or stamp his feet, even though he doubted he could be seen. The two of them had left the kitchen. He'd bought a hooded parka at a Goodwill store before he left Bradford, but it wasn't warm enough, and now he was paying the price for buying somebody else's lousy castoffs!

Who would live in a frigid dump like this? He'd take California mudslides and earthquakes any day. His legs were cramping and his friggin' feet felt like blocks of ice!

But in the end, it would all be worth it.

Slowly pushing to a standing position, he smiled despite his discomfort. Then he opened his coat, reached low and made yellow snow to let her know—without letting her know—that he'd been here and seen her whoring in the man's kitchen.

Excitement lifted him high, pulsed through him as hot sweat flooded his armpits and he righted his clothes. He wanted her dead. *Dead, dead, dead!* Inhaling, he closed his eyes and visualized her naked body, experienced a sublime buoyancy and a pleasure he hadn't felt since Maryanne.

He just had to get her alone. Away from the guy.

Not that Rogan intimidated him. He'd looked big and tough when he'd rushed out to check the shed door Danny hadn't latched right, but Danny knew he could take him easy. He just didn't feel like it.

He was saving his energy for her.

Clutching the cold metal wood rasp he'd taken from the shed, he made his way through the firs, glad the moon was high. He'd hidden his car behind the decrepit barn a couple hundred yards down the road. That's where he'd be staying now. Earlier, he'd seen a cop car go by real slow. There'd been prowl cars cruising by the whore's father's house, too, which told him that she'd received the cards and told the police to be on the lookout for him.

That is, he thought in amusement, *if* she wasn't convinced he was back in L.A. Right now, she probably didn't know which end was up.

Danny hooted at his cleverness, then, startled by the echoing sound, shut himself up and concentrated on following the tracks he'd made on the way in. It was an easier trek than his tight, trackless walk along the side of Rogan's shed, where the overhang kept the snow from collecting.

Grinning, he glanced back through the trees to the spotlight-drenched log house, watching pale smoke curl from the chimney and thin snow spangle the yard. He loved this! Loved watching her when she thought she was safe living inside a sweet little picture postcard.

"But you're not safe," he whispered.

Losing his smile, Danny pulled himself up to his full five feet eight inches and channeled Arnold Schwarzenegger.

"Ah'll be back."

Abbie quietly climbed the stairs to the loft, her short silk robe cinched tightly and her heart beating fast. Oddly, somewhere inside she felt calm.

After seventeen minutes of staring at the digital clock on the desktop, she'd suddenly realized how important each minute was, and how many of them she'd already wasted. Instead of calculating the number of minutes she might have left, she needed to celebrate the minutes she had. Life was a gift. And seventeen precious minutes had passed that she would never have again.

Carpe diem.

It was too late to seize the day. But if Jace allowed it…they could seize the night.

A board creaked beneath her bare foot as she approached the top of the stairs, and Abbie winced. She didn't want to announce her presence. If she did, they'd have to talk—have to make a decision based on their very separate lives and realities. And tonight, she'd done enough thinking for both of them.

Topping the stairs, she stepped onto the smooth, cool oak flooring. She just wanted to slide into his bed, slide into his arms—

Abbie cried out as a hand snaked out of the shadows to clamp her wrist and yank her forward. An instant later, she was lying flat on her back, with Jace straddling her, and her wrists pinned over her head.

She stared, wide-eyed, and he released a soft curse.

The frosty wash from the spotlights didn't reach the loft, but indirect moonlight touched his lined face and lean naked body as his gaze slid from her eyes to the parted front of her robe. A quick glance down told Abbie that the narrow sash at her waist was the only snippet of fabric that hadn't shifted. But she didn't care.

Locking her gaze on his, she saw the desire he couldn't hide, and every emotion she'd ever felt for him swelled inside of her. "Hi."

"Are you all right? Did I hurt you?"

She shook her head. But then…how would she know? Adrenaline was sharpening her other senses to needle points, and her mind wasn't on pain—only pleasure. Breathless, she drank in his primal male beauty, let her gaze drift from his broad chest to his lean rib cage and hips, then lower to where he was coming alive for her. She sent him a tiny smile. "I guess you were expecting me."

Jace went from his knees to a crouch, then pulled her to her feet. His turbulent gaze searched hers again, and more of those moments they shouldn't be wasting ticked by.

"You sure about this?" he rasped, his voice thick. "Nothing's changed. We still live in different worl—"

Abbie pressed her fingertips to his lips. "I'm sure. Now…no more talking." But something *had* changed. She couldn't say when it happened—when she'd finally finished falling for him and actually fell. But without a blare of trumpets or startling flash of insight, in those seventeen minutes downstairs, she'd come to the deep, satisfying realization that she loved him. In two short weeks, he'd taken over her heart, filled her mind and become the most important person in her world. Ultimately, what she would do about loving him depended on Jace. But for now…whatever the night had in store would be enough.

Taking her fingers from his lips, he kissed the tips of them, one by one. Then feeling his way, he untied the thin satin belt at her waist and slid her robe from her shoulders. It landed in a puddle at her feet.

With a blast of air that was part relief and part resignation, he took her in his arms, molded her to his body and brought his mouth down on hers.

Chapter 13

Abbie sighed against his lips, breaking the kiss only long enough to inhale deeply, then meet his marauding mouth again.

When had kissing become such an utterly visceral experience? she wondered. When had her thighs trembled and her tummy lifted so deliciously with barely a touch? She circled his neck, her mind spinning a rich tapestry of sensual images as Jace's tongue mated with hers. She slid her hands into his thick black hair, felt herself sink willingly into that mind-numbing whirlpool where nothing mattered but this moment. A moment in which she felt breathless and tense and needy and jubilant all at the same time.

They moved languidly against each other, glorying in every touch and letting desire build, giving their hands the freedom to go where they wished.

Jace reacquainted himself with her curves and hollows,

the faint scratch of his callused palms giving her nerve endings even more reason to thrum and curl. He threaded his left hand through her hair and deepened their kiss, pressed his right hand to her bottom and fitted her more closely to his arousal. There was no mistaking the immediacy or the intensity of his need.

This was what she'd longed for, Abbie thought, her mind floating. Intensity and immediacy, yet the restraint to savor.

Sliding his tongue into her mouth again, he backed her toward the bed, a tiny groan rustling in his throat as she explored, too. She stroked his chest, dallied with a nipple, then smoothed her hands down his taut midsection and trim hips. Finally, she encountered something even more intriguing to stroke.

A new shudder racked through him. Tearing his mouth from hers, Jace buried his face in her neck. "That's nice," he whispered. "But let's not rush things, okay?"

She did it again.

Sighing, then chuckling, Jace lifted her into his arms and carried her to his bed. "Behave, or this will be over before we get started."

Rumpled sheets still warm from his body welcomed her, and Abbie drew in a scent that was inherently Jace's. Then she reached for him, and he stretched out beside her to kiss her temple, her mouth, her chin, her collarbone.

She craned her neck and gave him clear access to the throbbing pulse in her neck and anything else he wanted to kiss. She sighed. He wanted to kiss everything.

She let her fingers play in the soft hair at his nape, breathed in deeply as he rained moist kisses over the swells of her breasts.

Then his warm mouth found a nipple, and lovely, drizzling chills sailed the length of her.

It was sweetness and it was torment. Every soft pull created a thrill that went straight to her core, tantalizing her with promises of completion and making her blood thunder in her ears. By the time he moved to her other breast, the sensation was so acute, she couldn't take the stimulation any longer without fulfillment.

Tugging him up to her, she whispered breathlessly, "Please tell me you've been to a drugstore or a seedy gas station lately, and we won't have to improvise."

Jace kissed her soundly again, then reached for a packet in the drawer of his nightstand. A moment later, he was levering himself over her and plunging inside.

Abbie dissolved into buttery warmth. She'd been so close for so long, the tingling began almost immediately. She slid her hands low, let her palms ride Jace's hips, felt every muscle and nerve ending she owned reach for the pleasure that was quickly approaching. Her muscles contracted around him as she broke from the commanding pressure of his mouth and filled her depleted lungs with air.

Then she was climbing and he was murmuring something she couldn't quite hear over the roaring in her ears.

The first wave crested and crashed in a flash of blue fire behind Abbie's eyelids, then radiated outward in a tingling swell that reached every part of her. Her toes, her fingertips, the roots of her hair. Pressing her forehead to Jace's shoulder, she inhaled his musky scent to keep that boneless feeling with her for a little longer.

She wouldn't have had to delay its departure. Braced on his elbows, Jace kept loving her, kept murmuring sweet words that made her smile.

The second staggering wave took her by complete surprise. But when she parted her lips to draw a breath, he sealed his mouth to hers, and trapped it inside until the shudders finished rocking through her.

The third wave took him with her.

With a low groan Jace drew a ragged breath and plunged fiercely, deeply, emptying himself and filling her, finding his own pleasure while Abbie's mind spun and she gloried in the sheer power and beauty of him.

Then...time hung suspended. Spiraling aftershocks slowly worked through them, leaving their limbs weak and their bodies blissfully sated. Outside, the chill wind was picking up again, but here, feeling a little more of his weight as the quiet stole over Jace, too, Abbie was contented and warm.

She touched and stroked, felt the sandy prickle of his beard against her lips as she kissed his throat, slipped her fingers through his hair and held him loosely, kept their bodies close.

Slowly, Jace lifted his head, and in the dusky half light, Abbie smiled up into his handsome face. There was so much devotion in his eyes, it gave her hope.

This was it, she realized. This was the moment she'd longed for since that first night in the gazebo...the moment of completely letting go and giving herself physically, emotionally and spiritually to a man. But not just any man. To Jace. It was the most amazing moment of her life.

"Incredible," she whispered.

He smiled, his dark hair rumpled and sexy around his face. "For me, too. I don't want to move."

"Then don't," she whispered. She drew him down for another soft, tonguing kiss. "Stay for a minute."

"Can't." He nuzzled her neck, sending a tickle down the side of her leg. "I need to take care of business before a few of my guys make a break for it. No babies, re-member?"

No babies.

Abbie stopped stroking his hair, her contentment flagging as their earlier discussion came back to her. He'd explained his reservations, told her that marriage and children were out of the question…but that was before they'd glimpsed each other's souls. No man could look at a woman the way he'd just looked at her without feeling more than friendship, could he?

Grinning, kissing her one last time, Jace moved away.

And suddenly Abbie was afraid that if they didn't stay close, they'd lose this indefinable bond between them. She gave him a few moments, then followed him into the master bath. The fixtures were white, but splashes of burgundy and hunter green were all around.

"I missed you," she said, sliding back into his arms.

"I'm glad," he murmured. "We can shower together."

"What a nice idea. You can wash my back, I'll wash yours…and then I'll find a way to thank you for showing me such a good time. The score's three to one, my favor. I'm afraid you were shortchanged."

His grin stretched. "No, I wasn't. But that said, I think you just made me an offer I'd be an idiot to refuse."

Later, nestled in his arms, Abbie listened to Jace's slow, steady breathing behind her. And as she stared into the semidarkness, she found herself wishing that there was no anxiety mixed with the contentment she felt. After he'd drifted off to sleep, sated once again, she'd turned her attention back to his no-babies comment.

True, she'd brought up the subject of birth control first—before they'd made love. But somehow, she hadn't expected him to even think about it after they'd drained each other. That should've been the time for touching and whispering in the dark.

Naturally, he'd had to deal with the reality of the situation, but he could've simply said he needed to take care of business and left it at that. But…he hadn't. And now she wondered if his offhand remark had been a gentle reminder that their relationship was short-term.

So, what are you going to do about it? a tiny voice questioned. *Can you change his mind? He was clear about what he wanted—and didn't want—when you discussed it. And realistically, is this what you truly want? Without stars in your eyes, without the memory of loving him humming through your system, could you leave the practice you worked so hard to build for a small town office and a few driving-under-the-influence clients?*

Both questions stopped Abbie's breathing. And suddenly she knew that not all of the anxiety she felt was due to Jace's no-marriage, no-children view of life. She had reservations, too. But how could that be when she loved him? Or was this love? Her emotional judgment had shown signs of wear lately. She'd misread Collin, and she'd horribly misread Danny Long.

Squeezing her eyes shut, telling herself that it was too much to think about right now, she slid her arm back under the blankets, then covered the warm broad hand on her waist. She linked her fingers through Jace's. At this moment, spooned together with the wind flinging beads of snow against the window, she felt cherished. She wouldn't allow anything to steal her happiness tonight.

Jace stalked out of the warehouse where a third of the red oak inside kiln number three—twenty-eight thousand board feet of someone else's lumber—had basically become firewood. It had gone into the kiln without having the ends waxed, dried too fast, and their losses could run into the thousands of dollars.

Crossing the snow-speckled lot, he strode into the office where Ida was still looking worn out. The moment she'd come in, he'd told her to go back home—then inadvertently insulted her by reminding her that she was no spring chicken. Now *she* was ticked off at him, too. He'd set a new record today for blowups and apologies.

He'd left while Abbie was still asleep, showered and dressed downstairs, then locked her safely in the house. Then he'd snuck out like…like a coward who couldn't face the day-after expectations.

Last night had been the most emotionally and erotically satisfying night of his life. But when the heavy breathing was over, he'd known he was in trouble.

How many times had he warned himself to be smart, keep his distance? But, no, he'd let the little general in his jeans do his thinking and at the first hint of sex, he'd buckled like an unfolded lawn chair and let her in.

Now he had to get her out. Starting with her job and ending with their different views on family, they had nothing to build on.

Ida called to him from the fax machine as he went by. "Pardon me, Attila," she snipped with her nose in the air. "You had a call while you were out."

Jace sent her a deadpan look. "One of my Huns?"

"No, one of your honeys. Abbie's on her way."

Jace felt a nerve leap in his jaw. First of all, she shouldn't be driving herself around without knowing where Long was. Secondly, he didn't want her here. He had enough problems to deal with.

"I told her we'd love it if she'd handle the phones again today," Ida went on sweetly. "After all, I'm a poor, decrepit, wrinkled old prune of a woman who needs her rest."

She pulled the sheet out of the fax machine and moved crisply to the file cabinet to drop it in a folder. "Looks like there'll be no dinner or hanky panky for Harold tonight. I'm obviously not up to it."

Jace froze in shock as he tried to wrap his mind around her reply. "Harold?"

"My gentleman friend," she replied, plunking herself down in her seat. "We met last month at the Rotary's Monte Carlo Night." She pinned Jace with a look. "And before you topple over, my Edward's been gone for fifteen years, and by the green on grass, I'm entitled."

Jace sighed, smiled then ambled around her desk to kiss her cheek and apologize. "I'm sorry. You're not old, you're a wild woman. And if you don't want to go home, please stay with my gratitude. I know we don't tell you often enough, but this place would crumble without you. I just don't want you to work if you're—"

She pointed an index finger at him, nearly poking him in the eye. "Stop before you get yourself in trouble again."

The door opened and Abbie came inside. She was all loving eyes and soft smiles, and for an instant—just an instant—Jace's insides got all stirred up again.

Ida grinned and waved at her, then commandeered Jace's attention again. "With Fran still out, I need some help. If your lawyer girl can handle the phones and take messages, I'll be able to catch up on my paperwork."

Jace watched Abbie slip off her black gloves and snowy scarf as she walked toward them. Once again she was wearing her black-and-gray herringbone coat, and high black boots, and once again she looked like she'd stepped out of a fashion magazine.

"Put her in Pete's office," he answered, relieved that she was now inside where he could keep an eye on her. Then he sent Abbie a cool nod she obviously didn't understand and went into his office.

He'd just pulled his phone close and picked up the receiver when she entered, snatched it from his hand and banged it back in the cradle. Her fiery brown eyes demanded answers. "What's going on?"

"I'm trying to make a phone call."

"That's not what I—" She stopped short. After a long, thoughtful moment she spoke again. "All right," she said quietly, her posture going rigid. "I'll let you do that. If you ever decide I deserve a straight answer, I'll be in Pete's office."

When she'd gone, Jace released a ragged breath, planted his elbows on his desk and combed his hands back through his hair.

Obviously, they'd have to talk later, but right now, he had to concentrate on business. Picking up the phone, he pushed her as far out of his mind as humanly possible and dialed Linwood Lumber. Twenty-eight thousand board feet of lumber. Ruined.

He had some groveling to do.

Abbie hung up the phone in the forester's office, made a note on the tablet beside her, then set the sheet aside. It had been two hours since Jace had subtly let her know that last night was last night, and this was a brand new day.

Well, so be it. Maybe this was for the best, she told herself, though the boulder on her heart wasn't convinced. She'd had doubts about where their relationship was headed after last night, too, but she'd never dreamed it would lead to a cold, sterile nod.

Ida entered, breaking her thoughts. Despite her fatigue, there was a twinkle in her eyes. "How's it going, honey?"

"It's going," Abbie replied, handing her the stack of messages.

"But not too well, I take it?" Pursing her lips, Ida shuffled through the notes, arranged them in some kind of order, then spoke again. "Be patient with him. This will all sort itself out."

When Abbie looked surprised, Ida reached out to tap her chin. "Whisker burn. Makeup doesn't cover it."

Abbie felt her cheeks color.

"No reason to be embarrassed," Ida went on with a grin. "I'm happy for both of you. Jace needs a good woman in his life, so he can *have* a life."

Abbie shrugged, pretending his attitude didn't matter. He'd had two hours to explain his mood, and for two hours, she'd been feeling like a fool. "Sorry to pop your balloon, but I'm temporary."

"You don't have to be. You could stay."

"I don't think so. We want different things out of life. I care about him, but I'd be crazy to sacrifice my career for something that has no chance of working out."

The lines on Ida's face deepened. "Forgive a nosy old lady her opinion, but life isn't always about careers."

Abbie silently agreed, but at the moment, her career was a convenient rock to hide behind so she could save face.

The phone rang. Excusing herself, she took the call, listened to some good news, then said goodbye and hung up. In spite of everything, she was happy for Jace. "That was the company's attorney," she told Ida. "The Flaggs have dropped their lawsuit."

"Wonderful!" Ida exclaimed, snatching up the phone and depressing the intercom button. She handed the receiver to Abbie. "Tell him. Tell him right now. Maybe that will lighten his load."

Maybe it would, Abbie thought when Ida had gone. If nothing else, it would give them the opportunity to talk about a neutral subject—then possibly segue into more important issues. But after paging him several times without success, she went to see Ida. "He's not answering his cell phone, either," she said.

Grinning, the older woman rolled her eyes. "I'm not surprised. It's back there on his desk." She nodded toward the front door. "Go find him, honey. I'll take care of the phones for a while."

A minute later, pulling her coat over her jeans and white sweater, she headed outside where a brilliant sun sparkled off the dusting of snow they'd gotten last night. Squinting, she waited for a flatbed truck to rumble by, then headed for the sawmill. Jace's black SUV was still parked beside the office, so if he hadn't heard her page, he had to be in the mill. Soon she was ascending the metal steps and opening the door.

It was cavernous inside, and the banging of logs and screeching of saws reverberated off the walls of the steel building. Everywhere, conveyors and rollers shoved wood through various stages of cutting, and the air was thick with the smell of sawdust.

She looked. Then she spotted him near the re-saw station where a huge band saw was squaring debarked logs.

Like the rest of the employees on the floor—and the man near the instrument panel at the re-saw station—Jace wore ear protection and safety glasses. He was standing on the landing above a short set of steps, and she saw, rather than heard, him lift his voice to be heard over the slamming cacophony.

Quickly closing the distance between them, she took the rough-cut stairs to the landing.

She didn't know how it happened or who yelled first— Jace or the employee he'd been speaking to. But suddenly, her boot caught on a raised nail head, adrenaline shot through her and she stumbled.

In a blur of movement, Jace grabbed her arm and kept her from falling onto the conveyor.

She'd never seen him look so angry.

Moments later, they were moving at top speed and he was hustling her out of the mill. His face was livid and his eyes sparked with fury.

"What in hell were you trying to do in there? Get yourself killed? Isn't a California nut job enough excitement for you?"

"I was trying to deliver an important message!" she shouted back. "I paged you, but obviously, you didn't hear me. I even tried your cell phone but you'd left it on your desk."

"*Nothing* is important enough for you to come traipsing through the mill without an escort. Everything under that roof is dangerous, and I'm not just talking about the saws. Good God, all Ty and I need is another lawsuit."

Picking up curious looks from the men in the yard, Abbie jerked out of his hold and stopped walking, halting his progress, too.

"Here's your message," she said. "The Flaggs have dropped their lawsuit. And if you think I'd sue you for something that was my fault, you don't know me at all."

"*You* wouldn't be suing. My bosom buddy and lifelong

friend Morgan Winslow would." Jace pulled off his safety glasses and lowered his suddenly shaky voice. "You'd be too messed up to do it. Do *not* go in there again."

He was angry, but he was angry because he'd been scared for her. She couldn't continue to be upset about that. "I won't."

"Good." He scanned the white sweater and designer jeans she wore, then frowned at the brand new grease smear on the flap of her coat. "You should get that to the cleaners right away. Hopefully they'll be able to get the stain out. I'm leaving now to run a few errands. If you want, I can drop it off, then stop at home and get your jacket."

"Home?" she asked, wondering if the word held any significance for the two of them.

If he understood, he chose to ignore it. "To my house," he replied. "Isn't that where your jacket is?"

Abbie glanced away before he could see the quick sheen of tears in her eyes, then headed for the office. Jace followed.

"Thank you, but I won't need it. I'll make sure my car's warm before I leave. Right now, I have to get back inside. Ida's probably wondering what's keeping me."

"Abbie…"

She met his churning gaze, watched the breeze toss his hair and ruffle the shirt tucked into his jeans.

"We'll talk tonight."

"About my ruined coat and my trip to the sawmill?"

"No." He opened the office door, waited for her to step inside, then slipped her coat from her shoulders. "I'll tell them to put a rush on this," he said. Then, without another word, he walked to his SUV.

The morning wore on, but answering the phone and

drinking coffee wasn't enough to keep her mind from her screwed-up life. She knew what she wanted. She wanted Jace. She just didn't see how that could happen. Especially when Ty and Pete returned from a logging site just before noon, and Ty suggested that he and Abbie do lunch.

She nearly said no. Then she saw something serious—or maybe curious—in his blue eyes, and she wondered if she was in for another chewing out after her trip to the mill.

"You spoke to Jace," she guessed as they drove away from the business. While he wore a denim jacket over his chambray shirt and jeans, she was coatless, and he hadn't suggested that she put one on.

He grinned. "Spoke? Does yelling count?"

"He yelled at you?"

"He's yelling at everyone today—then apologizing. I hear you were on the receiving end, too."

"My fault," she admitted, fiddling with the flap on her black shoulder bag. "I nearly fell onto some sort of conveyor near the band saw."

"Well, I can see why that might've set him off." Staring through the windshield, he went on. "He's been different since you came back. Less wired and gung ho about things." Grinning again, he glanced over at her. "Of course, he's also been an emotional wreck. Do you have the key to your dad's post office box with you?"

"Yes, why?" Since the second card had shown up, she and Jace had been dropping the mail off at her dad's house. It had become a near tradition.

"Jace asked me to take you to his place for your jacket, then handle your daily mail run. He can't do it today."

Can't? Or won't? Abbie exhaled softly. Apparently, he was angrier than she'd thought—and not because of her trip to the sawmill. He'd been thinking, she decided, mulling over their relationship, just as she had. Since nothing cataclysmic had happened after they'd fallen asleep in each other's arms, she had to believe he'd opened his eyes this morning and decided that fourteen years of mistrust couldn't be wiped away in two weeks. Not even after a night of passion.

Suddenly, Abbie felt very alone. "Ty, if it's okay with you, let's just pick up the mail and drop it off at Dad's. I don't need my jacket, and I'm not really hungry."

Tiring of his little game of cat and mouse, Danny munched a chocolate bar as he drove along behind the dark gray Silverado truck. Almonds crunched between his molars. He kept a few cars between them in the noon traffic to make sure he wouldn't be seen, though with his ball cap pulled low, longer black hair and tiny sunglasses, she probably wouldn't recognize him, anyway. He smiled then, thinking that despite the other guy driving her around today, she liked *black* hair. And right now, his looked a lot like Rogan's.

Maybe they'd party a bit before he introduced her to his Louisville Slugger. He'd tried to think of the best place to do it, a public place where people would see and be really upset. Someplace where it would make a big splash. He'd liked the shocked looks on people's faces when they'd talked about Maryanne. But Abbie's father was gone, and she'd been away so long, no one in her hometown cared enough about her to be good and horrified.

Except Rogan.

The Silverado pulled into a parking space beside the post office. Biting off another hunk of chocolate and almonds, glad there were cars ahead of him, Danny cruised by slowly. He drank in her long legs in her snug jeans as she left the truck and quickly walked up the steps. Watched her breasts bob under her white sweater. And he felt a familiar itch.

Yeah, maybe they'd party. He'd stroked off the days on the calendar, and let the anticipation build, but it was finally time.

Tomorrow was his birthday.

It was still light when she and Jace left the business and he followed Abbie back home. They hadn't spoken much as they'd walked to their respective vehicles, but he seemed to have left his tension behind and she was grateful. She was also curious. Immediately after they'd come inside, he said, "Be right back," and went out again. A minute later he was back and kicking off his boots.

Wrapped in green florist's paper, there was a bouquet of pink roses, greens and baby's breath under his arm, and a grocery bag in his hand.

"I found these lying in the driveway, and thought you might want to do something with them."

"Just lying in the driveway," Abbie repeated cautiously. "How strange."

"That's what I thought. I'll scare up a vase for them. There should be one or two around here. Betty likes to fill the place with lilacs when her bushes bloom."

"What's in the bag?"

"Steaks. Found them next to the roses. Maybe we should have them for dinner."

Abbie smiled a little. "Maybe we should." Then, because she wasn't sure if the flowers were an apology or something more, she murmured her thanks and carried them to the sink. A few moments later, Jace handed her a tall glass vase, and soon the bouquet was in the middle of the kitchen table.

"You said you wanted to talk," she murmured when he didn't say anything for a while.

"Yeah, I did. But maybe we should wait until after dinner. Ty said you weren't interested in having lunch."

Her cell phone rang.

Frowning, Jace glanced at her purse. "Go ahead," he said when it continued to ring. "I'd rather we were interrupted now than after we got into it."

And suddenly Abbie knew one of the words he'd be saying when they *got into it* was goodbye. Nodding, she retrieved the shoulder bag she'd looped over a maple chair, then took her cell phone from the side flap. The caller ID displayed a familiar number.

"Dad?" she said, wishing the interruption had come from someone—*anyone*—else.

He shouted over the noisy conversations in the background—loud enough for Jace to hear. "We're at the airport, Abbie. We decided to come home early. Didn't you get the message I left for you last night?"

Her mind swam. No, she hadn't gotten the message. Last night she'd been busy making love to her father's arch foe, to put it in superhero context—not checking her dad's answering machine.

"Dad, I don't understand. When you couldn't reach me at the house, why didn't you call my cell phone?"

"I didn't think it was necessary," he grumbled. "I imagined that you'd get the message last night when you got in—or at the very least, this morning. I just phoned the house again. Where are you?"

Abbie met Jace's grim expression and knew he was interested in her answer, too. She would tell her father everything when she saw him, but for now there was no point in getting him all charged up. He was already annoyed because she hadn't been at the airport with a Welcome Home sign and a running car. "I'm with a friend, Dad. Just sit tight, and I'll see you in an hour."

Abbie folded her phone, slipped it back into her shoulder bag and placed her purse on the table. "I have to go," she said reluctantly. "I have to pick them up."

"I know."

"Jace—"

Her jaw sagged when he took his vest from the hook near the door, slipped it on then took his keys from his pocket. He met her gaze, a challenge in his eyes. "Grab your jacket, and let's go."

Chapter 14

"Jace, please, not tonight. I have every intention of telling him I've been living with you, and I don't care how he feels about it. Just let me welcome them home first."

"Don't worry," he answered. "I'm not planning to ride with you. I don't need your father's company any more than he needs mine."

And that would never change, Abbie realized.

"I'm just going to follow you to the airport. If there's snow anywhere in the state, it finds Bradford, and you're not used to winter driving anymore. Morgan won't even know I'm around."

"All right, thank you," she said. But she knew he wasn't worried about snow. He was worried that she might pick up some unwelcome company along the way. And for that, she was grateful.

"One more thing. You mentioned having the newlyweds stay somewhere else when they came back. That might not be a bad idea."

"Miriam's home hasn't sold yet," Abbie called on her way to the closet. "I'll convince them to stay there."

"They'll think that's strange unless you give them a reason."

She sent him a weary look as she slipped her jacket on. "Luckily, I have a good one, but they're not going to hear it tonight. They don't need to hear grisly news directly on the heels of their honeymoon cruise. Let's go."

Fifty minutes later, they were leaving Route 219 and taking the three mile access road to the tiny commuter airport, Jace's headlights in Abbie's rearview mirror. The night sky was dark and thick with clouds, hiding most of the stars and the fine crescent moon.

Abbie pulled to the side of the road just short of the terminal, then lowered her window and waved Jace alongside of her. He put his window down.

"I'll see you later," she said, wondering if there would ever come a time when her life wasn't complicated. "After I drop Dad and Miriam off."

"You're coming back to my place?"

"Yes." Her father would hit the roof, but now, more than ever, she and Jace needed to talk. Without intending to, she'd made him the outcast again—and only minutes after he'd brought her flowers. "I'm not sure how soon I can break away, but I'll be there." She tried to smile. "I still haven't eaten, and someone promised me a steak dinner."

He didn't smile back. "Okay, then I'll see you later." He nodded ahead where lights blazed around the terminal, and cars dotted the two parking lots flanking the small brick building. "I'll turn around over there and head back."

"Jace, thank—"

But he'd already raised the window and was heading for the lot beside a mammoth hangar.

"Great," she breathed, then pushed her foot down on the accelerator.

The sunburned honeymooners were waiting just inside the lobby's sliding glass doors when Abbie pulled under the portico, their luggage at their feet. Shutting off the car, she hurried inside to greet them.

They looked tired, but Miriam still smiled and opened her arms to Abbie. Her dad was another story. Though he returned Abbie's hug and kiss, years of reading his eyes said there was an interrogation in her future.

She didn't have to wait long for it.

"I'm still surprised that you didn't get my message," he said sternly as she helped them load their luggage into the Expedition. "Is there something wrong with the answering machine?"

Abbie met his gaze candidly. "No, it's probably working fine. I've been staying with Jace since you left."

It took less than an instant for her words to register. If it had been snowing, water would have sizzled on his head. "Abigail, you know how I feel about this."

"Morgan," Miriam interjected, touching the sleeve of his dark overcoat. "She's a grown woman, and she's entitled to live her own life. Let her do it."

"It's okay, Miriam," Abbie replied, then faced her father. "I had a good reason for moving in with Jace, Dad—and a better reason for staying."

"No doubt," he snapped.

Headlights flared, and Jace's dark SUV pulled out of the parking lot, rolled past them, then picked up speed as he continued on to the access road. Abbie's throat constricted, watching his taillights disappear. He hadn't left immediately. He'd waited until she was safely surrounded by people.

She met her father's angry eyes again. "Ready? We can talk about all of this later." *Much later.*

Thankful that Miriam hadn't begun to move her things to her new home, Abbie followed her still-fuming father through Miriam's pale blue, cream and lace living room to the thermostat on the wall.

"I looked forward to sleeping in my own bed tonight," he growled, squinting to see the numbers as he turned up the heat.

"I know," Abbie returned, regretting the necessary lies. "But it won't kill you to crash here for the night."

"It might, but we won't know that for sure until tomorrow, will we?"

Abbie expelled an exasperated breath.

Miriam had gone to her room to slip into a caftan, then put the kettle on for tea. Their luggage still stood in the foyer of the pretty Victorian because as Miriam had said, there was no point in unpacking if they'd just have to pack up again tomorrow evening. Still, she was eager to see *the surprise* Abbie had in store for them—the surprise that would've been ruined if they'd shown up before it was ready.

The excuse was childish and unimaginative, but it was the only thing Abbie could think of to keep them from going to the house. If she told her father they were here for their own safety, he'd press and thunder until she explained.

He'd make it impossible for her to leave tonight if she told him what had been happening, and she needed time with Jace.

"Dad, I'm going to say good-night now, and see the two of you tomorrow for breakfast. I'll bring all the fixings. How does eight o'clock sound?"

When he got red in the face again and started to object, Abbie went on. "Look, you're both dead on your feet, and the last thing you need to do tonight is relive the very thing that wore you out. I'll see your movies and digital photos tomorrow. Besides," she teased, "technically, you're still on your honeymoon, and I wouldn't dream of butting in on your lovey-dovey time with Miriam."

Not amused, her father drew a long, uptight breath. "Will you be staying at home tonight?"

She wouldn't lie to him again. "No. All of my things are at Jace's. What would you like for breakfast? Bacon and eggs? Pancakes and sausage? French toast?"

The thoughts racing through his eyes were unspeakable, but he answered politely, obviously knowing that objecting was a waste of time. "Just a croissant from the bakery. Miriam might like something sweeter, though. You can ask her."

"I will." She kissed his cheek. "'Night, Dad. I'll see you in the morning."

Jace wasn't waiting at his place for her. As she left Center Street for the lights of the empty town, a familiar black Explorer clicked on its headlights, pulled out of a parking space near the Market & Main Diner, and followed her back to the log house on Maxwell Road.

The garage doors opened automatically as she approached the two-stall structure, and she and Jace both pulled inside and parked. He was out of his car before she was, opening the door for her and taking her hand.

Something—a sense of urgency, or the knowledge that

their lives were about to change in ways they might not like—charged the air between them.

Jace took her in his arms and in the stillness of the garage, he held her tightly, and she held him. Abbie closed her eyes, giving him her weight, feeling his strength and his tenderness. And a wonderful peace came over her. This was where she was meant to be. Where they were both meant to be.

"I didn't think you'd come back tonight," he murmured.

Abbie smiled against his warm throat. "Then why were you waiting for me in the street?"

"No idea," he whispered.

Moments later they were climbing the stairs to the loft. In the back of Abbie's mind, she still wasn't sure where they were heading, but she'd finally decided that love was worth more than any job in any town...and she was prepared to do whatever it took to find it with Jace. Even if it meant there would be no children. Love began with a man and a woman. That was the core. Now, with the lamp in the downstairs living room lighting their way, they kissed and disposed of the buttons, zippers and fabrics that were keeping them apart.

The next morning, Jace followed her to the bakery where she bought croissants and a variety of donuts. A few early risers glanced their way as they softly kissed goodbye beside their cars, but Abbie didn't care, and apparently Jace didn't, either. Then he went on to work while she stopped at the corner convenience store for milk and eggs, then continued up the street for breakfast with her dad and Miriam.

She and Jace still hadn't talked. The warmth and deeply emotional level of loving they'd found last night had been too special, and maybe too fragile for words. So they'd communicated with touches. A lovely glow suffused Abbie when she remembered the long hug that had begun it all. It had said, *I'm sorry and I'm confused and I want you, but the uncertainty of our situation is too much, so can we just be for a while?* And so they were. There'd been no time for discussion this morning, either. They'd chosen instead to make sweet, sleepy love again.

Miriam and her father both looked well rested, happy and contented when they all convened in the kitchen. Part of Abbie almost regretted that. Because immediately after breakfast and their travel tales, she'd be ruining their day.

Her father didn't take the news well.

"You went to *him* for help, but never bothered to tell *me?*" Still wearing blue silk pajamas and a burgundy pin-striped robe, he paced the dusty-blue carpeting in his bare feet, disturbed and insulted.

The grooves on his brow deepened. "Abbie, I might have a difficult time accepting some of your choices, but by God, I do try. To be kept in the dark when a killer is stalking the only child I have is absolutely unacceptable. Did it never occur to you that *I* would've wanted to watch over you?"

"Dad, I told you. I didn't want to ruin your honeymoon, and I didn't want you to postpone it. And until the cards started coming, I had every intention of staying at the house. But then things started happening, I got scared and Jace offered his spare room. We both agreed that if Long was coming for me, he'd have no reason to think I was living there."

Sighing, Morgan brought his hand to his forehead, massaged it for a moment then turned back to Abbie, determination in his eyes. "All right, then this client of yours won't have any reason to think you're living here with Miriam and me, either. I'm home now. I'll see to your safety until this business is settled."

"I don't think so, Dad. When I left this morning, I told Jace I'd see him later."

He started getting red in the face again. "If safety was the reason you moved in with him, I can provide that here. He lives three miles out of town in the woods, for God's sake—without a decent security system and a thousand trees surrounding the damn house. Anyone with half a brain could get to you there." He jerked out a hand to make his point. "Look around you! Look where we're standing. We're only five minutes from cops with guns!"

Silently, Abbie counted to ten. "First of all, we're not even sure if Long's in the area. The L.A. police still believe he's somewhere in the city."

Morgan batted the air. "Bull. If you believed that, I would've slept in my own bed last night. This whole mess—the things he said to you after the trial, your psychologist friend's assessment, the musical cards—and maybe the graffiti—tell me that this man is a wacko, and I want you *here*. With me."

Then, to Abbie's amazement, her father's eyes got damp and his voice grew husky—and he didn't like it. "It's what your mother would've wanted, Abbie. She'd want me to watch over you *here*..." He lifted the gold cross she'd taken from her old jewelry box. "While she watches over you from above."

Feeling her own tears sting, she put her arms around him, the first time she'd done that with tenderness in a long, long time. He'd always been such a tough nut, always been the big, brash and unflappable head of the family while her mother was the caring heart. But today he'd decided to be both, and it had cost him some of his dignity. She'd heard him cry when her mother passed away, but he'd done it privately in his room, and it had crushed her that they couldn't cry together. But these tears for her were unprecedented and they touched her deeply.

"I know," she murmured over the lump in her throat. "I know she'd want that." Blinking, she eased back and squeezed his hands. "But she'd also want me to be with the man I love."

Surprise sagged his thick features. Then, sighing and shaking his head as if things couldn't get any worse, he released her and walked to the window to peer out on the street. Abbie followed.

"You love him?"

They didn't look at each other. Instead, they stared through the lace curtains at the bare maples lining the curb, and the early-morning activity across the road as people hurried with their youngsters into the library.

"Yes."

"Does he love you?"

"I don't know."

Morgan turned to her, resistance back in his dark eyes. "What about Collin?"

"What about him? And before you tell me again that you've always hoped we could get back together—please don't. I made a terrible mistake with Collin."

"I always liked him."

She moved away from the window. "Dad, you didn't know him. You only knew who he was on our wedding day, and on those few occasions when we got together for holidays. Collin was—and is—smoke and mirrors. Jace is the real thing. He's strong and solid. He understands what's important in life."

"You're talking about children."

Abbie stilled, then moved to the mantel to straighten a gold framed photo of Miriam and her father. "I'm talking about helping and caring for the people around us—sharing the bad and the good and making sense out of life. The way you and Mom did." She faced him again. "The way you and Miriam will. Dad, I'm not going back to L.A. I haven't talked it over with Stuart yet, but I'll be offering my resignation." She released a short, humorless laugh. "I'll probably be disbarred when Long's picked up, anyway. At least this way, leaving the firm will be my choice."

Morgan took her elbow and searched her eyes. "You've only been home for two weeks, and with him for less than that. *Two weeks,* Abbie. That's not long enough to make a life-altering decision. Don't burn your bridges. What if he *can't* love you? What then? The man's life is his work. He spends more time at that lumber yard than any of his men, and always has."

Abbie smiled faintly. "That's a lot of information, Dad. The night of the Mardi Gras celebration you said you didn't know a thing about him."

"Yes, well," he blustered, "people talk."

Her smile warmed and her heart followed suit. "And they say nice things about him, don't they?"

Morgan's expression stiffened again, his brief flirtation with deeper emotions tucked away once more. "Considering who his mother was, I imagine some people respect what he's done."

"Do you?"

Throwing his hands in the air, he whirled on her. "What do you want from me, Abbie?"

She lifted her voice passionately. "I want you to admit

that the only reason you won't bend where he's concerned is *me*—me, and that night in the gazebo. More than that, I want you to *accept him* if this works out. And don't say you'll do it without meaning it," she warned. "I don't ever want to be put in the position of choosing between Jace and someone or something else again."

When he didn't comment, she softened her voice. "He's a good man, Dad, and if he doesn't love me, at least I know he cares. You didn't see him, but he followed me to the airport last night to make sure I got there safely, and he was waiting for me in town after I dropped you and Miriam off—when he had no idea how long I'd be, or if I'd even show."

Abbie held his rigid gaze for several long moments, held her breath, hoping that her father would at least *attempt* to put his bitterness aside. Because if he wouldn't, as painful as it would be, her choice was made.

Finally, he nodded grudgingly. "I'll try. But I want something in return."

Abbie released the breath she'd been holding. "All right. What is it?"

"I want you to move in here with us until this debacle is resolved."

Chapter 15

Hiding his tension, Jace walked their easygoing forester to his truck. It was quitting time for the office personnel, but a rush order had come in for ninety-six hundred board feet of green cherry, so a few of the guys were working overtime tonight.

"You're sure you won't be using these?" he asked, accepting the tickets Pete handed him. "The varsity doesn't make the state basketball semifinals every day."

"I'm sure. A family thing came up, and Carmella and I won't be able to make it. Take Abbie. She probably hasn't been inside the old high school for years."

"Probably not."

Thanking Pete again, he said goodbye and watched him pull out of the lot. Then Jace climbed into his own vehicle, tooted to Ty, who was walking toward the mill, and followed Pete's truck to the head end of the drive.

The manila folder Ida had handed him this morning nearly slid off the passenger's seat when he made the left turn onto the road, and he snatched it back. Inside was the data and reservations roster for the Friends dinner, which made him wonder again—as he'd wondered when Ida'd handed it to him—where Abbie would be on Easter Sunday.

That's when his stomach had begun to churn.

Regardless of their closeness last night, things had a way of changing when Morgan was involved. And despite her age and independence now, Abbie still loved and respected her father.

Sooner or later, depending on Long, she'd be heading back to L.A., and it was idiotic to imagine that she wouldn't. Compared to big fees, sunshine and movie stars, what did Laurel Ridge have to offer? He blew out a sarcastic breath. Half a year of crummy weather, an elk herd and an undefeated high-school basketball team.

Jace squared his shoulders. If she wasn't here for the dinner, so be it. As she'd said, nothing that had happened between them had put rings on their fingers, so he'd be fine with whatever turned up.

Yeah? a dry voice asked. *If everything's fine, why are you spending so much time rationalizing?*

Easy answer. Because she'd spent the last nine hours with her father and he hadn't heard from her all day.

A jolt of adrenaline hit Jace fifteen minutes later when he saw Morgan Winslow's big fancy Lexus idling in the wide turnaround near his garage. Memories flashed—memories of being sent packing, memories of humiliation.

His muscles tensed. If Morgan was here to take another shot at his parentage and shaky social status— "Bring it on," he muttered.

Flicking a button, he raised the garage door, swung by the Lexus and cruised inside the first bay. A moment later, he was walking to Morgan's window. The window slid down.

"Morgan," Jace said coolly but politely. The sun was gone, but the hot-pink sky behind the trees was mirrored on the Lexus's gleaming black hood.

"Rogan," he returned in the same aloof tone.

"You wanted to see me?"

"Not particularly." Winslow's gaze slid over Jace's vest, jeans and boots. "But since you're here, I should thank you for watching over my Abbie while I was gone."

His Abbie? Jace felt his nerves roll into tight little balls. "She needed help. I was glad to do it. I hope that didn't bother you." Truthfully, Jace hoped it had burned a hole in his gut.

"Not at all. But I'll take over now."

The hairs on Jace's scalp prickled, and suddenly he realized that the most obvious reason for Morgan sitting in his driveway—for Morgan *waiting* in his driveway—was Abbie.

Slowly, he turned toward the house.

"Yes, she's inside packing," Morgan said. "We talked, Abbie and I, and we decided that she'd feel safer staying with me and Miriam."

Jace never heard another word. The uncertainties he'd been battling all day blew through him like a hot, searing *clarifying* wind. He strode to the house.

The instant he walked into her bedroom and met her eyes, he saw the uneasiness there. Except it was no longer her bedroom. Everything was back to the way it once was—no more creams and perfumes on the tiny dresser he'd built, no silky hunter green robe draped over his computer chair. It was just an office now.

"Jace," she said. "I just tried to call you, but there was no answer. I tried your cell phone, too."

He reached for the case on his belt, then scowling, came up empty. He'd left the phone on his desk again. But that was neither here nor there. She was running again, planning to let him know with a phone call that she was leaving. Well, he wouldn't let her see him bleed. He hadn't allowed it the first time and it wouldn't happen this time, either.

"No problem," he returned indifferently. "I figured you'd be leaving after spending the day with your dad."

She'd apparently been here for a while because the only things left were her laptop, a small bag of laundry and a suitcase. "Need some help getting your things to the car?"

"Jace, don't do this," she pleaded. "Dad's feeling left out right now, and I'm just humoring him. He insists that with Miriam's security system and the police just a few blocks away, I'll be safer staying with him for a while."

"He's right. And as always, he's offering the best deal." He picked up the laundry bag and her suitcase. "Is this it?"

Her dark eyes flashed. "No, this is not *it*. If you'll stop acting like a spoiled child, I'll tell you—"

"No thanks. I like myself just the way I am." He nodded at her laptop on his computer desk. "Can you grab that?"

"Dammit, Jace, what are you doing?"

His control splintered all to hell. "I'm giving you back to Daddy—just like I did fourteen years ago. Those years are like a blip in time for you, aren't they? All he has to do is snap his fingers and you scurry back to keep him happy."

She was so exhausted after just going over the whole thing with her father again, Abbie threw her hands in the air and agreed with everything he said. "That's exactly right. Whatever my dad wants, he gets."

Grabbing her laptop, she strode into the hall, then through the great room and entryway before she faced him at the front door. "And why do you care, anyway? You made it clear that you only offered your spare room because I had nowhere else to go. Well, I have a place now. You can finally get back to building your business and impressing the town with your accomplishments."

They locked gazes, and Abbie prayed that he'd step into the silence and tell her that his feelings had changed—that he'd changed his mind about everything—the business, commitment, maybe even children. She prayed he'd tell her he was wired and upset because he didn't want her to leave.

Instead, he opened the front door.

"Fine," she said, hiding her hurt as she stepped outside. "I'll call you later when you're ready to discuss this rationally."

"Sorry, but I'll be too busy to be rational later." He carried her things to the top of the steps and set them down. "I'm going back to the mill tonight."

"Is that supposed to hurt me?" she asked. Then she sighed. "Know what? You're as stubborn and pigheaded as my father is, and one of you is more than enough for any woman to deal with. Goodbye, Jace."

His gaze went wide, then slowly gentled, and for a moment she thought he'd reach for her, or apologize—do *something*. Then her father rolled the Lexus closer to the house, and he shut down again.

"Those who won't learn from history are doomed to repeat it," he said quietly. "Take care, Abbie."

Danny's heart raced as the Lexus crested the drive and Rogan slammed the front door. Scrambling from his nest inside the trees, he snatched up his candy wrappers, grabbed his Goodwill sleeping bag and crashed through the underbrush. When he got to the road the Lexus was already out of sight. But that was okay.

Running across the road, then into the tree line, he picked his way toward the dilapidated barn where he'd been living like a rat, watching her and Rogan and waiting for this day. *Trying to figure a way to separate them.*

Who would've thought they'd do it *for* him?

He was parallel with the rear of the barn now. Staying low, he crossed the open field, hopped inside his car and started the engine. Then, cautiously, he rolled out of the dusky seclusion to check for cars. Except for a few houses closer to town, only Rogan lived on this road, so traffic was minimal. Finally flicking on his headlights, Danny bounced onto the road and headed for the Winslows' white-brick palace.

Twenty minutes later, after cursing a massive jam-up near the brightly lit high school, Danny crossed the bridge bearing his handiwork and slowly rolled past the Winslows' gated driveway. Despite its length, he could see most of the house through the trees.

A blistering rage nearly lifted the top of his head off, and he slammed on the brakes. The lights in the house were the same timed lamps he'd seen when he was here before. Winslow had taken her somewhere else!

Balling his hands into fists, he pounded the sides of his head, his scream bouncing off the windows and doors. Where was she? Where? To everything there was a season! A time to live and a time to die! This was her time!

But then…he thought, slowly unclenching his hands and taking several long, deep breaths…if he couldn't find her, maybe killing *him* would work until he could get to her. He'd watched them. No matter how they'd left things, from the way they'd slobbered all over each other, Danny somehow knew that losing Rogan would hurt her a lot.

Then he remembered what Rogan had said before she'd finally taken the hint and left.

He knew where he'd be tonight.

Bone tired, Abbie climbed the stairs to Miriam's pretty blue-and-white French country guest room after another toe-to-toe argument with her father about Jace.

After dinner, as a courtesy, Chief Frasier had come by to share what information he had, and to assure them that they would continue to patrol Center Street and the Winslow home often. Then he and the part-time officer who'd accompanied him had left to handle the traffic pouring into town for the basketball semifinals.

Abbie swallowed. With so many strangers in town for the game, Danny would be able to come and go at will. If he was even in the vicinity. The uncertainty was wearing her down. She wanted her life back, and she wanted it on her own terms, without worrying that someone was waiting in the shadows. More than that, she wanted to talk to Jace, but once again, he wasn't answering.

Taking her cell phone from her purse, Abbie called his cell again, then tried the RL&L office a second time. There was still no answer, but this time she waited through Ida's recorded voice and spoke after the tone.

"Jace, it's Abbie," she said. "Please call me back on my cell. It's a little after nine right now. You have the number." Then, because she was half-afraid he'd forgotten it, she repeated the number and said goodbye.

She was dozing, fully clothed, on the queen-size bed's puffy blue-and-white coverlet forty-five minutes later when her cell phone rang. Quickly, she checked the caller

ID. Her heart leapt when she recognized Jace's cell number. "Jace, hi," she said, refusing to hide the relief in her voice. "I'm so glad you called."

Static and the screeching din of saws on the assembly line muffled his voice and she had to stop him. "Jace, wait. I can barely hear you. Can you step outside for a minute?"

"I am outside," he returned, his voice breaking up. "It's noisy all over. What did you want?"

"We need to talk about this afternoon. You have to let me explain."

"Not over the phone. Can you come out here? I can't leave right now."

That startled her. "You...want me to come to the mill?"

"Oh...right. Maybe you shouldn't. I just wanted to get things straightened out. We can talk tomorrow or the next day."

But Abbie was shaking her head before he finished. She couldn't let another hour go by without seeing him, without laying her heart on the line and asking him how he honestly felt about her.

"I'll be there in a few minutes. Dad and Miriam just came upstairs. I need to give them time to settle in before I leave. If not, he'll either be in the car with me, or insist on a police escort."

The saws and rumble of the assembly line filled the air space, almost seeming to grow louder—as if he'd moved even closer to the noise. "Be careful," he said.

"I will. See you soon."

Jace drove from the mill, feeling more unhinged than he had in years. Fourteen of them, to be precise. The scoreboard in his mind was flashing, and the numbers were nothing to cheer about. Morgan 2, Rogan 0.

Well, the score was about to change. Four hours of head-pounding tension and at least a week of denials and rationalizations were enough. He needed her in his life. Period. Needed her with every breath in his body. Without her...

He didn't even want to think about the alternative.

Now, with some space and time to think, he knew she hadn't been slamming the door on their relationship. She'd simply been between a rock and a hardhead, and trying to please everyone. And he'd gone off half-cocked like he always did when he felt defensive. Yell first, think later.

The lights of town appeared, but seeing a long string of traffic leaving the high school, he veered onto a side street to avoid it. Apparently the game was over.

He and Abbie should've been at that game tonight.

He reached for his cell phone—then scowled when he realized he still hadn't picked it up. He'd wanted to call and tell her he was on his way, but no matter. Face-to-face was always better than a phone call.

The expression on Morgan's face when he pushed aside the curtain on the door and saw him made Jace's night.

"I want to see Abbie," he said when Morgan opened the door. Behind him, Winslow's new wife was descending the stairs in a pink robe and slippers.

"She's asleep," he replied coldly. "So were we."

"Then wake her up."

Morgan's sunburned face brightened even more. "Go home."

Sighing and tossing a look at her husband, Miriam turned around and started back up the steps. "Just a minute, Jace. I'll get her."

He and Morgan were still perfecting their glares when she rushed back downstairs, a sheet of tablet paper flapping in her hand.

"Abbie's gone." She handed Morgan the note but spoke to Jace. "She said you called for her to come to the mill."

The blood drained from Jace's face and his legs went weak. "I didn't phone her. I wouldn't have asked her to go anywhere alone without knowing if—" The bottom fell out of his stomach. "Call Chief Frasier," he ordered, already descending the steps. "Tell him I'm on my way to the mill."

Abbie pulled into the parking lot, her brows knitting when she didn't see Jace's SUV parked with the four other vehicles in the lot. Noise still issued from the sawmill, though, and dim auxiliary lights were on inside the office. She started for the mill, then remembered her promise to steer clear of it.

As expected, the office door was unlocked. Walking inside, she pulled off her driving gloves and called Jace's name. Called again.

She'd nearly reached the short hall leading to the restrooms and the private office when her cell phone rang.

Plucking it from her purse, she saw Jace's number in the ID window again, then smiled as she unfolded it and brought it to her ear. "Hi. I'm here. Where are you?"

"Right behind you, counselor."

It wasn't Jace's voice.

Abbie whirled as Danny Long stepped out of the shadows, a baseball bat at his side. His hair was longer—and black. But his eyes and expression held the same smug look she'd seen that day in the courtroom.

With a nonchalant smile, he flipped Jace's cell phone to the floor.

Abbie bolted, her nerves on fire as she raced for the office. She slammed the door, reached for the lock—and gasped when she realized there *was* no lock. She heard Long's pounding footfalls.

Adrenaline surging, she ran to the double-paned window—unlocked it and thrust it open, tried to work up the window screen.

The door banged open and in three long strides, Danny was on her. He swung the bat—caught her across the legs. Screaming in pain, Abbie hit the floor. She scrambled away, kicked out at him, got to her feet and lunged for the door.

Danny rammed into her, knocking her onto the desktop. Then suddenly, the bat clattered to the floor and something sharp and pointed pressed into the soft tissue under her chin. She stopped fighting. Sprawled on her side on the desktop, she glanced down at the long wood rasp Danny held to her throat.

She started to pray.

Breathing hard, Danny rolled her onto her back, then knocked everything off the desk and climbed on top of her. He sat on her thighs, the gagging odors of perspiration and neglect assaulting Abbie's nostrils. Spotty patches of blond peach fuzz sprouted from his chin.

"That's better," he murmured, his leering smile making Abbie's stomach heave. "Now we can have that talk you've been so eager to have."

Filled with loathing, she stared up at him.

"Well?" he prodded. "What did you want to talk about?"

"How about prison and the death penalty?"

"Sorry. Double jeopardy. Can't be tried twice for the same crime. By the way," he added, wiggling the rasp. "This belongs to your boyfriend. Nice of him to leave his cell phone for me, too."

"You were here when I called?"

He smiled. "Waiting for him, but then you called and plans changed." He laughed, then let his voice slide into a mocking falsetto. "*Jace! Oh, Jace, I'm so glad you called! Thanks for leaving your new cell number.*"

His blue eyes turned to ice and he yanked down the zipper on her jacket. "No, I don't want to talk about prison. I want to talk about justice. *My* justice. I want to talk about an eye for an eye."

"Then you'll be letting me go," Abbie said, her mind racing—trying to remember how things were arranged in Jace's desk drawer, trying to think of something that would stop him. "I gave you your freedom."

Danny pulled the sides of her jacket open. "Not by choice."

"Vengeance is mine sayeth the Lord!" Abbie shouted.

"The Lord helps those who help themselves!" Danny shouted back. He popped the top button on her white blouse. Then he saw the gold cross at her throat and his eyes went wild and crazy. It was just the distraction she needed.

Abbie yanked open the desk drawer, grabbed the letter opener and punched it into his thigh. Screaming, Danny dropped the rasp and jerked onto his knees.

Abbie jammed her knee into his groin, shoved him off her. Another cry tore from his throat as he hit the floor. Scrambling from the desk, she rushed from the office— burst into the chill March night just as Jace's black Explorer roared in.

"Where is he?" Jace shouted, leaping out.

"Inside!"

A crash and the splinter of breaking glass joined the vibrating noise from the mill. Jace tore into the building, reached his office just in time to see Long's slim frame disappear through the smashed-out window.

Sidestepping the bat on the floor, he barreled out of the building and stopped to look around. In the distance, sirens wailed. Then Jace spotted Long, half running, half staggering toward the sawmill. Light glinted off the front fender of a car parked behind the building.

"Jace, no!" Abbie shouted as he took off after him. "Let the police handle it!"

"No! This ends tonight!"

Danny turned, saw him coming and ran harder, grunting with the pain and effort.

But with healthy legs, Jace took a diagonal route toward the car and like a rider turning cattle, sent Long off in another direction. He headed for the loading dock's open doors.

Long scuttled up the rough wood steps, raced inside. Now Jace was only a dozen steps behind him. Without earplugs, the machinery and conveyors were nearly deafening.

Jace glanced around the mammoth room, dipped to look under the three-foot-high conveyors. Every operation was linked to the next, and raised walkways ran alongside the log- and lumber-moving belts.

The attack came from behind, swift and fierce.

Crying out, Jace buckled as something crashed across his shoulder blades. He whirled, pain splintering through him. Long swung again. Jace stepped into the arc and grabbed the angle iron. Wrenching it from Long's hands, he threw it, ringing, across the concrete floor. Long bolted again.

Dead ahead was the resaw station. Danny rushed up the steps and knocked the startled operator aside—leapt over the oncoming logs and onto the raised track.

His wounded leg didn't hold him.

Screaming, Danny fell into the shallow track moving lumber toward the band saw, and horrified, Jace bounded up the steps to the control panel. He slapped the red Emergency Stop button, then stared down and felt his stomach pitch. He'd stopped the saw blade and conveyor. But the steel rollers that moved the trimmed logs along had sensed a new log coming. Long lay pinned against the guide rail. *But he was still alive.*

Suddenly aware that all operations had ceased and his men were running toward him, Jace yelled for an ambulance.

Even as the words left his throat, Jace heard Chief Glenn Frasier shout, "They're on the way."

"Are you sure you're all right?" Jace asked as they held each other near Ida's well-stocked coffee station. The RL&L office was brightly lit now, and two untouched mugs of coffee sat on the table beside them.

Abbie nodded, the loss of adrenaline leaving her weak and making her aware of the throbbing in her right leg. "I'm okay." She looked up and touched his face. His wonderful, handsome face. "You?"

His tired smile matched hers. "The same, I think. Haven't had time to check."

Thirty minutes ago, as Chief Frasier and Patrolman Harris were taking their statements, the paramedics had left in a silent ambulance. Danny was no longer a threat to anyone. Now the officers were interviewing the men who'd witnessed Long's fall. Jace had tracked down Ty, and he was on his way. The grounds were like a three-ring circus with flashing lights and slamming car doors.

Her dad and Miriam had been there briefly, too, but

after assuring them that she was fine and would see them tomorrow, she'd insisted they go home. It was a shock when her dad walked over to Jace, who'd hung back while they talked, and asked to shake his hand.

"Can we end this here?" he'd asked, and grimly, Jace had nodded.

Now Abbie snuggled closer, loving his warmth, inhaling his scent and thanking God for second chances. "I hope Frasier finishes soon."

Jace's voice was a low rumble. "Me, too. I want to get out of here. I have things to do."

"Like what?"

He stroked her hair. "Like buy an engagement ring and beg the woman I'm holding to marry me."

Abbie jerked her head up to meet the tenderness in his eyes.

"She'll probably tell me to take a long walk off a short pier. But then I'll tell her that without her, I'm nothing, and hope she sees that I'm telling the truth." He smiled. "Then I'll tell her that I'm willing to move to California to be with her." He drew a hesitant breath. "What do you think she'd say to that?"

Tears filled Abbie's eyes and she was nearly overcome by emotion. "I think...I think she'd tell you that she'd already decided to leave her law practice and stay right where she is—with you—for as long as it took to make you love her. The way she loves you."

Jace crushed her in his arms, and they clung to each other. "You're sure?" he murmured against her temple. "You probably haven't noticed, but I can be a complete ass sometimes."

She kissed his neck, sighed against his ear. "I *have* noticed, and yes, you can be. But I'm sure. Oh, Jace, I'm sure. I need some time, though."

"I know. We can take it slow. We've only been together again for a short time."

"That's not what I meant." She eased back, everything she felt for him in her eyes, in her voice. "I'd marry you five minutes from now if it were possible. But before that happens, I need to go back to L.A. and own up to what I did."

His face lined. "He's gone now. It doesn't matter. No one will ever know for sure."

"You're wrong. *I'll* know."

Jace held her close again.

After a while, Abbie lifted her head, her smile returning as she counted her blessings and a new wave of confidence in the future floated her heart. "Hey…don't you have something to say to me?"

"Can't think of anything," he said teasingly.

Abbie traced the curve of his lower lip. "Come on, Rogan," she murmured. "I showed you mine."

Then he smiled, and the devotion in his eyes was unmistakable. "I love you. I think I have since the day Jim called me into his office and ordered me to help you with your term paper. I've loved you ever since I saw you in those faded fanny-hugging jeans."

Abbie laughed softly. "Fanny-hugging?"

"Yep," he whispered, parting his lips over hers. "But now that's my job."

Epilogue

A week later, Abbie and Stuart left the judge's chambers, then strode down the hall, their footfalls echoing off the glossy floor tile.

"Well, my girl," he said, smiling. "Now you can get on with your life."

There'd been some censuring on Judge Wilcox's part, but in the end, Abbie had felt almost validated for leaking information to A.D.A. Garrett. Though the judge stopped just short of admitting it, she and Stuart both knew he wouldn't have let her withdraw as Danny's counsel with the trial only a day from ending. Judge Wilcox hated waste, and to him, that's what the court's time and the county's money would've been. After angrily cautioning her to keep her oath in mind from this day forward, he'd thrown them out of his office.

"Stuart, thank you so much," Abbie said gratefully.

He nodded his graying head, then squeezed her hand as

they walked. They were a Mutt and Jeff team, Stuart several inches shorter than she was in her heels. "I'll miss you," he said.

"I'll miss you, too. But we'll only be a few hours away by plane. I hope you'll visit."

"Oh," he chuckled, "I imagine I'll be seeing quite a bit of you with a wedding and babies in your future."

Abbie stopped walking, stopped breathing. Her heart began to race and tears stung the backs of her eyes. "Babies?"

Stuart's pale gaze twinkled behind his rimless glasses, and he nodded toward the end of the long hall where Jace stood, silhouetted against a long, arched, sunstruck window. "He gave me the honor of telling you. Apparently he thinks it would be a travesty to deny a child a mother like you."

Abbie's whisper was barely audible. "He said that?"

"Not precisely," Stuart replied, "but, yes. Now, if this pleases you, perhaps you should let him know it."

And, tears streaming, Abbie ran for that sunlit window and flew into Jace's warm, wanting arms.

* * * * *

Hidden in the secrets of antiquity, lies the unimagined truth...

Introducing

ROGUE
ANGEL™

a brand-new line filled with mystery and suspense, action and adventure, and a fascinating look into history.

And it all begins with DESTINY.

In a sealed crypt in France, where the terrifying legend of the beast of Gevaudan begins to unravel, Annja Creed discovers a stunning artifact that will seal her destiny.

Available every other month starting July 2006, wherever you buy books.

GRA1

Page-turning drama…

Exotic, glamorous locations…

Intense emotion and passionate seduction…

Sheikhs, princes and billionaire tycoons…

This summer, may we suggest:

THE SHEIKH'S DISOBEDIENT BRIDE
by Jane Porter

On sale June.

AT THE GREEK TYCOON'S BIDDING
by Cathy Williams

On sale July.

THE ITALIAN MILLIONAIRE'S VIRGIN WIFE

On sale August.

With new titles to choose from every month,
discover a world of romance in our books written
by internationally bestselling authors.